One Last Ride

Coming Soon....

Sparks

In the riveting sequel novel to 'One Last Ride', Jake allows love into his life but one last time. In the midst of his renewed faith in 'forever' tragedy strikes and turns his world upside down. Struggling to find his way he discovers a new life beyond any that he might have imagined for himself. Will he once again trust in love, or will he turn his back on the best thing that ever happened to him?

ALSO COMING SOON!!!

FULL CIRCLE

When in our youth we discover the hungering for adulthood, frequently we find changes we truly weren't prepared for.

Annabelle finds herself torn, tormented even by the whirlwind of altercations she's facing, while desperate to find balance between youth and adulthood. In those overlapping moments, innocence is lost, desires met, and futures altered forever.....

One Last Ride

T.R. Williams

One Last Ride Copyright and published 2013 by T.R. Williams. All rights reserved. Printed in the United States of America. No Part of this book may be used or reproduced in any manner whatsoever without written permission except in the case of brief quotations embodied in critical articles or reviews. For book signing dates, autographed print copies and/or more information please contact:
trwilliamswrites@gmail.com

Design and photography by
T.R. Williams
ISBN 978-1-940-69002-5

Dedication

This, my first novel I lovingly dedicate to my late mother and father. Who, though they will never see my work, believed in me and my dreams of writing when I was barely ten. For instilling in me an unwavering sense of humanity and for showing me that through it all true loves fire cannot be extinguished, for this I am eternally grateful.

To my little sister Shar, thank you for all the adventures we shared roaming the mountains from dawn till' dusk. The 'cave', and all our memories stir creativity in me still today, a lifetime later. You were the best belated birthday present I ever could have asked for.

To my husband Britt, for the decades we've faced in this unpredictable accumulation of experiences we call life. Thank you for taking that bold step after my life was devastated and purchasing me my first computer. Who could have known that having freedoms taken away by that horrific wreck might pull me back on course. Your belief in me means more than spoken words could possibly express.

Though unconventional to say the least, I also wish to dedicate this to Mr. Bulhozer. If you had been paying attention to the road that fateful evening I may have never slowed my life enough to realize that I had missed my calling to write. I forgave you the day I typed the first words of this novel.

To a very special friend Tigger, (though this may come as quite a surprise)... for being my muse of sorts. You hold a very special place with me still after all these years and forever will. You are living proof that with just a few words spoken you can alter another's life. Forever I'll cherish the time...

Sincere Thanks

As I embark on this journey, I recall the words my 8th grade teacher wrote in my yearbook of how one day I would be doing precisely this. Thank you for believing in me, for offering inspiration in the gift God instilled in me. I found my destiny once again after decades of wandering lost in the desert of life. Finally I'm making good on your request for an autographed copy of my first novel.

Great grandpa Taylor, God rest your soul. I wish to offer up thanks for teaching me to be fully present in all I do ... for the love of gardening, fishing, music and especially violin. I vowed to name my first born after you. She's a different type of baby, but here she is grandpa. Save a place for me on the riverbanks in Heaven. XO

Above all, thank you Lord for the opportunity to follow the path you set for me. For being my one true compass; the beautiful light I focus on in the darkest of times. I'd be roaming about the desert lost, rather than knowing I have eternity with you. Though the journey is never easy, you always make right on your promise in the end, 'all things work for the good.'

Authors Note

In the blink of an eye life as we know it can change. The unspoken constant which one so relies on to stay grounded, centered even, can be ripped away in an instant... leaving behind little that resembles the life lived before. Each faces adversity with much diversity, moving forward through the vexation with independent reactions and emotions, each walking away with our own unique scars.

Surrendering to the current of change is often the greatest challenge one confronts in troubled times. Fighting the current can often leave one's life in the ashes of yesteryear, rather than the on the horizon of a brighter tomorrow. We are creatures of habit, who in general prefer to remain 'as is' unless moved by force. Rare are those who welcome change.

Holding fast to the truth that higher authorities have our backs is key to the success in this transitional period. Embracing that which has come to pass, (regardless of how against the current our emotions might attempt to carry us), as well as all that lies ahead can often lead to the most amazing journeys. Leaving ourselves open to the new path life offers up can often prove to be even more exciting than one could ever imagine. But first there must come acceptance and release of control... this being of utmost difficulty for most.

Life is not intended to be simply a round of work, no matter how interesting and important that work may be.
A moment's pause to watch the glory of a sunrise or a sunset is soul satisfying, while a bird's song will set the steps to music all day long.
- Laura Ingalls Wilder

Prologue

Living exceptionally varied lives, Liz, Toby, and Taylor never imagined being faced with such a life altering reality. All they'd known and relied upon came crashing to a screeching halt that fateful day they lost their mother. The wake of such devastation leaving nothing unchanged.

Running Donna's restaurant since the fatal accident had taken a toll on the three of them. Facing the ever growing mound of unpaid bills, hundreds of unreturned phone calls, staff scheduling, ordering, and employee issues drained every last drop of their life energy. Somehow, regardless of the dire circumstances, they had toughed it out and seemed to have things under control merely a year after Donna's had been placed in their hands.

Walking away from their own lives in order to save the bar and grill Donna had so painstakingly built from the ground up, hadn't been their idea of a dream by any means. But their undeniable love of the restaurant, for how it had kept them fed and off the streets after the loss their father, this they could simply not ignore. The raw truth that their mother had invested every last dime of their fathers' life insurance money in the restaurant, allowing her to keep the family together, left them no other seemingly logical option, but to keep her dream alive.

Though they'd grown up in this quaint mountain town, never had they imagined returning here. Most of their memories were in this town, from this place. Cherishing the countless times they had done their homework at the bar after school, helped wash dishes, learned to run the cash register, to choose fresh produce, and especially the secrets behind their mother's award winning recipes; these experiences had in many ways formed the people they now were. Each had even worked there during their years in high school. Donna's had been their second home, so regardless of all they had sacrificed, they couldn't simply throw it all away.

Their mother had never spoken of her wishes if something were to ever happen to her, nor had the three of them ever thought to inquire. When the fated call from the estate attorney came, briefly informing them that they had inherited equal shares of Donna's, their mothers desires were made crystal clear. The stipulations were that they would partner or Donna's would be sold and ran under a new name. The shock of losing their mother had yet to sink in before decisions that would affect their lives, their very futures would need to be made. Banding together for the first time, the three of them had left their own worlds to save their mother's life work.

The words of their grandfather rang ever true. 'When faced with the unexpected twist and turns of life we must learn to fully welcome adventure, growth, excitement, and opportunities beyond our own understanding.' Each would soon find that such leaps of faith often bring a lifetime of new ventures, awakening hearts to passions beyond our wildest dreams. Such change would soon open the world to the three of them as never before. In losing their mother, they'd gained not only a restaurant, but a new and unforeseen destiny.

Chapter One

The ringing phone startled Liz sending the tray of salt shakers she'd been filling tumbling over, toppling to the freshly mopped tile floor behind the bar. Frazzled she reached to lift the receiver. "Donna's Place," Liz answered gruffly. A familiar voice exploding from the other end of the line so abruptly, she nearly dropped the receiver.

"Hey sis! You won't believe what I just went and did!" Excitement oozing from Taylor's every word.

Rolling her eyes, Liz sighed with disdain. "I can't begin to guess Taylor. Let me see, you got married, dyed your hair blue, no wait you tattooed your forehead? Knowing you there's no limit, so just tell me already!" Frustration spewing with her every word.

Though their relationship had never been based on much beyond matching strands of DNA, Taylor longed to bond with her big sister in every opportunity possible. Though her heart was in the right place, Taylor knew deep within her soul that what little they shared was most likely all they ever would. In all her thirty years, never had Liz yielded and still Taylor hadn't ever grown accustomed to her sister's inability to get excited about most anything in her life.

"I bought that motorcycle I've wanted since I was eight, can you believe it?" Taylor's heart soared as she paced back and forth across the soft cream carpet in her living room, brushing off her sister's discouraging tone.

A long stretch of silence hung between them before Liz spoke once again. "Really? Well I hope you don't kill yourself on it, we need you here you know!" Shrugging the phone between her ear and shoulder Liz wet a bar towel in the sink, kneeling to wipe up the salt melting on the still damp floor beneath her feet.

Saddened, Taylor shook her head, sucking in a long deep breath, attempting to suppress her frustration. The familiar sound of Liz's earring clanking against the phone agitated Taylor even more. This being Liz's signature inattentive move, signaling she was truly uninterested in anything Taylor had to say and was most likely no longer listening. Once again she had put herself into such a disappointing, no win situation. Rolling her eyes, she subconsciously scolded herself. Meandering down the hallway toward her bedroom, Taylor laid back onto the bed sighing, searching for the right words to reach Liz on some level.

"Taylor hold on, Toby's here. Why don't you tell him your big news?" She said sarcastically, before roughly shoving the phone into Toby's hand. "I don't have time for this," Liz huffed under her breath, "I have a restaurant to run."

The muffled handoff reignited the flutter of excitement Liz had nearly extinguished. Taylor knew her little brother would definitely join in on the celebration.

"What's the big news kiddo?" Toby asked excitedly, sparking a new wave of ardor within her.

Taylor stood, moving down the hall again as she began explaining the details of her new street bike. "Can you believe it Tob? I finally did it! I bought my dream bike after all these years. I am so excited, I can't wait to take her out!" Taylor's voice cracking at the mere thought.

"You did what? You bought yourself a motorcycle! That's fantastic Tay, I'm so excited for you! Hey, now when we go to the coast I can actually take a real woman, not my pipsqueak twenty-six year old sister on the back of my bike." Their shared laughter warmed Taylor's heart. Possessing such a special friendship meant the world to her.

Smiling, she cleared her throat trying to act tough. "Last time I checked I am a 'real woman', even if I'm petite, thank you very much! And might I add, you never complained before when we traveled together young man," withholding a giggle behind her feigned brusque tone.

"That's because you look so darn fine in those leathers. Having you with me always seems to get the women drooling over me. I appear to be more of a challenge I suppose." Toby offered smugly grinning.

"Oh I get it, the truth is out. You used me as your chick bait did you? Well now you can troll alone like the rest of the single biker boys. I am officially out of your hair big guy." Though joking, Taylor felt a pang of sadness deep inside for the changes her independence would bring. Riding together had afforded them many priceless memories, times she'd forever cherish... adventures she would never forget.

"Let's not put words in my mouth now, that's not the only reason and you know it sis. I loved our times on my bike. You're a fantastic passenger, and an even better riding companion. This however, is awesome news for you girl. Congratulations again!" Toby's love for Taylor exuded from his every word.

The sound of glass breaking echoed through the phone, followed by loud waves of shouting.

"What was that Toby, are you guys alright?" Taylor's stomach flipped hearing such cacophony.

"Hold on sis, there is a fight breaking out on top of the pool tables. I'll be right back, don't go anywhere!"

Before she could reply the receiver banged against bar. Taylor could hear Toby yelling over the rowdy crowd, as they egged on the angered men. Pleased that she always seemed to miss the boisterous nights at work, she smiled to herself.

Moments passed before the sound of the phone being picked up pulled her from day dreaming of the cruises she would take on her beautiful machine. Being on a bike satiated her with the deepest sense of utter freedom; such immense satisfaction she had found nowhere else. A profound peace flowed through her when she was on two wheels. The truth that when she rode she was somehow closer to God filled her with such a deep sense of exhilarating liberty, freedom, and serenity.

"Hello. Is anyone still there?" The deep warmth of an unfamiliar male voice on the other end streamed through the line, strangely filling her belly full of fluttering butterflies.

"Yes, I'm here." Unwarranted chills washed over her as she spoke. "I take it Toby isn't done with bouncing the trouble out just yet?" Taylor replied casually, disguising the thrill of hearing this mystery man's chocolaty smooth voice.

"Not to intrude, but did I over hear that you bought a new bike?" Genuine interest flowing from his words.

How could it be that this stranger was truly interested in hearing her news without even knowing her name? Utterly shocked she stammered, swallowing hard. "You did, I did, I mean, yes." Her palms suddenly felt clammy, her heart pounding wildly within her chest. Confused as to how this stranger could evoke such reactions through telephone lines with merely a few words, Taylor searched for a sensible reply. "I'm sorry, but do I know you?" She inquired trying her best not to come across overtly suspicious.

"I don't believe so, I just noticed the phone still lying there on the bar and figured you must be wondering if anyone was coming back to hear more of your exciting news. With the ruckus stealing your sunshine, I took the liberty. I hope you don't mind," his soulful warmth pouring through the line.

Confused over her unexpected responses to this stranger, Taylor continued. "Not at all, actually it seems I might have been waiting for quite a while. I probably would have hung up soon anyway. I guess you saved me from celebrating alone."

"Good, I'm glad to hear it because I am beginning to enjoy myself for the first time all night," his immense tone altering slightly, revealing a softer, ever more magnanimous dimension.

This stranger seemed to possess a natural gift for twisting her up inside. Though unsure how to proceed, she too was finding their conversation quite enjoyable.

"I really hoped that you were still waiting on the line once I made my stealth over the counter maneuver to snag the phone," he said laughing under his breath.

Taylor's stomach flipped in hearing his words echo in her head, a flush of warmth washed across her cool skin. Who was this man? What power was this that he had to evoke such feelings from her with so little as a few seconds over the phone?

"I'm Garrett by the way, Garrett Larkin," he said, as if he had read her mind. "I started riding in my grandfather's side car when I was barely even tall enough to see over the windscreen. Motorcycles have been a passion that seeped deep into my core that very first ride. In an instant I was hooked. The mention of a bike and I tuned in, though it might seem that I was eaves dropping. I guess that proves I'm truly obsessed. So much so that I owned a motorcycle before I ever sat behind the wheel of a car. I suppose you might say it was destiny for it to have grasped my soul so deeply and to have stuck with me so after all these years."

Garrett's sated depth swirled through the phone lines mesmerizing Taylor. His answers flowing with such open truth, a welcoming rarity of effortless conversation, bringing nothing underhanded and/or pretentious. His raw intensity took Taylor's breath. Such an unexpected turn of events had her reeling. Life always seemed to have a way of perpetually keeping her on her toes, this experience being no exception.

"And you, what name did your parents grace you with?" Garrett inquired with a colorful spark in his voice.

In all the wonderment of this mysterious man and his intriguing ways, offering her name had escaped her. "They called me Taylor my first day and it kind of stuck," she answered feeling quite the fool, "my grandfather was my name sake actually. Appropriately, as he was my favorite human being. He still is, though he passed on years ago," she answered laying back onto her sofa. Tugging a chenille throw from the back of the couch she slipped her legs beneath it, pulling it up under her chin. "When I was little I was teased a lot for having a boy's name, but I have grown to love it. Besides what's in a name, right? If I can ride a motorcycle, then certainly I can sport a boy's name."

Hearing Garrett chuckle made her smile. No one had ever fully appreciated the under-current of humor dwelling within her. What was this all about? Where did he come from, this friendly, intelligent, interesting man waltzing into her life as if from a dream, stirring up emotions she had long ago laid to rest? Just who did he think he was being so kind, so real, so interested, so, so, wonderful? Her head spun with thoughts

16

and feelings she hadn't allowed herself in so long that she barely recognized them for what they truly were.

The conversation turned to their favorite areas to ride, where they would like to travel, favorite people, love, loss, life and all that it entails. Time slipped by and before either noticed Liz had yelled out 'last call'. Momentary silence fell between them at the realization that they had been on the phone nearly three hours.

Stunned, Garrett cleared his throat. "I guess I should get going and let you get back to whatever you might have had planned, now that it's, well closing time and all," chuckling with embarrassment. "Thank you for the enjoyable evening. Finding you on the other end of the phone turned out to be quite a lovely surprise."

Taylor smiled, pleased that he shared in this feeling. She hesitated, sad for the evening to have passed so quickly. "It's been my pleasure Garrett. And with all the commotion I doubt anyone even noticed the phone being tied up," Taylor paused before continuing, "thank you for sharing in the excitement of my new toy with me. It was nice to have a fellow biker to celebrate the occasion with." Silence fell between them once again. Hesitating to say good bye, Taylor savored the moment knowing better than most, that times as sweet as these don't come along everyday… quite possibly ever.

"Taylor, if you are interested, there are a few of us taking an evening cruise up to the look out next Sunday. The ride would give you a chance to show off that new beauty of yours. That is, if you aren't already busy."

Squeezing her eyes closed, she sank deeper into her billowy couch, her face fully flushed. The mere thought of meeting Garrett face to face pleasured her heart with feverish thrill. Stammering she forced an answer. "I… um, I would love to. Where are you all meeting?" Beaming with elation that this would not be the last of their new found friendship, holding her breath in anticipation.

"We're meeting around five here at Donna's."

"Alright then, sounds like a date, I mean a plan," quickly correcting herself, her eyes popped open. "So I will see you then Garrett Larkin," Taylor answered, trying to play it cool, silently praying he hadn't realized she had said the 'D' word.

"Sweet dreams Taylor... until then." His velvety words spoken in hushed tones streaming through the line to her.

"Sweet dreams to you Garrett," she said softly in return, grinning. Laying the receiver down Taylor closed her eyes, replaying the night in her mind. The moments shared with Garrett had warmed her heart through and through. It had been so long since she had felt such intense energy from another, especially a man. Experiencing such tantalizing gratification between them, though having never met, made the thought of encountering him even more thrilling.

She had grown so tired of being judged by the male adaptation of a sexual sliding scale. Relationships based on appearances had misleading connotations that often made it difficult for Taylor to verily know a man outside the physical realm. Tonight had been refreshing. Their encounter renewed her spirit, even reopening the doors of endless possibilities. This mystery man had proved to Taylor there was still hope for her in the realistic continuum of intimate relationships. Acknowledging the possibility to reconnect with her most intimate self, to revive the dormant vessel she had become, brought overwhelming peace upon her. The opportunity to break free of the painful past she'd clung so tightly to, cleansing her soul of the heartache weighing heavy upon her spirit and be fully open to all awaiting her seemed all but a miracle. No more redesigning herself to meet impossible guidelines set upon her by childish men and their selfish motivations. Garrett liked the very heart of her just as she was, sight unseen... such a thrilling revelation.

Standing, Taylor yawned, stretching tall before laying the throw over the back of the couch, making her way down the hall to her bedroom. Undressing in the cast shadows of moonlight, she slipped between the sheets, snuggling bare skinned beneath the soft covers. Smiling to herself she envisioning Garrett doing the same, imagined the line of his face, the curve of his shoulder, his shape beneath the sheet, the rhythm of his breathing nearly audible. Taylor let her imagination carry her off. Holding fast to every word they had shared, she tucked the details into the recesses of her soul.

Something had changed in her this night. Somehow Garrett had broken through the walls she had so effectively built up. This stranger had awakened her from the emotional coma she'd wandered about in for so many years. The mere thought of letting a man in once again made her skin crawl, until tonight… until Garrett. Taylor ran the night over again in her mind as she slipped into the sacred space of dreaming.

Chapter Two

Anticipation often casts a wicked spell, this being no exception. The moments of each day seemed to drag on forever, leaving Taylor to wonder if the rally with Garrett would simply never arrive. Washing and polishing her bikes' ivory paint nearly every day, it was a miracle she hadn't scrubbed the copper flames clean off. The wonderment of meeting this mysterious new acquaintance continuously building with every breath. She found herself cruising main most evenings when not putting in a shift at Donna's. Those moments spent stretching the engines legs along the out skirts of their sleepy little town helped clear her mind, helped to somehow make the seemingly endless days more tolerable, if only temporarily.

Sunday dawned with a glorious fiery fuchsia sky as the sun ascended into the clearest azure blue glory. Dew drops glistened on the tips of the frosted green pine needles like diamonds, misty sunbeams streaming through the bows of the trees in pearly ribbons. Bird song filling the air, the fresh scent of damp earth and fragrant flowers awakening the senses.

Taylor awoke with increased longing to soak it all in. A quick cup of coffee before a long walk to try and clear her head. Reminiscing once more over the lovely time shared talking with Garrett she daydreamed of how his eyes might sparkle when he laughed, how the corner of his mouth might curl, if he had dimples or even a cleft in his chin. She imagined the feel of his hands, the scent of his skin. Shaking her head she stopped mid stride, clearing her mind of any further thoughts. "Get a grip girl!" Shaking her head, laughing. Saving herself from any further torture, she headed home to shower.

Making her way to town she tended to the list of errands she'd bartered Liz for so that she could have the evening free to finally meet her mystery man. Scanning the list of stops she organized a plan to tackle the near overwhelming manifest. One by one she made her way through the list, fueled by the sweet anticipation of the night ahead.

Arriving at her last stop, Taylor opened the hatch on her SUV squeezing in the cart load of supplies before pressing the button, watching it close. Walking the cart back to the store front she felt a sudden chill. Folding her arms over her chest she smoothed her hands over her elbows trying to shake it off. 'What is this? I cannot be cold, it's ninety degrees out. I'm sweating for goodness sakes!' Taylor thought, trying to brush it off as if it hadn't happened. Quickly opening the car door, she slipped inside, pulling it closed behind her. Pressing the key into the ignition something caught her eye. Fluttering across her windshield were the most exquisite butterflies she had ever seen. Snow white pearlized wings glistened in the sunlight as the two of them danced across the glass stretched before her. Mesmerized she sat staring, entranced in holy reverence of the vibrantly spectacular beauty of the moment.

Suddenly remembering her favorite bedtime story of the snowy white butterflies that her father would tell her as she huddled beneath her covers just before she'd slip off to sleep.

'The snowy butterflies will forever watch over you sweet girl, just as mommy and daddy will.'

Though she couldn't recall the rest of the story, his words resonated as she watched stunned. Twirling up into the air above her, circling one another, they danced round and round vanishing suddenly as mystically as they had arrived. Had it merely been a figment of her imagination, or had this been some kind of sign?

'Mom, dad... was that you?' She whispered. Her mind searching still yet for some semblance of comprehension.

Pulling her cell phone from the console, her trembling fingers typed the number for Donna's, desperately needing to touch base with reality. She needed to speak with her family, she needed Toby and Liz.

"Donnas' Place, Toby speaking."

Hearing her little brother's voice brought forth a wave of emotions rushing from the depths of her soul. Unable to control herself, she felt her eyes sting with tears. Struggling to find a way to express to him what had just happened, her mind growing more confused with every passing second. Swallowing hard, quickly wiping her tears away, praying Toby wouldn't notice the tidal wave of emotions brewing, she cleared her throat before speaking.

"Hey little brother, I'm heading back. Do you need anything that's not on my list?" Garnering a weak attempt to mask the unexpected onset of emotions stirring within, refraining from the mention of the true purpose behind her call.

"I think we all are set girl. Your voice sounds kind of strange, is everything alright Tay?" Toby's honest concern melted her heart. They'd always shared a much deeper bond than simply being siblings, somehow always knowing if the other was in need or hurting. God had blessed them with the depth of connection twins have been said to possess, for this she was exceptionally grateful.

"Do you recall the bedtime story that dad used to tell us?"

"You mean the tale of the snowy white butterflies? Sure Tay, why? What on earth made you think of that?"

"I will explain it later Tob." Taylor pulled it together momentarily, hoping to disguise the unexplainable surge of melancholy stiring beneath.

"You sure everything is alright sis?" Toby questioned her once again.

"Everything is great. Are you kidding, I have date with my motorcycle and the moon tonight, life doesn't get any better than that big guy." A sense of calm washed over her with the reminder of the enterprising night to come.

"And with a handsome mystery man no less. You can't have forgotten that my darling sister." Toby teased in a low whispery tone, offering a weak attempt to sound sexy.

"Yes, and especially that, though I don't want to get my hopes up too much. Just because we can talk on a phone for hours on end doesn't mean we are going to ride off hand in hand into the sunset, though that would be exceptionally nice," pausing she savored the thought of how many wonderful ways the night could truly unfold. "I will see you when I get there then, love you kiddo." Trying to hide the truth raw that she secretly wished they would stay on the line even a moment longer, she said goodbye. An unexpected wave of insecurity had her feeling ever more uneasy. She hadn't felt this since the day her mother had passed. The reality of such offering even more restlessness.

"Love you sis, see you in a bit," Toby said quickly, hanging up before she could stop him.

Squeezing her eyes tightly shut, she slumped in her seat with her cell phone still pressed to her ear. 'Pull it together woman, what is the matter with you? There's a great night on the books and here you are in such a state,' Taylor attempted to talk herself back to reality as she turned the key over, pulling the shifter into drive. Heading toward the highway she did her best to push out the looming cloud of apprehension hanging over her.

Suddenly, Taylor noticed that traffic seemed heavier than usual, even more so than it had earlier in the day. Realizing that in all her anticipation of the night she'd forgotten it was a holiday weekend. Heavy traffic and plenty of road congestion was to be expected with town being such a fairway to several tourist draws.

Rounding the curve of Haley's corner she noticed the seemingly endless line of cars in front of her quickly slowing. On such a busy weekend it was likely there'd been an accident ahead. Worry played on her mind, what if the delay made her late for her big plans? What if she missed meeting Garrett after all the day's anticipation? Reaching for her cell phone she froze, recalling there was no way for her to contact him, as they'd not exchanged numbers. Then as quickly as it had slowed, traffic proceeded to pick back up. Shaking it off, she breathed in a deep breath, pressing on.

Before she knew it she was headed toward Miller's Grade. Applying the gas slightly in anticipation of the hill, tightening her grip on the steering wheel, she felt the shift of the transmission beneath her. A quick glance at the continuous row of cars behind her then back to the car just in front of her, when her eyes caught sight of an eighteen wheeler speeding down the grade. The roving truck floated back and forth over the center line as if no one were driving. Before Taylor could blink the semi struck the compact car in front of her just in back of the driver's door. Chunks of jagged fiberglass erupted like popcorn three feet above the tiny car, an unconscious woman momentarily visible through the gaped open driver's door. Her limp body dangling from the ravaged car, flailing as it spun, then vanishing from sight behind the massive trailer.

Taylor's mind began assessing how she could possibly help the driver in the car. Imagining that the truck driver would most likely over correct and fly off the opposite embankment, she pondered that he might need even more attention. Her head filled with endless scenarios, when in a flash the horror of the inevitable pulled her back to reality. The truck, still barreling toward her offered no attempt to steer away. The raw truth starring her in the eye... she was next.

The massive truck grill filled her windshield, her eyes glued to the horrified truck driver's pale face staring down upon her. His boney white knuckles clinching the steering wheel, braced with terror.

Taylor's thoughts turned to those she'd leave behind, all the wasted time, the things she so longed to say and do, but hadn't. Silently she mourned her unfinished life... Garrett.

A sudden screaming of subconscious filled her mind, 'relax, you have to relax!' With no place to go she dropped her hands to the bottom of the steering wheel, moved her foot from the brake pedal, drawing in a long slow breath as she felt the monstrous truck plow through her SUV.

The explosive concussion of impact ripped all four of her tires from their rims at once. Lurching forward her teeth crammed into the steering wheel. Her face and neck suddenly set a-fire with an intense stinging sensation, quickly followed by the blasting force of the airbag smacking her face, throat and chest with the velocity of a baseball bat then quickly deflating. Within seconds the SUV was air born. The intensity of reverberating explosive inertia shattering all the driver's side windows. Such tremendous side force fracturing the windshield into a sagging, crackled web. Millions of glass shards filled the air within the cab. Slivers of debris peppering Taylor head to toe with fiery stinging.

Unable to grasp the reality of what was happening she squinted, trying her very best to remain emotionally focused. Suddenly blue sky shone through her obscured view from the windshield. With a sudden pivot the SUV jolted, violently flipping over, abruptly landing hard on its tail before careening down the rocky cliff below. As obstinate as a derailed roller coaster, the crumpled heap heaved into several consecutive flips. Taylor's already tender flesh set afire with the pelting of rocks, dirt and continuous unpredictable waves of even more splintered glass. Waves of shrapnel repeatedly raining upon her bleeding flesh with each flip. The heap of supplies she carried pummeling her head like rocks in an avalanche, splitting her lip, her eye brow, blackening her eye. With one last end over end spiraling flip the SUV slammed with a heavy heave to the earth, abruptly landing on its top. Fiery pain shot through her side and into her arm. Dizzied by the whirlwind, she tried to focus, her head still spinning.

Taylor fought to ignore the screaming taunts of her mind, trying with all her might to quiet the looming fear that this unimaginable horror might be her final resting place. The daunting reality that at any moment she might draw her last breath. A flash in her mind of all the markers lining the highway. The dozens of wooden crosses; remembrances of those lost in just this manner brought bile rising in her throat. Each hot ragged breath forced from her lungs sending inconceivably all-consuming pain shooting through her constricted torso. From the fiery heat of her throbbing ribs, blood bubbled forth, trickling its way to her face, filling her nose. Spewing the blood forth she tried to turn to investigate the culprit. Stunned, she found herself unable to move, she was pinned, utterly confined to the wreckage. Taylor glanced around with limited range, realizing her hair was stretched taught to the scalp. Somehow it had been sucked through the shattered web of the windshield and now lay burred beneath the rubble of her SUV.

Something glimmered in a tiny beam of light streaming through the shattered glass window, catching Taylor's eye. Protruding from her left arm, a large shard of glass was plunged clear through, rendering it useless. Straining she scanned her broken body, seeing the window regulator arm impaled deep beneath the shredded flesh of her chest. Her ragged breathing proof of her shattered ribs twisted her stomach into knots. With each shallow breath blood continued to gurgle from her side. Doing her best to stay calm, to simply focus on staying present in her own head, steadying the rhythm of her shallow breathing.

From out of the deafening silence the deployment of her airbag had allotted, Taylor heard angelic singing drifting closer and closer. Once again acrid bile rose in her throat at the reality of angel's song growing nearer by the second. Choking on the forced acceptance that her time on earth quite possibly was over, her stomach sank.

Before she had a moment more to assess her own viability, someone began violently rocking the wreckage of her SUV. Momentarily unable to speak, her limp body swayed painfully in the constraints of her safety belt. No longer at her waist, having nearly slipped from it in the midst of the violent flips, the safety strap tugged at her bruised thighs. Powerless she dangling upside down like a rag doll as the strangers repeatedly rocked her. Knowing she had to stop them, Taylor sucked in as much air as she could muster. Then let out a single, barely audible warbled cry. "Please stop, you are going to kill me!" Squeezing her eyes tight. "Please God stop them, please!" She prayed. Within seconds the rocking stilled.

"She's alive! I can hear her praying! Hey, we need help down here, we have a live one!" The stranger's voice echoing up the canyon lovelier than a lullaby, taking her mind from the angelic voice still beckoning her. Taylor held her breath fighting back tears, relieved that help would soon arrive. "Thank you God, thank you, thank you, thank you!" She said aloud, grateful her desperate pleas had been heard.

"There's someone still alive in there?" Yet another voice called from outside the crumpled door. But they had better hurry, there's smoke!"

The stranger's tormenting words plunged through her already fragile psyche. 'Smoke!!! Where there's smoke...' Repeating the words in her mind Taylor's heart skipped a beat. Panic shot through her ravaged body. So desperately she wanted to claw her way from this twisted tomb.

The feel of a warm hand on her ankle shook her back to reality. Just then Taylor realized she could feel something poking her. Stickers were shoved into her sandal. She could feel that her foot had somehow found its way through the window and now lay in the three feet tall weeds surrounding the wreckage. Taylor expelled a ragged sigh of relief, silently celebrating that she wasn't paralyzed.

The angelic summoning grew louder still with each moment. Holding her breath, awaiting impending doom.

"We're down here, we need help!" With that the stranger moved his hand from her ankle, taking hold of her fingers, his voice wavering with fear. "Hang on Miss, help is on its way, just stay with me, just stay awake."

Such kindness comforted her. Squeezing his fingers as tightly as she could muster, trying not to move, fearing her back might be broken Taylor held as still as she could. The reality hitting her hard. One wrong turn and she may never walk again; God forbid never ride again.

"We're getting help for you, they're on the way, just stay very still," the man said laying down on his stomach in the tall weeds to get a better look inside the wreckage. Releasing Taylor's hand, he reached in and turned the key off and with that the angel song ceased. In an instant Taylor realized it had been Madeleine Peyroux on her stereo summoning her all along, not heavenly beings. Calm filled her weary body, sighing a breath of relief she mustered a smile, hopeful her time on earth hadn't come to its end quite yet.

"They're hurrying as fast as they can Miss, hang in there we are going to get you out of here, I promise," the kind stranger took her hand once again, pressing her cold fingers to the warmth of his palm.

Sucking in another ragged breath, her pleas just above a whisper. "Please call my brother, he's waiting for me. Toby won't know where I am, he'll be so worried! Please call him... Donna's Place," Taylor said, mustering all the strength she could through the blood clotting in her throat. Tears pooled in her eyes, mixing with blood, tinting her vision with rose hue.

Waves of harsh unnatural crunching accompanied by excruciating pain beneath her skin seemed to worsen with each new breath. The true extent of her injuries began to set in as her once adequate numbing levels of adrenaline began

29

wearing thin. The fear of paralysis began to taunt her frazzled mind once again. Followed by haunting thoughts of never knowing the pleasure of meeting her mystery man, of never again feeling the pulse of the road passing beneath her, Taylor's head spun with 'what ifs'. The fear of never feeling the buffeting wind moving against her body again, the thrill of the speed, the perfect ecstasy of harnessing such power. Was it possible that she would simply die here alone in the confines of this crumpled heap, covered in dirt, glass, and weeds; splattered with gore and never have the chance to love again? The horror of it all came crashing in around her as she helplessly hung there, awaiting her fate.

Taylor's heart sank at the mortifying reality that they may have to cut her hair off to free her from the wreckage. After losing a bet with her father she'd agreed to grow her hair for three years, vowing to never cut it again after he died.

Blood gurgled rhythmically with her breathing, trickling in an even wider path, now flowing over her chin and more profusely into her nose and eyes. Worry taunted her that if this continued she might possibly drown in her own blood. Squeezing her eyes closed, she prayed for strength. Grasping for even a tiny bit of reality, struggling to stay conscious. 'Why do I merely call upon you when I'm in dire straits Lord? I'm sorry. I trust you, whatever you have ahead for me... I trust that you are in charge. Thank you Lord. In Jesus name, Amen.' Calm washed over her, offering a moment of refuge from the calamity at hand.

Time ticked on... an eternity seemed to have passed when the glorious thumping of helicopter blades closed in, circling above. A sudden rustling in the surrounding weeds pulled her from her thoughts. Help had finally arrived and she was still alive. Biting her stinging lower lip, she fought off a wave of torrid emotions. The stranger squeezed her fingers once more. Taylor strained to see out the corner of her blood filled eyes.

"My brother found the phone number and called Toby," the stranger's words filled her with relief. "He's in touch with dispatch and will be meeting you at the hospital. Can you understand me?" Peering inside the SUV, he met her eyes.

"Thank you so very much. God bless you."

The stranger squeezed her hand one last time, smiling shyly before slipping away.

With a startling crack, a large shard of windshield was pulled down. The air soon after filled with chatter emitting from the rescue teams radios as they began to assess their excavation plan. A shielded face peered through the newly made hole in the windshield, momentarily staring at Taylor.

"I know it's bad. I'm not sure, but I think my back may be broken and my hair is caught in the glass. I think it's under the car." Hoarse whispers spewing forth. "Please... please save it if you can. If I don't make it I want to look a little like myself for my family's sake," pleading, Taylor's voice caught in her throat. Her dark brown eyes misting over at the thought of being buried battered, torn and bald; barely a resemblance of her former self.

"I'll do my best," the deep melody of his voice somehow bestowing peace in the midst of the chaos. Laying his gloved hand gently on her bruised shoulder, he met her eyes through his face shield silently offering reassurance before he began hastily digging clods of dirt from under the sunroof. Grateful for the gesture she closed her eyes again focusing on the soothing rhythm of her rescuers breathing.

Within seconds another fireman lay beside her just outside, peering through the twelve by fifteen inch hole in the driver's side window, half buried in thistle and foxtails.

"We are going to take you out of the side here Miss. I need you to stay as still as you can. Just relax and try to breathe normal. Air Rescue is setting down just up the canyon. Once we clear you from the wreckage we will take you to the helicopter by hand. Do you understand what I am telling you?" The fireman's confidence exuding hope.

Taylor shook her head, confirming that she understood before he moved from her view again. Returning her attention to the rescuer working diligently to free her hair, she winced aloud in pain.

"Can you tell me your name?" The warm depth of his voice resonated through her agony, helping her to refocus.

"Taylor." The harsh graveled sound of her fragile voice seemed somehow foreign to her.

The digging ceased momentarily, before he continued ever more feverishly to free her hair. The second fireman resumed making small talk with her, offering a much needed distraction from the situation at hand. "Can you tell me the date Taylor?" He asked, attempting to keep her preoccupied.

Taylor searched her memory, but nothing formulated. "I can't seem to remember."

"That's alright, just relax, we're almost there." The first fireman huffed, continuing to dig frantically beneath her.

After much effort her hair was freed. Reaching inside the wreckage he gently laid the tangled web beside her, smiling as he once again softly touched her shoulder.

"Thank you for your kindness," she said in a garbled hush, wincing as the expended energy brought worsening waves of sharp emanating pain.

His kind smile, though barely visible beneath the face shield, warmed her shivering core, soothing her soul.

"You're more than welcome Taylor," his smooth voice so familiar, so comforting, had her mysteriously mesmerized.

Momentarily he slipped from view, just as the end of a back board was snaked through the small hole in the side of the SUV. "Alright, here we go Miss. Let's get you out of here," the second rescuer said, peering in to her once more.

Before she could think her safety belt was cut and several hands braced her head, neck, and hips as they slowly lowered her to the headliner of the twisted cocoon. The sweet man that had freed her hair placed his gloved hands through the shattered windshield once again, holding her head firmly he strapped a wide Velcro band across her forehead, then carefully slipping a rigid plastic brace around her neck, securing it with much care. Shielding her eyes he finished stripping away the remaining sheath of shattered glass from the windshield. Leaning in above her, laying his arm softly across her tender body, he cleared from the remaining tangled web of the restraints. Shivering beneath the heat of his breath falling on her cold damp cheeks, the warmth sending chills racing over her ravaged flesh.

"Here we go. On one, two, three!" With numerous hands about she was lifted again, then gently slid onto the unyielding rigidity of a backboard. Moving from the interior he stepped around the side taking the head of the litter.

"Ready, again on one, two, three!" With his command she was lifted once more and they began the rigorous ascent out of the rocky ravine. Focusing on his face, she tried to push the excruciating pain from her mind as they negotiated the aggressive terrain. His kind eyes, the loveliest shade of golden olive green. Dark brown wisps of sweat soaked hair escaping his helmet lay against his sun kissed neck. Though unable to see his face in all, she knew he was most handsome. 'Perfect timing Taylor, guys like this are all but extinct, unless of course your elbow deep in dirt and weeds, bathed in your own blood, splattered in glass and hanging on to life by a thread.' Her mind taunting her. 'Why is it that my timing is always off?' she thought, sighing.

A warm smile stretched across his face as he lifted his shield. His dreamy gaze met hers once they'd reached level ground, before continuing the remainder of the haul. "We're nearly there," he said confidently offering her much needed assurance.

She tried her best not to stare, but there was something familiar about this man, something so very comforting and somehow heartwarming. The undeniable feeling that she had known him before, had her mind reeling.

"Hang in there, we'll get you on your way as fast as possible."

His kindred spirit tugging at her heart. Though Taylor was nearly positive she had never seen this man before, she felt mysteriously drawn to him. As a moth to a flame she was entranced, utterly captivated.

A sudden blast of air pushed hard against them. From the corner of her eye she spotted the Air Life copter standing at the ready just ahead. Watching as the pilot and two females sporting blue flight suits hurried to her side pushing along a chrome rolling liter. The pilot set the brake with his boot as the back board beneath her was laid over top of the rolling gurney and strapped down. The team lifted her with a heavy jolt setting the wheeled legs below the liter to a higher position. Once the brake was released they were rolling quickly toward the heavy buffeting of the whirling blades.

"Just a little further, we are almost there. It's going to be a bit rough here for a second Taylor, just try to stay relaxed as best you can," his sincere kindness cutting through the excruciating pain. Holding fast to his words kept her from losing the final strand of her composure.

The quickened movements furthered the crunching, pain ridden fury raging within her body, bringing with it nausea and dizziness. Barely holding on to consciousness, reeling in silent torture, repeating his kind words over and over in her head. 'Just a little further... almost there'.

A crowd of onlookers had gathered along the road. Aggressive news people screaming out vulgar questions of alcohol being involved with the accident summoned qualm from deep within her belly. Squeezing her eyes closed, she said a prayer, silently willing it all away. A line of highway patrol worked to hold off the crowd as they approached the helicopter. Powerful turbulence pushed off the choppers blades blasting her, making it nearly impossible to keep her eyes closed as the doors of the air ambulance swung open.

"They have you from here Taylor. Be strong. God speed." Squeezing her hand one last time, he stepped from the group ushering her into the helicopter. With a heavy heave from behind, her weary body was transferred into place, sending fierce waves of stifling pain shooting through her. The doors slammed shut abruptly, violently jolting her. Fighting tears she turned her eyes to the side window. There stood her fireman just beyond the aircraft, helmet in hand. In the chaos of the moment their eyes locked, time slowed to a crawl. His kind gaze offering unspoken courage. Sending her away with a slow wave and a concerned smile he watched unmoving as she lifted from the ground. Closing her eyes once more, attempting to hold fast to the moment... to him standing there, wanting never to forget those eyes.

During the thirty minute ride to the trauma hospital Taylor listened intently to the seemingly endless diatribe of vitals and probable injuries being called in by the medic on board. The morbid details of the accidents aftermath filling her mind, nearly overwhelming her. Attempting to silence the noise, she slipped away subconsciously, drawing on the moments her hero had extended such needed comfort. Dwelling on the peace he'd brought her amidst the utter horror; the internal strength her firefighter had offered in such a harsh time of absolute helplessness. What kindness and compassion he had shown her, though she was no more than a stranger. If she made it out of this alive, Taylor vowed there and then to find him and thank him for being her saving grace at the utmost critical of times.

Suddenly dizzied, she moaned at the sight of two brilliant pearly snow white butterflies fluttering about the helicopter. Her vision narrowed, then in a flash she blacked out, slipping into the silent abyss of unconsciousness.

A tiny effervescent pearl appeared in the vast darkness. Growing nearer she realized the pearly apparition stirred inside with movement, a movie of sorts playing upon its shimmering shell. Seeing herself taking her very first steps, then as a toddler standing on her daddy's feet as he moved with the music. Then seeing herself on the first day of school, her first dance, first kiss and that long awaited day of pulling the family car from the driveway all on her own. The pearly globe dimmed then once again brightened with the sight of Taylor riding against the wind, dressed in full leathers seated on her bike, a smile stretched across her face. In her rearview mirror she spotted a dark rider close behind. Moving along the curve of the highway they rode. Following behind he moved in close, swaying through the turns, perfectly in sync with her as they traveled along. Her heart swelled with joy as her dream carried them away from reality, further and further into the mountains. With a sudden burst of power the dark figure opened the throttle, quickly passing her. Turning to look over his shoulder at her, he offered the warmest smile, nodding before speeding into the far distance leaving her all alone on the deserted road.

Taylor felt a sudden throng of pain, ripped from her sweet dream, she was conscious once again. Faced with the ever mounting intensity of agony she lay motionless, wishing she had been left to follow the mysterious man into the horizon. A single tear trickling down her cheek at the thought of the harrowing journey ahead.

Chapter Three

Gasping, Taylor was awakened further by waves of intense pain racing through her as she was slid with the backboard onto an emergency room bed, completely shocked at the manic buzz of people surrounding her. Alarmingly bright lights hung in circular fixtures above her, illuminating her body like spot lights. The crew of twenty masked, scrub laden attendants poked and prodded her battered body as if she were a science project. Leaving her strapped to the table, they proceeded to stab her with multiple needles, cutting her clothes from her bloody body, leaving her fully exposed, all the while violating her every orifice. None of the masked humans seeming to notice she was fully aware of their evasive invasion, and if so certainly none seemed to care. Bedside manners had no place here. Such insensitive humiliation frazzled her, leaving her ever more frustrated than the persistently mounting pain. The sudden ringing of an alarm alerted across the emergency room, immediately clearing the frenzied crowd around her. Closing her eyes she sighed, grateful for momentary peace.

"Well hello Taylor, it's so wonderful to see you awake, how are you feeling?" A petite dark haired nurse said as she leaned across her pulling a heavenly warm blanket over her nakedness.

"I, I'm alive." Taylor's parched lips stuck together, her right eye blurred with every blink, a murky pink fog clearing then seeping in once again.

"Well that is a start dear. You're a lucky lady to be here after what you've been through. Quite a blessing that you survived, someone upstairs was definitely watching over you." Making her way around the rolling bed, she gently tucked the blanket in around Taylor. "Are you warm enough? If not I can bring more heated blankets."

"Yes… please, more… please. I cannot … seem to… to, to get warm," Taylor stammered, struggling to move the words from her head to her mouth. Forming sentences had never before taken such effort and concentration.

"After all you've lived through it's to be expected my dear. I will be right back with more."

Alone again the reality of her damaged body brought crushing waves of insecurity. Taylor sunk into herself, wanting to disappear. Squeezing her eyes tightly closed, sending up a prayer as tears poured down her battered cheeks.

"Here you are my dear." The nurse layered three toasty-warm blankets atop her, tucking them snuggly against her. "Oh honey, I know it's a lot to take in right now, but you will get through this, I promise." Reaching for a tissue, she gently dabbed Taylor's cheeks, brushing away her tears. "Let's get you cleaned up a bit, alright?" The nurse said turning away, noticeably touched by Taylor's emotions.

Unable to muster a word Taylor smiled, knowing then she'd somehow survive this tormenting reality. Breathing through the excruciating pain ruminating within her every cell she tried to push past the ever present desire to cry out as the kind nurse wiped the layers of bloody debris from her face and neck. Spotting a tiny stream of fresh blood trickling from Taylor's eye the nurse held open her eyelid. "There's the little culprit. I wondered where that was coming from." The nurse spoke slowly, pulling the tiniest shard of glass from Taylor's eye.

"Thank you," she whispered, forcing a smile through quivering lips. "That's mu... much better."

"You have visitors waiting to see you." The nurse said smiling as she continued wiping the warm, damp cloth across Taylor's gritty cheeks.

"There she is," Toby's voice shot through her. "Can I touch her?" Pausing before approaching the bedside.

"Yes, just don't move her. Her spleen is still bleeding, we are trying to spare her surgery. If the blushing slows enough on its own we won't have to remove it, so the less movement the better. I can only allow you a moment. They will be repairing her arm and chest soon." Leaning over her, the nurse laid a corded button into her palm. "I'll be right over here, press this if you need anything." Ever so gently patting her arm she stepped away allowing Toby to move in closer.

"Well you sure know how to get attention sis." Toby forced a laugh, holding back tears. "You really scared us half to death you know." His eye's reddening more, leaning down he kissed her still bloody hand. "I couldn't live without you Tay. When the call came in I actually screamed at the guy, I called him a liar. It took a minute for me to accept that this wasn't just a cruel prank." Toby's voice wavered with emotion.

"He stayed with me until help came. I told hi…m you'd be worried." She labored with the words, the puncture in her lung still not fully closed making it difficult to catch her breath between words. "I… I am… so sorry," she stammered again, her eyes filling with tears.

"Stop it, don't be ridiculous! It's not like you wrecked on purpose. They arrested the guy that did this for drunk driving. From what they said he passed out at the wheel. They felt he would have kept on going if he hadn't lost two tires after running you both down. His sheer stupidity nearly took you away from us sis." Toby turned away wiping his tear streaked face on his sleeve. Sniffling he sucked in a ragged breath before meeting her red rimmed gaze again. "Thank God you are still here Taylor." Leaning over her, Toby ever so gently pressed his lips to her abrasion streaked forehead, then lifted her hand to his lips, gently laying it beside her before stepping back. Fidgeting he stuffed his hands into his pockets before speaking again. "I have to go, they'll only allow one of us to see you at a time. Liz is out in the hall waiting, but I will see you again real soon okay Tay?" Shifting uncomfortably he took another step back. "I love you so very much, stay strong girl." With that he blew her a kiss, quickly turning he covered his face with his hands, walking briskly out of her line of sight before losing his composure.

Taylor swallowed hard hearing the effects of her situation on her little brother. Not only had the ramifications of that truck drivers poor decisions devastatingly affected her very existence, but those she loved as well.

"You already had the day off, you really didn't need to do this Tay." Liz joked sheepishly, offering a poor attempt at humor.

The fact that Liz never gave up trying to be humorous intrigued her. Though this was neither the time nor place, she understood Liz's intension offering a smile none the less.

"I'm... so very... sorry sis." Sucking in another breath she pushed the words forth. "I... had no... nowhere to, to go. He was there... before I could... think. Cliffs... either... side." Blood began gurgling from her side once more as she strained, forcing the words from her heavy chest.

Watching the blood seep through Taylor's blankets Liz shivered. "Shhh, silly girl, I am just teasing you. I am so glad you are alive, I love you." Liz cleared her throat, stepping aside for the nurse.

"I hate to break up the party, but the plastic surgeon is here Taylor. Once she's sewn up and there's a bed available we will be moving her from the emergency room into ICU, then you'll be able to visit more freely." The nurse turned her face to Liz, moving the large light directly over the top of her as she spoke. "She's in very capable hands. I promise to take the best care." Offering kind words as she ushered Liz away.

"We aren't going anywhere sis, Toby and I are right outside, we will see you in a little bit, okay? We love you." Liz's voice cracked, her eyes filling with emotionally charged tears. Quickly waving, she turned hurrying away before Taylor could find words.

Taylor hadn't been prepared for Liz to show so much affection. Such love from her sister brought a new wave of unexpected, thought provoking emotions. Tears burning her eyes once again, as the surgeon moved a rolling stainless steel tray of surgical tools close beside her.

"I will need to clean the wounds before I can close you, this may take a while. Just try your best not to move," he said laying her black and purple arm across her breasts exposing the gaping hole in the side of her chest, further opening the shredded wounds on her upper arm, inhaling loudly as if to say he had his hands full. "I'm going to have to numb you first. You will feel a series of stings." His formal tone making her even more uncomfortable than the thought of all those fiery needles. She closed her eyes, thinking how nice it would be if only they all could have her nurse's disposition and sense of compassion.

The hours ticked away as she lay motionless. The sound of shrapnel falling into the metal tray as the surgeon dug out chunks of glass, rock and shards of metal from her pulverized flesh. Facing further fiery pain with dozens more numbing shots as the surgeon began the extensive process of stitching Taylor back together. Two miserable hours later he tied off the last layer of sutures, rinsing his work with saline, moving to clean the jagged tears in her neck and cheek. "I put in three layers, a total of one hundred and fifty stitches. You may have some nerve damage. Though the extent of permanent damage may not be apparent for quite a while, as some nerves may regenerate," he said flatly as he flushed the wounds, dabbing them dry before wrapping gauze bandaging around her arm. "The numbness will wear off in an hour or so. You may want to request pain reliever as soon as the first twinge starts. With multi-layer sutures there will be internal scarring that can sometimes restrict mobility. I'll suggest therapy to lessen the chances as soon as you are cleared by your doctors. Until then you may want to limit your activity to allow proper healing. Again, I suggest you get in to see a physical therapist as soon as your primary doctor will allow." His words cut as harshly as the shards that had left their mark, leaving Taylor reeling momentarily in the harsh truth.

"Thank you." Taylor managed as he was walking away, unsure if he even cared to hear.

"I heard what he said, but I sadly can't allow pain meds I hate to tell you dear." Her nurse stepped beside her again, brushing a chunk of bloody hair away from Taylor's swollen cheek. "With a spleen blushing like yours, there's a chance of increased bleeding with pain meds and we don't want to preclude that lung from continuing to close on its own either. I know you are quite uncomfortable, but meds would only cause more damage and impede your healing." Shrugging, the nurse offered a weak smile. "I'm so very sorry. We will do all we can to keep you as comfortable as possible, but for now this is all we are allowed. Time is your best friend at this point. You need plenty of rest and time to heal."

Taylor's heart filled with dread feeling the immense pangs of her nerves reawakening. The searing pain emanating from her freshly stitched wounds proved that this would be a very long haul. Weeping in silence at the reality of her awful predicament, the ugly truth weighing heavy upon her soul.

Ten hours passed while Taylor lay in partial traction, wracked with pain, tormented by repeated flashbacks. The explosive impact playing over and over in her head.

Taylor was nearing the eleventh hour in the emergency room when an ICU bed finally opened. The shifting, rolling and horrific bouncing that the journey to intensive care afforded, nearly broke her well before the elevator doors opened on the twentieth floor. Forty minutes of bed shifts, blanket exchanges and bandaging had her bruised body throbbing with her heartbeat. Multiple I.V. lines ran from her to numerous bags hung just above, likening her to Medusa. Sporting a classic pastel blue backless robe, along with the noteworthy ensemble of a nasal cannula, catheter bag and four cumbersome monitors rounded out Taylor's new fashion statement, the thought of which made her laugh.

Another hour passed before the door creaked closed, thankfully leaving her alone in the quiet of her private room. This day would forever be etched in her mind. This, the day that she lived beyond all odds, this day that she pushed past such overwhelming pain and torment. Her life had been difficult, but this experience had offered her realms beyond prior difficulty. Taylor had now lived through more than she might have ever believed possible. Until now there had been no proof to insure that she had been blessed with the courage to survive such aftermath. Never had she known the level of immense pain a body could endure, the depth of misery, the challenges of simply existing moment to moment. She wasn't one to complain or let others see her sweat, but this was near intolerable. She prayed that this wouldn't be her breaking point, though she wanted nothing more than to cry out in the midst of her misery, to simply give in to the insanity.

At each turn in the road Taylor had met the demands placed upon her with strength and vigor head on, but this day she wished she were not so alone on the journey. She longed for big strong hands to hold her and tell her that this too would pass and that she was still as lovely as ever, scars and all. She longed for someone to stay by her side through the night watching over her, a guardian angel sent just for her. She wanted nothing more than a man of her very own, that would care for her in times like this, love her through it all.

Drifting off, she replayed Garrett's comforting voice in her head. The echo of his laughter lulling her into a deep sleep she so needed, so desired. Dreams of him dancing upon her subconscious. The feel of his arms around her, his hand in hers, his warm breath on her skin took Taylor away from the painful trauma of her reality. His words filling her with joy, with precious, glorious serenity. Slipping further from her reality with every passing second, Taylor soaked in the glorious affection her dreams afforded.

Chapter Four

Time in ICU passed slower than Taylor thought possible. If she hadn't known better she would have sworn the clocks were moving in reverse. Every chance she had to rest had been interrupted by nurses, phlebotomists drawing blood, various people checking her blood pressure and temperature, among many other ghastly deeds. Countless unnecessary visits from unknown people accessing the rooms creaking cabinets, as well as several disruptions from janitors moping the floor had Taylor realizing there would be no rest for the weary here.

The frigid air pumping through the ceiling vent just above the bed had her chilled clear to the bone. The stale air, accompanied by the overwhelming scent of disinfectant had Taylor fighting off nausea. Seconds of momentary silence shattered by the haunting sounds of whimpering, moaning and often inhumane screaming erupting from the burn unit across the hall had her nerves frazzled. Taking in three hours of uninterrupted sleep in a week had her nearing insanity, often contemplating if she'd simply died and gone to Hell. The devastation upon her life began drawing her down to the depths of sinking darkness. The daily fight to remain grateful for this life wore on her very soul. Grasping for answers as to why she had to face such adversity, she prayed for clarity and understanding.

Though she'd been led to believe that she was allowed visitors, the reality that no one had been to see her tugged on her heart strings. She longed for a break in the monotony of monitors buzzing monitors... beeping and the constant spewing of her oxygen line. Most of all she longed for the company of her siblings. Taylor missed all of Liz's crazy quirks, and even her frustrating dissatisfaction with life. But she especially longed for Toby's sweet balance of love and teasing. How she so cherished him. Though she longed to see their smiling faces, sadly each day passed without any sign of either of them.

Boredom left her with nothing more than day dreams to keep her grounded. Most moments she spent looking toward each new day, filling her thoughts with riding. Though the mere concept of long heated showers, steamy bubble baths; of sitting on her porch sipping freshly brewed coffee kept her striving to push on as well. There was a great big world awaiting her out there, if she just held on.

Taylor watched as those that didn't survive what personal Hell they'd faced were rolled away from ICU, shrouded in white linens. The reality struck her that this time would pass for her, yet sadly for others this was where it all ended. There in the wake of such intense reality she vowed to never again take the little everyday blessings for granted. From that moment on she would fight off the evil whispers beckoning her to give up. Such negativity taunting her to see only the bad. Focusing on getting back to her life; the real day to day was all that mattered. This new inspiration kept her fighting, pushing forward toward her future.

Hearing the doctor's glorious words as he stood beside her bed telling her she'd be moved to the rehab hospital and begin physical therapy came not a second too soon. The very next day she was transported by ambulance, the swift journey affording priceless freedom.

Languishing in the glory of a hot shower, savoring the taste solid food, she sat relishing sweet sips of her favorite honey sweetened Chamomile tea. Above all, she cherished the feel of a real bed topped with fluffy down pillows cradling her still tender body. Sitting on the bedside she smoothed her fingers across the crisp white linens, over the fluffy chenille bedspread, pleased for some semblance of the real world, and even more so to simply be alive. Knowing how very blessed she'd been through the worst pain and suffering, having heard those still small voices reminding her that life was so worth fighting for, offering much needed comfort. For this she was most grateful.

"Wow, look at you, still a hottie even sporting cotton P.J.'s and bandages," Toby's voice as sweet as angels' song to Taylor's ears.

"Toby! I missed you so much. When you never came to visit, I... well I, thought you'd forgotten me." Tears filled her eyes, spilling onto her bruised, scab spattered cheeks.

"Oh sweet Taylor, you silly girl, I could never forget you. We were told you were better off not having visitors, otherwise I would have been by your side every possible moment... you must believe me. I called every day to check on you, did they not tell you?" Toby asked, furrowing his brow.

Shaking her head, Taylor silently admitted that they hadn't.

"We wanted to see you, believe me. That's why I came as soon as you were transported. Well it doesn't matter now. None of that matters, there is nothing more important than you getting well." Toby's eyes misted over as he sat a glistening crystal vase filled with white roses, snowy star gazers and creamy gardenias onto the round table in front of the bay window. Making his way to her he knelt before her. Inhaling a deep breath Toby smiled, taking her hand in his. "I missed you so Tay, you have to know that. Having you away was as if there was half of me was missing."

"I missed you too Tob, it just seems as if I have been gone so long." Leaning her elbow against the nightstand, kissing him on the cheek, she lay back into her sheets with a new found peace washing over her weary soul. "Where's Liz?" She asked, gently pulling the covers over her. A new wave of concerns clouding over Taylor's eyes at Toby's hesitation to answer. "Is everything alright?"

Stuffing his hands into his pockets, Toby took a deep breath before speaking. "She said there is too much to do for both of us to be here all at once. But don't worry, she'll be by to see you in the morning before the grill opens." Toby shifted his eyes so as not to meet Taylor's suspicious gaze.

"She must be pretty upset with me for disrupting her schedule. I know how very much she despises that," she said sighing.

"You put that to rest, do you hear me? I've been covering all of your shifts! She hasn't had to work one minute extra! There is no justification for her being upset about anything, I made certain of it. I promise there is nothing for you to worry about." Toby tightly clasped her hand between his staring intently into her eyes. "Nearly losing you has been hell on the two of us. We're just simply grateful you're alive. Losing you would have surely been the end of both of us Tay. Nothing matters except that you heal and come back to us." Toby had never been more serious with her in all their lives.

Smiling, she squeezed his hand in return. "I'm glad I made it too. For a while there, I hate to admit I was selfishly ungrateful. I'm ashamed to even speak the words, but I actually… well, I questioned why God let me live if I was to be so miserable." Sighing again she continued. "I know it's terrible; how despicable it was for me to allow such nonsense to stir in my head, for not simply trusting…believing that the darkness would lift. Like mom always taught us, we have to keep looking forward, reminding ourselves that never again do we pass through this moment. Through misery we learn to take each experience as an important lesson. Challenges build upon our character, allowing us to come through with richer perspectives. But I found it's much more difficult to trust the man upstairs when things are falling apart. And then to be all alone through the most difficult time in my life, well it made for a distinctively pathetic combination. The path ahead seems so dim when it no longer resembles what you have grown to expect from life. It is not easy staying positive when all sanity is ripped away and you're buried beneath such overwhelming circumstances. When you're forced to make a painful pilgrimage, to turn an unfamiliar corner, a new page even, it's difficult to get a grip on reality. In the most miserable battles we face, something wonderful can be manifested, I know this now Toby. Though my life is veiled by present circumstances, I must learn to simply trust that everything will work out and that the man upstairs has everything in control. I was inhibiting the real miracle by taking for granted the simple presence of air in my lungs. I was fearful of suffering when there are those that aren't blessed with a second chance, those poor souls who don't survive. I was being ridiculous, unfit to have been graced with even one more precious day." Her voice cracked, emotions stirring within the harsh reality of her admittance.

Toby patted her hand, sucking in a long deep breath trying to take in all she was saying.

"I realized today that though none of this will be easy, through this I will grow and find more compassion for others.

Rather than saying 'why me', I owe it to God to thank him for the life lesson and more so for sparing me. I'm allowing my heart to be filled with hope Toby. I owe it to Him, to take this as an awe inspiring signal from the universe that a better future awaits me. I need to trust that this accident will not define me, that the purpose of it all was more a catalyst for an amazing awakening, the dawning of a new life. I realize now that I need to show gratitude for these endless chances to grow, though I am so often tempted to lash out at the challenges set before me. I'm slowly finding a way to savor every simple moment, good or bad Toby. I'm learning to get past the desire to escape any and all hardships. I'm gradually beginning to understand mom telling us that we are like diamonds, designed by a higher power to grow more beautiful with pressure and adversity. I finally get that I will be restored and if I allow the good to outweigh the bad I will be a better person for it. I need to be thankful for the opportunity to have a tomorrow, regardless if I am damaged. I am alive Toby and I have my whole life still awaiting me once I'm healed." Taylor squeezed her eyes closed smiling.

"Wow Tay, I must say you seemed to have pieced your life together quite well for going through all that you have. No more runaway emotions, resistance or critical self-analysis. You should be proud of yourself, this is a huge step. You're spectacular Tay. It's amazing that through this you are seeing everything so clearly now. This accident seems to have simultaneously rewoven the unraveled yarn of the past and provided a new and better platform for the adventurous woman still lurking within that fragile body of yours. Mom would be so very proud of you Tay. You haven't given up, refusing to allow life to get the best of you. That is a truly difficult road to hoe, yet you are beating this, hands down. And just think, soon you will be out there ridding your bike, the wind blowing that long beautiful hair. I can see you now riding along grinning ear to ear." Toby winked, kissing her cheek trying to lighten the moment.

"Thanks Tob, you always know how to make me feel better, especially for listening to me, for really hearing me. You're the best friend a girl could have…" stopping, turning her ear to the window, closing her eyes again. "Do you hear that glorious sound?" Taylor asked grinning. "Open the window please," her face beaming with joy. "How I have missed that beautiful sound."

Toby moved to pull the curtain back, unlatching the oversized window, pushing it open. The rumble of pipes poured in, echoing from across the pond below her window. Taylor sat tall in her bed, straining to see. Just off the edge of the grass sat a dark cherry red motorcycle, its rider dressed in all black. Taylor wiggled, moving closer to the edge of the bed, attempting to get a better look. Sitting there unmoving, a tall man starred back at her across the spans toward the open window.

"I think he can see you Tay, he just waved. Looks like you may have a secret admirer," Toby said confused, "or were you expecting company?"

"No, he's probably just waiting to pick someone up. But I am certainly enjoying his visit."

The exhaust rumbled even louder as the rider prompted the throttle. Still staring in her direction he slowly lifted a hand once more in her direction.

53

"He just waved again! Did you see it that time?" Toby's voice rose with amazement.

After a momentary pause the mysterious biker seated himself, kicking the shifter into gear, riding away just as quickly as he had arrived.

Taylor's heart pounded with sheer delight. Frozen in place, her mind raced. 'Could it be?' She thought to herself, then quickly dismissing the idea as fast as it had arrived.

"Well that was certainly odd, wasn't it?" Toby asked, pulling the window closed before turning back to her.

"And yet so very wonderful," smiling she drifted off in thought, imagining that she truly had a secret admirer. Hopeful that it might quite possibly be Garrett. Though she doubted it, she held fast to the dream. Closing her eyes she lay back into the sheets once again, imagining the feel of the throttle in her palm, the vibration of the motor moving through her core. She had so tried to suppress the deep desires brewing within her, the borderline obsession she had for riding. Secretly harboring how devastated she had been at the heart wrenching possibility of never being allowed to ride again. She decided in that moment that she would let nothing stand in her way, of taking her life back... nothing.

"Tay, are you alright?" Toby inquired moving to her side, patting her hand softly.

Snapping out of her daydream, back to the reality of her circumstance. "What? Oh, sure I'm perfectly fine, I was lost in thought." Taylor shook her head, clearing her mind of riding, of the mystery man, if only for a moment. First she had to master walking without a cane, then she could think of riding again... 'baby-steps,' she thought to herself.

"I hate to ask, but do you honestly think you will ever ride again? Or should I just sell your bike now?" Toby inquired, as if he'd read her mind, weakly attempting to stifle his brewing laughter.

"Touch my bike and die little brother," she quipped with fiery spunk. "I will walk again and you can bet I will ride again soon after!" Taylor stopped, painfully sitting up she met Toby's eyes again. "I am right, aren't I Tob? They haven't told you something different have they?" The blood drained from her once flushed cheeks. "Toby talk to me!" Panic rose with each word. "Tell me the truth please!"

"No they haven't told me anything, relax girl I was just messing around with you. I assume that your chance of rehabilitation is really up to you at this point. It won't be easy, but I bet if you work hard you could be back to being yourself one hundred percent again, no problem. You're the toughest woman I know." Toby kissed the back of her hand. "You just wait, before long you'll be back in the saddle showing me up on two wheels. Take it one day at a time sis, everything will work out all in time, you wait and see." Toby smiled, lovingly tapping his finger on the tip of her nose as their father always had.

The sound of the motorcycle moving along the ridge below the hospital echoed across the spans of lawn. Closing her eyes again, soaking in the glorious sound, listening as it vanished in the distance. 'Come back, take me with you.' She thought to herself.

Just then a nurse stepped through the door. "Visitation is over you two. Taylor has an early appointment with her physical therapist, she'll need plenty of rest," she offered flatly, staring at Toby.

"Well I guess that's my cue. I love you sis. I'll see you tomorrow." Toby gently kissed her on the forehead waving goodbye, making a funny face behind the nurses back as he slipped out the door.

Holding back laughter, squeezing her eyes closed she drifted off into the depths of her mind to the freedom of her bike once again, leaving reality far behind in the proverbial dust of her imagination.

Chapter Five

Weeks ticked by and Liz had still yet to visit. Though she mailed cards and had lavish flowers delivered, Taylor's heart was saddened by the ever growing distance between them. Regardless, she refrained from calling her, knowing it would merely put them both in an even more awkward position. The encompassing reality of the car wreck had yet to sink in for Liz; to totally rear its ugly head in its entirety. Nonetheless, she wasn't about to go poking around, stirring things up. Taylor still prayed that time might help bridge the full-fledge ravine standing between the two of them. Regardless, Liz's absence wore heavy on Taylor. Knowing this was simply her way of dealing with life since they'd been orphaned, Taylor tried to let go of all expectations and be thankful for what little attention she had received from Liz. A lifetime of experience with such, had proved to her that any form of confrontation would simply be taken as no more than Taylor being an antagonist.

Months passed in slow succession of one another as Taylor made the journey back to her life. Aspiring to make the best of her survival she pushed on flourishing. The 'phenomenal transformation' the local paper had touted, showing Taylor move from reclusive invalid to determined warrior, gave her a deeper sense of accomplishment than she ever thought possible. This along with her own personal cheering section of hospital staff had Taylor mindfully appreciative of each passing success.

Upon returning to her room following yet another grueling session of physical therapy, Taylor showered and changed into her cotton pajamas. Taking pride in this being the first time she hadn't required the help of nurses since her arrival; the first time that she hadn't needed her cane. Smiling to herself she marked it as yet another milestone, moving one step closer to her freedom.

"Well my, my, did you do all that without any help Miss Taylor?" Nurse Tina asked in her infamous Jamaican accent, raising an eyebrow. Smiling she moved to the window, pushing back the curtains as she did every evening so that Taylor could watch the sunset over the pond. Unlatching it, she slowly opened the window.

"Yes, can you believe it, I did it all by myself," she answered, her heart swelling with pride.

"Well good for you. I have a feeling you'll be back on your feet in no time, living life in the real world once again. I can bring you more magazines tomorrow if you would like. As for tonight I am on my way."

"So early?" Taylor inquired, tilting her head to see the time on the clock above the door.

"Yes my dear, it so happens that I have a date. So I will see you tomorrow. Have a fantastic night," Tina called out gleefully grinning, cheerfully waving as she quickly passed through the door.

"Have fun!" She hollered after her, "for me too," she continued under her breath, hearing Tina giggle as she headed down the hallway. Simply hearing the word 'date' had her daydreaming of Garrett, wondering if he even remembered her name after all this time. Sighing she sank into her bed, slowly drifting off in thought.

Sunlight beamed through the window lighting her room with waves of brilliant orange, reflecting onto her window from the shimmering water below. Watching sunset on the pond, how the twinkling water danced in the amber light had become the highlight of Taylor's days, falling second only to the near nightly sightings of the mysterious man on the black cherry bike. Whoever the stranger was, he had infused her day to day existence with much renewed excitement for the opportunities awaiting her on the other side.

Carefully she made her way to the seat by the window to watch the ducks playing in the evening light. Placing a pillow into the chair back she slowly lowered herself down and settled in to enjoy the festivities. Filling her lungs with the cool night air she closed her eyes soaking in the moment.

The soft rippling of water, lapping at the rocks scattered along the sandy shore lulled her as she drifted off in thought. The wind against her body, the purr of the bike beneath her, the sheer power of the throttle in her palm. Though the fantasy was always the same, she never tired of it. Her thoughts abruptly interrupted by the sound of a motorcycle coming up the ridge. The immediate recognition of the pipes took her by surprise. The throaty rumble drawing her eyes toward the curve of the entrance drive, then back to the grass, searching for the mystery man. The sheer excitement of seeing him escalated as the bike grew closer and closer. Her heart thumping as a bass drum beneath her ribs with the anticipation. At once on the horizon she spotted a dark bike coming up the road, the rider in fitted black leather chaps and jacket, tufts of steel grey hair dancing beneath a metallic helmet. Feeling silly she slumped in her chair. How ridiculous was it to fantasize over some stranger that she'd never met, and worse to imagine that she had heard his bike in every passing motorcycle.

In spite of her momentary bout of denial she stirred again, hearing yet another bike in the distance, as it ascended the curving grade just out of sight. 'Could it be him?' She excitedly wondered. Sitting tall in her seat she strained to focus on the horizon, forgetting her earlier thoughts. Across the pond rose her mystery man from the road beyond. Taylor's heart leaped seeing that he had come again. She'd been right, she had heard the familiar pipes of the bike that had been there countless evenings before. Reveling in the intensity of their shared moments, she sighed like a love sick school girl.

The chrome of his bike glistening in the setting sun quickened her pulse. Pulling closer to the edge of the water than usual the stranger put his feet to the ground standing, lifting his glasses staring straight toward her. Taylor strained to be free of the chair. Setting her feet securely beneath her, she stood. Staring back she slowly leaned toward the glass window pane, pressing her palm against the cool glass. Saying a silent prayer that one day she would meet this mysterious stranger face to face she gazed on, locked in a trance. Slowly his hand rose from his side as if to meet hers, palm to palm. A euphoric rush poured over her as they stood transfixed, unmoving. Dazed, Taylor felt an unexpected rush of wind brush against her body from off of the water, momentarily taken away by the thought of riding with him, of having her arms wrapped firmly around this man she knew nothing of. Allowing her mind to drift, her imagination pushed the limits. Swooning at the thought of riding with him, of collectively moving through the corners pressed tightly to one another. The mere thought of such leaving her breathless.

Curling his fingers to his palm, his hand lingered as if he had captured her touch from the air, holding tight to it before pressing it to his chest. Then with one swift move he slipped his glasses on, backing the bike away. Glancing over his shoulder toward her once more, he opened the throttle with a thunderous rumble before stealthily disappearing into the distance as quickly as he had arrived.

"Miss Taylor do you need anything before I start rounds?" Naomi's asked with her signature thick Southern drawl.

Startled from her mesmerized trance, she turned to Naomi, her palm still pressed to the glass.

"Are you alright dear? I'm sorry, I didn't mean to startle you so," she asked, her forehead crinkled with concern. "I'm not so sure that you should be standing unattended just yet." Rushing to Taylor, Naomi helped her back into the chair.

"Do you happen to know who that man on the bike is? He visits most every night. Do you know if he works here?" Still transfixed on the ponds edge, hanging on every last decibel of the rumbling pipes echoing up the canyon.

"I know he most certainly does not work here Miss Taylor. I wish I could be of more help but I honestly have no idea who he is. I can tell you however…" Naomi paused, leaning closer. "That mystery of a man is most certainly the talk of this place. I have my bets that he is here to see you, as all of the rooms on this side are empty… except for this one. That's very interesting, don't you agree?"

Taylor sat stunned, hanging on her every word. "Me? Really? I'd hoped he might be, but honestly thought it impossible."

Naomi carefully watched Taylor for a moment, unsure if she should have said anything. "Alright then, if you need anything just ring the nurses' station my dear. I will be back to check on you later," her words fading.

Lost in the moment she sat motionless, her eyes transfixed on the pond. Offering a quick wave to Naomi as she stepped from the room.

Taylor's therapy schedule seemed to be never ending as she wound down the final days of her stay in rehab. Monotonous repetitions of strength exercises and stretching had convinced her that much more and her legs would simply fall off. Little by little her strength had grown, and with each passing day Taylor felt more like she had before the accident.

Once cleared of her final strength and balance testing, she'd been approved for release within the week. The reality of such news brought thrilling prospects. Though she would surely miss all her new found friends, as most of the staff had become like family, Taylor was more than ready to get back to her prior existence. Her final week sped by in a blur and Friday arrived before she knew it.

Taylor awoke early to shower. Quickly packing her belongings, she searched the room twice making sure she hadn't forgotten anything. With one last farewell glance across the pond, an orderly arrived pushing a wheelchair through the doorway.

"Ready for your ride out front?" He asked, taking her bags, hanging them over his shoulder. Helping her into the chair, he wheeled her from the room in awkward silence, making their way down the hallway and through the automatic doors. Watching the doors swing open, Taylor gasped. Before her stood every staff member she'd been in contact with during her stay, most with balloons in hand. The crowd launched into song. "For she's a jolly good fellow, for she's a jolly good fellow... she's a jolly good fellow, which nobody can deny!" The room erupted in cheers, tears flowing all around. "Surprise Taylor!" The crowd roared, excitement filling the air. "Speech! Speech! Speech!" They chanted, not a dry eye remaining in the house.

Standing from the wheelchair, her eyes brimmed with mixed emotions. "Thanks you guys, really, this is so sweet of you! I never expected anything like this. You have all been the best of friends through the worst of times. I miss you all already. Well except for P.T. that is, sorry Ben." She put her hand to her heart, bashfully meeting her therapists glance. The room erupted again in tearful laughter. "Seriously, thank you. I never could have come this far without each and every one of you." Smearing her hands over her tear streaked face she sighed. "Look what you have all done, I've been reduced to no more than a babbling baby!"

Laughter exploded again from the crowd just as Liz and Toby walked through the front entrance.

"My goodness, get that woman a Kleenex before she drowns." Toby's words catching in his throat at the sight of his sister standing on her own. Taking her in his arms he squeezed her tightly, Liz tearfully joining in. "You did it Tay! You are going to walk out of here just as you prayed you would," Toby whispered in her ear.

Saying her goodbyes had taken more energy than she realized. Before long she was reeling with exhaustion.

"Ready sis?" Toby smiled seeing the weariness in her eyes. Taking her hand in his, he beckoned her toward the exit.

"Yes, more than ready," sighing with relief that she was on her way home.

"Don't forget these my dear," Naomi stepped in close laying a thick collection of balloon strings across her hand. "Thank you. I will never forget your kindness," Taylor whispered into Naomi's ear, squeezing her tightly in a hug. "Be well my dear. And let me know if you ever meet that mystery man." Stepping back, Naomi quickly turned away sniffling.

Waving farewell, Taylor's legs felt strong beneath her as she made her way through the doors. Taking in a long deep breath she paused after stepping outside. Looking to the azure blue sky above, smiling to herself, realizing that she'd truly done it. She had survived against all odds, worked hard to regain her strength and now her life was being handed back to her. Squeezing her eyes closed she sent up a prayer of thanks. Tilting her face to the warm sun, she raised her hand releasing the dozens of balloons into the air. "Be free and fly." Feeling as if she'd been reborn, taking her first steps into the world, Taylor watched the balloons scatter; floating high into the sky.

"Thanks again everyone, for everything!" Taylor hollered out of the car window, blowing kisses as Toby closed her door climbing into the backseat behind her. Pulling away from the hospital they rolled past the end of the building, Taylor's eyes opened wide. "Stop Liz!"

Braking, Liz looked to Taylor surprised. "What's wrong? Did you forget something? Are you alright Tay?"

Across the pond something caught Taylor's eye. Chrome glimmering in the sunlight. There he was, standing beside his bike. He had come, her mystery man had come to see her off. Taylor's stomach flipped. Giving a nod he threw his leg over his bike. With a stirring growl the engine lit up. Taylor's heart skipped, her cheeks heated with a rush as he disappeared ahead of them. Taylor sank back in her seat flooded with emotions. "It's nothing Liz, we can go."

"Who was that?" Liz asked, completely perplexed.

"Just a secret admirer of Taylor's." Toby answered, reaching around the right of her seat lightly squeezing her shoulder.

Taking his hand in hers she lay her cheek against it, closing her eyes smiling. 'Mystery was right', she thought to herself, wondering if she would ever know who he really was as they headed down the grade not far behind him. Taylor leaned her head against the frame of the open window soaking in the echoing rumble of his pipes filling the air. Somehow this stranger was an expert at soothing her soul. 'One day I hope to know you... to meet you. Thank you for all the visits,' Taylor thought to herself as his bike accelerated, quickly shifting until he was out of ear shot.

Chapter Six

Pulling up in front of Taylor's place, Liz slipped the shifter into park. Taylor's eyes widened, filling with crocodile tears. In front of the freshly washed sparkling glass of the bay window she spied her garden thriving in full bloom. The lush emerald freshly trimmed lawn smelling of a spring day. Just outside the garage stood her bike, gleaming in all its glory.

"What did you guys do? Everything is so, so beautiful!" Covering her face, emotions gushing, tears now spilling freely from her already reddened eyes. She had never truly known how wonderful it would be to finally return home again. Overwhelmed by such kindness Taylor struggled not to blubber, trying hopelessly to contain the fountain of emotion building within.

"We all pitched in and kept up with the place. I thought you might like to see your girl all spiffed up too, so I gave her a good bath." Toby did his best to stifle his emotions, quickly climbing from the back seat to open her door, offering her a hand out. Taylor took hold of his hand stepping from the car, throwing her arms tightly around his neck, squeezing hard before stepping away. A single tear escaped Toby's eye, trickling down his reddened cheek. This touched Taylor more than all the rest put together. Such love and kindness was precisely the medicine she was in dire need of.

Once she was alone, Taylor made all those months of daydreaming a reality. A long steaming bubble bath and a perfectly delightful night's sleep in her very own bed had Taylor ready to brave a new day. 'Baby steps', she kept reminding herself of the advice her doctor had given her. 'A slow integration back into your life. It's most important that you don't overdue it.' The words echoed through her mind as she rose, putting her feet to the floor. That would not be a problem, as even the little daily deeds of dressing and brushing her teeth wore her out quickly. Taylor was reminded of how the cool smooth wood had always felt so very good beneath her feet as she made her way to the kitchen. Wrapped in her fluffy robe, a piping hot cup of coffee in hand along with one of Toby's freshly baked blueberry scones, and she was beginning to feel herself once again.

Staring off into the tree lined horizon from her porch swing Taylor daydreamed of riding again. Realizing she had never before been to those distant mountains, she definitively decided that this would have to be remedied as soon as possible. Her bike beckoning her from the confines of the garage. "All things with time Tay," she said aloud to herself. Patience had never been one of her virtues, but through this she was certainly learning.

In the distance thunderheads brewed. The sun slowly rose setting the sky afire with the dazzling warmth of the dawning day. Taking in a deep breath Taylor leaned her head back, smiling with the thought of the wind blasting by, the thundering power of her bike rumbling beneath her. Riding was all she seemed to focus on lately, subconsciously willing herself to heal as fast as she could.

Her thoughts drifted to Garrett. Having made such a connection with another, only then to lose the chance of meeting him had never settled well with her. The thought of having such promise vanish in the blink of an eye made her cringe. The reality that she may never know Garrett Larkin tugged hard upon her heart strings.

Lifting her eyes to the sky she sucked in a ragged breath, exhaling slowly. "Don't go there, pull it together girl," she whispered aloud. Standing she glanced around the lush greenery of her yard. There was no place like home, this she knew today more than ever before. Today dawned more than just a new day, this day offered her a new lease on life, a new brighter tomorrow.

Spending the following weeks puttering around the house had Taylor catching up on reading, going through her closet and sadly watching more television than she had in the entire three years prior. There was no denying how desperate she was to fully return to her life.

A quick shower and she was ready to get to it. Pulling open the garage door her heart fell seeing her bike again. Throwing her leg over she wrapped her fingers around the grips, squeezing the throttle back her heart raced. Trembling waves raced through her, though the bike was merely sitting in silence. Her eyes brimmed with tears, her body quivering so hard that she could barely even focus. This couldn't be happening! She had brushed off the warnings of her doctors. She couldn't be so weak as to have P.T.S.D., not in a million years. She tried convincing herself this had to be sheer nerves. She wasn't like those others... was she? Weeping she stepped from her bike, hurrying into the house, embarrassed of her prideful ignorance. Saddened that her life was not simply falling back into place as she had planned she curled up on her bed burying her face in her pillows and wept harder. A tidal wave of pain escaped her, leaving her fully spent as she drifted off to sleep.

A heavy knock startled Taylor awake. Peering through the darkened living room windows on her way to answer the door she realized she'd slept the day away. Peeking through the peephole Taylor's heart sank seeing a stranger wearing a dark helmet standing just outside. Garrett? Panicking she looked at herself in the entry mirror, seeing nothing less than a disheveled mess. Repeatedly he knocked, even more aggressively on the door, the reality of him being on the other side of the door jolting her. Slowly she reached for the knob, pulling the door open.

"Ride with me?" The deep melody of his hypnotizing voice sent shivers running across her dewy skin.

"Give me a just moment." Closing the door she ran to her room, threw on her well-worn jeans and a white cashmere turtleneck. Grabbing her riding boots, jacket and helmet she rushed back. As she stepped onto the front porch he started the bike. The throaty rumble of his Vance and Hines thrilled her. Looking back over his shoulder he nodded for her to join him. Stepping on the peg she threw her leg over. Garrett reached behind, pulling her arms tightly around his waist. Her thighs pressed against him, his warmth seeping through her jeans. Throttling up they pulled from the drive, maneuvering through the tree lined streets and onto the highway. Shifting they sped toward the distant mountains. Shifting again Garrett gunned it, Taylor squeezed him tighter, pressing him firmly into her. Her heart raced as they sped on faster and faster. Taylor's heart wildly dancing beneath her ribs. This night was more than she ever could have imagined.

The phone rang startling her from a deep slumber. Sorely disappointed that she had been dreaming, she reached for the receiver. "Hello," her scratchy voice muffled by the sheets.

"Get ready Tay, its Friday and you're coming down to hang out. I need a babysitter to control the crowd during our pool tournament, and you need to get out of that house my dear." Toby's sweet excitability always a welcome comfort, pulled her from the haze of slumber. "I'll be there in twenty."

Glancing out her darkened window she realized she had truly slept the day away. "Actually give me forty five Tob," Taylor said laying the receiver down without a goodbye. Shaking off the emotional waves resonating after such a dream, she stood moving slowly to the mirror. "You need a shower, a cold, cold shower," she said to her flustered red cheeked reflection.

Toby arrived just as Taylor finished blowing her hair dry. Meeting him at the door, jacket in hand, as he reached to ring the doorbell.

"Perfect timing sis." Grabbing her hand he excitedly led her to the truck. "Would you like to drive?" He asked, trying to offer the option, without pressing.

Taylor lowered her head ashamed of her shortcomings. "No thanks, maybe next time," seeing Toby smile as he let her into the passenger side door.

"You know you need to get back on that horse sooner than later Tay. There's no rush, whenever you're ready," climbing into the driver's seat, patting her shoulder.

The ride to Donna's was impossibly quiet and dreadfully uncomfortable. Taylor starred out the window replaying her dream over and over wishing she was still lost in the beauty of riding in unison with Garrett.

"Here we are!" Toby's forced enthusiasm turned Taylor's stomach. Parking, Toby hurried to help her from the truck.

Stepping ahead he made his way to the front door opening it as well. Looking around Donna's, soaking in the energy trying to get into the groove of things once again. The reality that she would rather be home painfully evident on her face.

The tournament went on without a glitch, proving Toby's suspicious ploy to get her there had simply been unnecessary. Most of the crowd had cleared by nine. The hub of rowdy players leaving her spent. "Tob would you be able to drive me back home soon?" She asked, feigning a long yawn.

"Sorry sis it's going to be a bit. I still need to get things cleaned up or Liz will wring my neck. You remember how it is. Hang tight and I'll bring you a drink."

Taking a seat, she moaned under her breath, 'I never should have agreed to this.' Tapping her fingers impatiently on the bar top she sat staring into space.

"Here you go beautiful, and here's some quarters. Play us some tunes would you?" Toby slid a roll of quarters across the bar, winking at her.

Moving toward the jukebox she saw someone step through the front doors from the corner of her eye. 'Oh great, at this rate we'll never get out of here!'

Frustrated she searched the songs looking for as many of her mother's favorite oldies rock as she could find. Choosing one last song she shrugged. "That ought to do it until we are out of here," her words echoing across the room.

Sliding onto the barstool once again, Taylor inhaled deeply. She so missed her freedoms. The realization hit hard at times like this. How she had taken for granted being able to come and go as she pleased, when she pleased. If she wished to have her life back, she knew that she must deal with her fears of driving as soon as possible, yet the mere thought made her heart pinch. Dependency on others had never suited her. Besides she wanted to ride, needed to ride nearly as much as she needed oxygen if she was ever to be whole again.

Pulling up a stool beside her, Taylor heard a husky voiced man order a beer. Clearing her throat, she diverted her eyes, hoping he wasn't planning to make a move.

Finishing her lemon sweet tea, she slid her glass across the bar. "Thanks Tob. Will it be very long before we can go?" Doing her best to keep her eyes from wandering in the stranger's direction.

"Not too long now sis. Here play one more song." Toby handed four more quarters to her, then went back to washing glasses.

The juke box cranked out CCR as Taylor searched for her favorite song. She never could recall the number for 'Turn Me On'. How she loved Norah's music, the smoky mood it always put her in. Just as she started to slip the quarters into the slot she felt someone step in close behind her.

"Play one for me pretty lady?" His deep groveled voice moved through her. Could it be Garrett? This couldn't really be happening. She had to be dreaming again. 'Pinch me, wake me before I have a heart attack in my sleep!' She screamed inside the confines of her mind.

"I would really love to hear B17, if you wouldn't mind." His heated whisper falling upon her hair. Leaning in so that his body was nearly pressed against her, he reached around slowly slipping each of four quarters into the coin slot just in front of her hip, moving ever closer to her with each quarter. The spicy warmth of his cologne tickling her nose, tantalizing her senses. 'No one should smell so delicious. Could this truly be Garrett?' Taylor questioned herself. 'But he doesn't sound like Garrett.'

"Thank you beautiful," he said stepping away, leaving her paralyzed, staring blankly into the screen momentarily unable to focus. Running her fingers through her long hair Taylor sucked in a deep breath attempting to pull herself together. Searching the song list she spied B17. 'Help me make it through the night.' Taylor knew the song well, being one of her mother's all-time favorites. 'Interesting choice', she thought smirking. Pressing her trembling finger to the button, she reluctantly chose his request. 'Relax girl, you can do this. What if it truly is Garrett?' Sliding her own quarters into the slot she chose her song before moving back to the bar.

Nervously she slipped onto the same stool she'd been seated on before, keeping her eyes straight ahead, trying her best to remember to breathe. 'Don't look at him, play it cool.' Convincing herself not to flee into the office, she folded her hands on the bar just in front of her, in a weak attempt at steadying the nervous tremors. Adrenaline coursed through her veins leaving her dizzied by the reality unfolding before her.

"Take that ribbon from your hair, shake it lose and let it fall…" the male singer drawled on. Taylor felt her stomach sink to her toes, swallowing hard. The words of the seductive song filling the room.

"May I have this dance?" The sexy rasp of his voice sending chills surging through her, rendering her speechless. Slowly she stood turning to him, taking in his massive size. The depths of his sea green eyes boring through her as he took her hand in his. Walking in silence he led her slowly to the middle of the hardwood dance floor, tucking her close into him with one slick move. His huge hand pressed tightly into the small of her back. Pulling her firmly against his broad chest, taking her other hand softly into his he lead her in a slow cowboy waltz across the floor.

Taylor felt fiery energy emanating from him, flowing onto her. This mountain of a man exuded sexuality from his every pore. Wavering between utter excitement and disquieted disconcertion, Taylor swayed to the music, a mere puppet in his brawny arms.

"Do you ever ride?" He asked in a deep, husky whisper.

Confused by his question, she smiled not answering, squeezing her eyes shut trying to halt the sudden spinning in her mind. If this was Garrett why was he pretending not to know the answer? If this wasn't Garrett, then who was this hunk of a man attempting to sweep her off her feet?

Swallowing hard she opened her eyes, turning her face up to his. Their eyes meeting once more, the intensity stealing Taylor's air. The corners of his mouth curled slightly at the sight of her flushed cheeks. That devilish smile had Taylor's heart revved up tight. He was trouble with a capital 'T'. She could feel it in her bones, yet her feet stayed beneath her, refusing to carry her away to safety. She must admit that she longed to know just who this tall dark drink of water might be.

"Excuse me?" Taylor played it safe, pretending not to know precisely what he was asking, stalling just a moment longer so as to pull herself together.

"Do you ride motorcycles?" His raw tone tightened, exposing a bit more of an edge beneath his charm. Having countless hours clocked bartending, she knew his type oh too well. The typical sexy playboy out to find a new adventure in every opportunity. She was no more than a mystery awaiting exploration to this tall, dark and dangerously handsome man. She wasn't about to be just another conquest added to his list. Yet she so reveled in his touch, lulled by the musk of his skin. Taylor loved how he exuded sheer power and self-confidence, regardless of who he was. What could it hurt, right? She longed to be on a bike again and this was her chance. "Why… are you asking?" She replied, offering a lusty smile that could only invite danger.

"Do you want me to be?"

The reality of his words fell heavy on her heart. This was a huge step to be taking, especially with a total stranger. Yet Taylor persevered. "Yes, I believe I do. Though I'm sad to say that it has been a while, I do ride," the words flowed from her so freely she completely shocked herself. Inviting such trouble surely showed she was well on her way to a full recovery… or so she tried desperately to convince herself.

"Well then, I guess it's set, we shall ride. I promise to take exceptional care of you. You can trust me, really." Smirking he gave her a slow wink.

"I bet you say that to all the girls." Taylor quipped back without thinking, surprising herself.

Before the reality of the situation sank in, Taylor was explaining the deal to Toby, her own words blowing her mind.

"Really? Wow sis, I have to say I am floored! Though I realize that this is truly a great triumph, I must admit it's kind of insane considering you don't even know this guy. Are you sure you want to do this Tay?" Toby asked frustrated, his voice huffing in hushed tones. Wishing now that he hadn't tricked her into coming down after all, Toby sighed, rubbing his forehead with worry.

"As you said little brother, I have to get back on the horse sometime, right?" Taylor smiled nervously, patting Toby on the back. "I won't be long. Wait for me? I still need that ride home."

"I'm not going anywhere! I'll be here waiting when he safely delivers you back!" Toby said in a bellowing voice, looking past her, staring the stranger square in the eye.

"I'll be fine lil' brother. Love you." Kissing him on the cheek she pulled her leather jacket from the coat hook just inside the backroom, slipping it on. "Watch my purse, would you please," she said tucking it below the bar, grinning.

"Hey dude, we're not above sending an armed search party if she's not returned back safely," Toby called out loudly, brandishing as gruff a tone as he could muster.

"No worries man, she'll be back safe and sound. And quite possibly even tonight," the stranger said, throwing his head back, producing an impressive laugh.

Taylor looked to her feet, holding her breath, unsure if she was doing the right thing after all.

"Ready darlin'?" Taking her by the hand, he led her through the door onto the sidewalk just outside.

"What a beautiful bike." Taylor's eyes lit up seeing the gleaming burnt orange chrome shrouded motorcycle.

"Not as lovely as you though," stepping to the saddle bag he pulled a half shell helmet out handing it to her, starring wantonly into her eyes, "here you are."

"Thank you." Her heart flipped as he leaned in to retrieve his own helmet from the seat. His muscular forearm softly brushing against her, sending chills racing across her skin.

"I'm Jake by the way… and you are?" He asked in a low purr.

"Taylor." Swallowing hard she replied as she slipped the borrowed helmet on. This guy Jake had a way of unnerving her she seriously wasn't prepared for.

Swinging his leg over the seat, he set the bike upright, turning the key, pushing the kickstand up with his boot.

"Jake," laying her hand onto his muscular arm, momentarily preoccupied by the feel of his bulging bicep she paused.

"Yes Taylor? Are you alright?" Truly concerned by the look on her face, he turned the key back.

"I need a favor."

"Anything darlin'," Jake turned to face her, genuine concern filling his dreamy green eyes.

"I, um, well... remember how I said I haven't been riding in a while?" Forcing the words forth, she glanced to her feet. "Yes, I promise that I am a veteran rider. You are exceptionally safe with me." Jake touched her chin bringing her gaze to meet his. "We don't have to do this tonight if you aren't comfortable," his softened tone warmed her heart.

"Thank you, that's sweet of you. I just need you to take extra care. I had a terrible accident not long ago and... well this is honestly only my first night back in real life. I haven't even driven a car yet. I am still... It's just that I'm still a bit fragile physically and though it pains me to admit it, even more so emotionally. This is actually my first ride since before the wreck as well." Taylor's voice cracked as she spoke the painful words.

"Well I surely feel very privileged to be your first, especially knowing now that you are a biker yourself." Jake leaned in close, their noses mere inches apart. "I will break you in gently my dear. I will take the best care, you have my word, biker's honor." Jake took her hand in his, pressing it to his warm lips. Holding her stare he sat unmoving, offering a kind smile, awaiting her response.

"Thank you Jake," Taylor's spoke just above a whisper, tears stinging her eyes. His gracious outpouring of kindness renewed her faith in the ride ahead. Though torn with desires and near paralyzing fear, her heart soared with joy for having this opportunity.

Turning the key again, the bike lit up. The seductive rumble of the pipes filled Taylor's heart to the brim with stirring exhilaration.

"Climb on my dear, the road awaits us," Jake grinned sweetly.

Taylor's pulse quickened as she stepped on the peg, swinging her leg over the seat, settling in behind Jake.

"Don't be shy lil' lady, snug on up, it's going to be a bit cold tonight. Wouldn't want you to catch a chill." Smiling at her in the mirror, he patted her knee. "Any excuse will do," Jake winked, shifting the bike into gear. "Here we go. If you get uncomfortable in the least, just tug on my shirt and let me know. I will cut this short anytime you want." Jake slid his helmet on, rolling the bike out of the parking spot, angling toward the road.

Taylor's blood pulsed in her ears like a raging river. Sliding her hands into the warmth of his pockets she laid her palms against the steeled muscles of his chest, her mind momentarily imagining how he might look under his clothes. Startled by such forward thoughts, Taylor blushed ashamed of her lustful hungers, thankful he couldn't hear them. She had promised herself, following the last debacle of giving in to her wanton desires, to never again allow such nonsense. She wanted more than anything to find her soul mate. To once and for all put an end to the vicious cycle of dating games, opening her heart only to find herself empty, ashamed and even more lonesome than before. This was safe. This was simply a ride with a beautiful man, no more, no less.

Closing her eyes she soaked in every second, every single delicious detail as they took each curve of the road. The lavish scent of spicy pine burning in a distant fireplace, the buffeting wind playing on her, the calming purr of the bike beneath them, the grooves of the road pulling and pushing against Jake's brute strength. His muscles shifting beneath her fingers awakened undeniable desires for the feel of a man she had fought so hard to quiet.

The thought of Garrett suddenly lulled her from the moment. Why couldn't this be him? Why was it that she had been so quickly caught up in this man, lost so in their conversation though they'd never met? Why was she so hopeful for something between them without truly knowing anything about him? Not that any of this mattered being that she had no way of finding him. Now, here she was replaying the words they shared over in her head as she sped down the dark road wrapped around yet another mysterious stranger. Awkward pangs of guilt played on her emotions for being here with another man, regardless of how ridiculous a notion it was. Confused by her off handed feelings, she pushed away the thought of Garrett. Forcing herself to stay in the moment she rode on, sliding further forward, pressing herself tighter against Jake's back. He patted her knee once again, pressing her thigh firmly to his leg before moving his hand to the grip again. Guilt washed over her as the desire to feel Jake's hands on her, his mouth, hot, wet against hers pushed out all sensibility, all thoughts of Garrett. Her primal needs were getting the best of her, she fought to keep her head, praying for strength.

Pulling off the main road Jake parked between two massive bull pines, turning the bike off. Taylor felt a lump rise in her throat. 'What were you thinking taking off alone with this stranger and on a bike none the less? Now here you are out here in the boonies, with no one to rescue you stupid girl!' Thankful he hadn't heard her words, though her mind was screaming.

"So you seem to be doing great so far beautiful. You're bouncing back quickly." Jake grinned proudly at her in the mirror. "I want to show you something," Jake said excitedly pulling his helmet off, hanging it from his grip once again. Slipping his gloves off, he lay them inside. "Are you alright Taylor?" Noticing that she was frozen in place, he turned sideways on the seat, looking her in the eye.

"I'm good, it's just a lot to take in all in one night," her words spoken half heartedly, "my first night back at Donna's, meeting you, my first ride... You're not taking me to the woods to torture me are you?" Taylor questioned him laughing nervously.

"I have to admit the thought crossed my mind as you do look pretty tasty and smell quite delectable. But no, I won't do anything without your permission, I promise you this. Though I can't guarantee that I won't try and kiss you, since we are being honest here. I keep hoping your curiosity is peaking and will soon get the best of you," Jake grinned again, showing off the multifaceted layers of his wicked confidence.

Stepping from the bike she slid her helmet off, handing it to Jake. Hanging it next to his he slipped from his jacket. Mesmerized, she stood watching his broad shoulders ripple beneath his shirt as he hung it from the other grip. Taylor's stringent sabbatical following her last disastrous relationship was under an attack of the fiercest kind. Jake was beautiful, funny, kind and thus far quite the gentleman, growing more intriguing with each passing moment.

Jake stepped from the bike moving so close to Taylor she could feel his steamy breath falling on her cheeks. "Come with me," he whispered intently. Taking her hand firmly in his, he led her carefully down a well-worn path beneath the boughs of the stoic trees. Someone must come here quite often she devised from the smooth trail beneath their feet, but where 'here' was she still had no idea.

In a clearing just past the tree line moonlight spilled from the sky, pooling on the ebony spans of water stretched across the horizon, onto the rock formations dotting the shore filling every crevice with eerie shadows.

"How perfect is this?" Jake pointed to the lush patch of grass that lay before their feet. "Come sit by me and soak in the moon for a bit?" His deep, throaty request beckoning her to a lion's lair she was certain. Slipping her leather jacket slowly from her shoulders, he kneeled laying it across the plush grass, then seated himself close by. Patting her jacket he silently summoning her to take a seat.

Stepping onto the grass patch Taylor lowered herself beside him. "Thank you," she managed through chattering teeth. Unsure if she was truly chilled or rather her nerves were wreaking havoc on her still fragile nervous system. Staring out across the still, sparkling water streaked with snowy white ribbons of moonlight dancing on the surface, Taylor felt her stomach tighten, her heart quickening.

"So tell me about yourself Miss Taylor. Where are you from? What do you do? Are you happy?"

"Wow that's a lot of questions," Taylor replied taking a deep breath. "Where do I start?" Taylor paused, pleased for the momentary safe haven of conversation. "I was raised here actually. My mother opened Donna's when my brother, sister and I were very young. I moved away years ago to pursue photojournalism. Before my mother died I had my own separate life away from here." Swallowing hard at hearing herself speak the truth of her mother's fate, such painful words never went down easy. "The three of us pulled together, to save the place. It's definitely not my dream… it isn't any of our dreams, but we felt that we owed it to mom. We each sacrificed a lot, and in the end we are making it work. I'm trying to adjust to real life once again, things have been a bit askew, complicated ever since my accident. I'm working at getting back on my feet. It hasn't been easy, but I know the dire importance of carrying my share of the responsibilities. Tonight, as I told you earlier, was a huge stepping stone on the journey back from that wreck. You've certainly helped that process along." Taylor's eyes sparkled in the moonlight softly falling all around her.

"Happy to be of service my lady. So is there a man in your life?" A glint of Jake's softer side momentarily shone through. Then within seconds he was back to business, not waiting for her reply before continuing on. "Does he keep you fulfilled? I mean you are a beautifully sexy, passionate being. You deserve to be pleased, to be explored and lavished with long sweet kisses and passion leaving you gasping for air. I could be this for you, if you don't already have a man in your life." Lifting her hand to his mouth he softly kissed the back of it. "We only live once and none of us are getting any younger my dear," Jake said just above a whisper as he leaned in close. Running the tip of his finger around the ridge of her ear, along her cheek, down the line of her jaw, slowly tracing the curve of her collarbone, stroking the nape of her neck. Taylor shivered as he lingered along the edge of her lace tank top, unnerved by the intense sensation spreading through her as fierce as an uncontrollable wildfire blazing through a dry open field. Squeezing her eyes shut she tilted her face to the night sky drawing in a deep breath. "Jake, stop. You really need to stop," Taylor pleaded in a breathy whisper. "I'm a freight train ready to derail here. Once you start this I may not be stoppable," slowly turning to him. "I've so longed to find the perfect man, to be his everything, to give him all I have. But honestly I have to admit I long ago buried my needs, my desires as a means of survival. There's a lifetime of passions lying dormant inside me Jake, I'm a ticking time bomb. You're stirring things within me and I barely know you. We need to slow things down."

"Your lack of response proves there's obviously no one in your life willing to fulfill your desires, to give you all that you deserve, so I am simply offering you this with no strings attached. Such a sensual, sexy woman like you should be devoured, pleased until she cries out over and over again, until she's utterly spent. Let me fulfill your wildest fantasies. You won't regret it, please say that you agree beautiful."

Taylor felt a tug deep within, her body suddenly heated. The reality of his proposal had her comatose sexuality awakening. Thoughts of his warm, wet lips against hers, his fingers laced through her hair, nibbling, a voracious feeding frenzy, man to woman. Tenderness building to waves of passionate feasting. Taylor's heart rate doubled at the mere thought of such closeness with a man. Realizing that by accepting his offer she'd be free of the shackles that her past hurts had afforded. She'd be free of the walls built as a way of protecting herself. Knowing too well that taking of such freedoms, of being able to openly share in such a sacred, forbidden fruit would alter her forever. Never again would she be able to return to the confines of her lonely, restrained existence. In partaking of such, never again could she accept mediocre relating. All the while, Jake would move on to his next willing subject, leaving her to deal with the insatiable appetite he so willingly awakened. The mere thought of fully realizing her deepest inner desires, of openly exploring her most intimate cravings only to once again be faced with the lonesome emptiness she currently knew oh to well, had her simply unnerved. This was why she had long ago promised herself and more importantly God, that her days of frivolous dating and carefree relating were through.

"Jake, I need you to know that I long to have this more than you can possibly comprehend. But honestly I cannot brave relinquishing my control without risking losing my sanity. The sheer thought of such impassioned experiences alarms me. I scare myself in simply knowing the depths of all I conceal within the restraints of my resolve. How would I ever again reign in all that was loosed? And all with no foreseeable future with you?" Taylor shivered at the feel of his fingers feathering across her chest, over the crest of her shoulder, along the most sensitive line of her inner arm, into the exquisite realm of her palm.

"But we would forever have the memories of exploring one another, pleasing one another." Jake moved closer, his breath fluttering hot on her ear, waves of deep chills washing over her. "Sweet memories of you crying out my name." His words like thick, warm honey drawing her deeper into the tantalizingly temptation.

"So what happens if you fall in love?" Taylor inquired, in a weak attempt to lighten the mood before giving in to the ever growing desire to feast his muscle bound body, leaving nothing but a rack of bare bones behind.

"I promise I won't fall. We will keep it simply physical. I will not allow myself to fall in love, I promise."

"Wow when you put it that way, how could I resist the utter temptation?" Nervously laughing aloud, Taylor felt her temperature lower slightly, thankful for the respite.

"You so excite me Taylor, this I cannot deny. Though you're sexy, it's truly that mind of yours that captures my heart." Jake's smile stretched ear to ear, looking her square in the eye. "Let me please you."

"So make love to my mind if you love it so, spare my body the dangerous journey," she bantered, maintaining a serious expression.

"Girl you are something else. You should be a lawyer. No, even better a used car salesman!" He snipped chuckling.

"Well thank you sir, I will take that as an off handed compliment," Taylor held his glance, smiling.

"I still want to devour every inch of that hot little body of yours, regardless of your exceptionally sexy brain though." Jake slowly ran his fingers up the length of her spine, into the fall of her hair, softly wrapping his fingers in the silky strands tilting her head back, exposing her neck to his warm, wet lips. Softly he nibbled along her throat. Kissing his way to her ear again then back to the ridge of her collarbone, before moving to the nape of her neck once more, softly sliding his hands to her ribs, taking hungrily to her bosom.

Taylor's head spun, a massive unannounced rush of adrenaline rising within her. This charismatic man had her melting in his hands, momentarily lost in his lavish attentions. "Jake…" a breathy plea escaping her.

"I love when you call out my name," smirking, he continued feasting. Softly slipping her blouse from her shoulder, kissing the round of it, lightly nibbling across the line of her neck once more.

"Jake, we need to stop please, I can't go here right now, please," Taylor gasped, attempting to catch her breath.

Disappointed, he covered her bare shoulder, smiling sweetly. "You can't blame a man for trying." Running his hands through his thick black hair, Jake sucked in a long deep breath, sighing heavily. "Well beautiful, you ready to head back before they send the troops looking for us?"

Getting to her feet Taylor pulled herself together. "I'm sure my brother is pacing the floor by now," smoothing her blouse with her palms.

"He's wound a bit tight, isn't he?" Jake stood offering her jacket to her. "That just shows how very much he loves you."

"That he does… yes, that he thankfully does," smiling at the sweet truth.

Walking up the path Jake cozied up close behind Taylor, pressing his body tightly against her. Moving his feet in sync with hers he slid his hands into the front pockets of her jeans, tickling her hip bones.

"What are you up to back there mister?" Closing her eyes, pressing her head back into his chest, soaking in the moment, savoring the long missed feel of a man's touch upon her.

Slipping his hands from her pockets, Jake ran his palms firmly down her sides, along the line of her hips, pulling her tight against him as they continued up the path. Their legs still moving in unison as they carried on toward his bike in silence. Slipping into their jackets, they tugged their helmets on. Throwing his leg over Jake scooted forward, watching as Taylor climbed on. Squeezing her eyes closed she delighted in the feel of his body so close to her. She had always treasured the feel of a man, the way it made her feel like a real woman. Her imagination ran wild with thoughts of them skin on skin, tangled, heated, recklessly feasting on one another without regard for rules and boundaries, time or reality. Jake's tempting offer very well could be precisely what she needed. Still the nagging possibility of the horrendous aftermath pulled her back from the edge of such temptation. The pact she'd made with God to refrain from such actions in exchange for Him guiding her to her soul mate resounded in her thoughts. After all she had survived through with the last man that was allowed keys to her heart, the utter devastation he had plagued her with though she had offered him all of her… this could not be allowed again. With Taylor the heart was one with the body, a combination not so compatible with playboys, regardless of their caliber. Lust was not in her DNA, it had only ever brought her lonesome sadness. Yet the roaring lion still reared its ugly head.

With the road passing briskly beneath them she felt her temperature rise once again. The feel of his wide shoulders, his broad back pressed against her chest thrilled her more than she would ever had imagined possible. Though the sensation had her mesmerized, she had to wonder if it was simply the idea, rather than the man that had her blood stirring so.

Garrett flashed in her mind's eye… what about Garrett? Her resolve weakened by the sudden intense surge of desire that washed over her. Squeezing Jake she imagined Garrett against her. An unexpected rush of guilty emotions filled her to overflowing, tears streamed freely from her eyes. There was no hiding the way she felt. Somehow she knew deep in her heart that with Garrett no substitute would do. Regardless of how Jake stirred her within, she knew that in truth it was simply her body reacting, matters of the heart had nothing to do with it. Finding resolve, her tears drying as they rode back to Donna's Place. Taylor was proud of herself for not falling once again into the trappings of lustful desire. Thankful that her prayers for inner strength had been answered.

Jake pulled the motorcycle up close to the front door, allowing Taylor to step from behind him. Sliding the helmet off, she caught Jake staring at her.

"Are you sure you won't let me ruin you for all others?" Holding her gaze he took the helmet from her, locking it in the saddle bag.

"I have to admit that is the most tempting of offers… very, very tempting. But for now I will have to pass thank you."

"Go with me to the lake sometime then, just as a friend. We can share a bottle of wine on the docks and talk, get to know one another better," winking, not waiting for her to answer, he pulled a pen from his tank bag. Lifting her hand he scribed his number on her palm, shoving the pen back in the bag. Pretending to tip his hat, Jake backed his bike from the sidewalk and opened her up as he pulled onto the street. The intense rumble of his pipes fired her up once again. Tilting her face to the illumination of the moon Taylor soaked in every last decibel until only cricket song filled the air. Opening her palm she stared at his number scribed on her skin, still pondering the prospect. 'What are you thinking Tay, don't go there. You simply must not allow yourself to go there again!' Shaking her head at the very thought of accepting such an insane offer, she turned heading inside. Grabbing ahold of the handle she started to open the door. Pausing she pulled her cell phone from her pocket, adding Jake to her contacts list grinning all the while at her lack of resistance for such charm. Typing the word 'Trouble' in rather than his name, she bit her lower lip at the sheer thought.

Chapter Seven

Several weeks had passed since her ride with Jake, and Taylor had taken on a few short shifts at Donna's, just enough to get her feet wet. She'd even began driving the rental car her insurance loaned her until she had her replacement funds in hand. A quick trip to the grocery store, Post Office, here and there and she was on her way to healing, her confidence growing with every mile.

Liz had phoned moments earlier, her frazzled words spewing through the phone line nearly faster than she could comprehend. "Come now! Everything is such a mess and I am down to three plates with orders across the board! Please Tay, I need you now!"

The phone slammed down on the other end, cutting her off before she could reply. Without thinking, Taylor slipped from her sweats, tugging her black work jeans and embroidered short sleeve work shirt on. Snagging her leather jacket and black square toe biker boots she headed for the door. Grabbing her purse from the coat hook she paused tempted to grab the bike keys, then refrained. Moving to the alarm pad she found herself hesitating before punching in the code. Pulling the front door closed behind her she fought amidst herself. "Not tonight Tay, you are not riding tonight." The powerful urge to be on two wheels had returned full force. Thinking better of it she headed for the rental car, knowing too well her nerve had still yet to catch up with her desires.

Steering into the parking lot of Donna's, her eyes bulged from their sockets. "What on earth!" Scanning the parking lot, not one parking space was left open. Glancing through the window she was even more shocked at the sea of people jammed into every inch of floor space. Tucking her rental car tightly into the stall behind Toby's bike Taylor turned off the ignition, pushing the door open stepping out. Her eyes locked on an incredible deep crimson bike parked close by. "What a beauty," stopping momentarily, mesmerized by the sleek line, the depth of the black cherry paint, the sparkle of its polished chrome. Snapping herself back to reality she hurried to the front entrance pausing as she opened the door to get one last eye full of the sleek machine before slipping inside. Frustration flushed her face as she pushed through the crowd, fighting her way behind the bar. Fully realizing in that moment precisely what she'd volunteered for. Manic, frenzied insanity exuding from the massive crowd of sweaty patrons crammed into the restaurant.

"Thank God you showed!" Liz screamed above the brain numbing beat exploding from the jukebox. "We need help bad!" The buzz of the crowd muffling her, making it difficult for Taylor to understand her every word. "Would you take the bar, I need to get back to the grill before Amanda burns the joint down!" Liz screamed even louder.

Waving her reply, Taylor grabbed a short waist apron tying it on. Stepping in beside Toby she began taking orders as fast as she could keep up.

Hours blew by before the crowd thinned. "Hey Tob I'm going to step out and get some air real fast if you've got this?" Taylor said unknotting her apron strings.

"Could you deliver this plate to the guy sitting by the fireplace before you go please? You'll save me the trip." Toby asked, handing her a heaping plate of buttered green beans, fluffy butter streaked mashed potatoes and a golden brown encrusted country fried steak before she could answer.

"Sure thing," she said under her breath. Flustered she sat the plate on a serving tray, retied her apron, grabbing a silverware set tightly wrapping them in an embossed paper napkin. Adding them to the tray she sucked in a deep cleansing breath, sighing long and hard in a weak attempt to relax. 'Too much too soon,' she thought to herself, frustrated with Toby for not respecting her need for a break after eight consecutive hours on her feet with no more than a sip of coconut water here and there.

Stepping from behind the bar she moved through the disaster splayed dining room, repulsed by the slop the local crowd had left behind before heading to a party up the canyon. 'So much for taking a break,' she thought to herself, making her way to the table.

"Here you are. Is there anything else I can get for you?" Taylor asked in the kindest tone she could muster as she sat the plate and utensils in front of the man sitting alone.

"No, this will do just fine. Thank you." He replied, just above a whisper, barely lifting his head.

Turning to face the utter chaos, to tackle the daunting task before her, she focused on the days that she might return to her writing, to her beloved photography. Retrieving the bus cart from behind the bar she yawned. This relentless night seemed to be dragging on and on. She longed to soak in a steamy candle lit bubble bath, wine glass in hand, fully emerged in the pages of an engrossing novel.

Clearing the glasses, bottles and plates from the last table, Taylor glanced back to the lone guest she had served. Her eyes lingering upon him a little longer than necessary, it struck her how very handsome he was. His deep espresso hair lay in soft feathered wisps along his shirt collar, smooth olive toned skin so warm to the eye. Watching the careful way he lifted his fork to his mouth, as each bite passed between his lips, each move had Taylor mesmerized. Staring as his jaw tensed and relaxed, savoring every forkful. His chiseled arm flexing beneath a thin cotton sleeve left Taylor dazed. Hopeful he'd turn her way, she imagined an intoxicating pair of hazel eyes set behind a lush mantel of silky black eyelashes.

"Sis? I thought you were going to take a breather?" Toby hollered from the bar as he scrubbed its sticky surface with a damp towel. His voice startling her from the trance she'd been lost while admiring their only remaining customer. Losing her grasp on the beer bottles dangling from her fingers, the crash of glass exploding on the floor echoed across the room, jolting her once again. "You alright Tay? You need any help?" Toby asked nervously as Liz rushed from the kitchen to investigate the noise.

Taylor's face flooded with embarrassment. Mortified she knelt behind the cart, nervously clearing the floor of shards. 'Please, please tell me you don't know I was watching you and lost my bearings momentarily,' she silently pleaded.

Wiping the last crumbs of glass from below her the rumble of a motorcycle arose outside. Seconds later the flash of a head light reflected off the window beside the front door, then faded just as quickly. Within seconds the thunderous roar of pipes filled the parking lot as the bike pulled away. Taylor froze in place, staring at the table where he had been. The beautiful stranger was gone. Her head suddenly dizzied with the details.

The dark cherry red bike that she had so adored when arriving earlier, a lone man that had been here all night. Could it have been Garrett? That smooth, deep voice had a familiar ring. Rushing to the far windows Taylor climbed across the leather seat of a booth. Straining to see outside, she peered through the neon sign. A gleaming red tail light flashed from the rear fender as he released the brake, pulling onto the street just beyond the edge of the parking lot. If it had been Garrett why didn't he introduce himself? Her heart sank as he disappeared in the distance, the glow of his head lamp slowly dimming until darkness enveloped it.

Sliding into the seat she replayed the night in her mind. He had sat at the bar alone all night, ordered two beers in five hours, barely touching either. She recalled that he had barely spoken and avoided eye contact with her all evening. Though several times she would have sworn she'd caught him staring, his kind hazel green eyes lowered every time she stepped close. How many times had he run his fingers through that silky dark brown hair, shielding his face from her? Could it be that he had he seen her scars and found her repulsive, simply deciding he wasn't interested after all? Though she did her best to cover them, their bright pink jagged edges were distracting. She had truly realized the depth of her disfigurement by the reactions she received from half drunk, unencumbered strangers. She wasn't perfect, not that she ever had been, but now she was simply damaged goods. Taylor's mind ran over the details once again before resolving to let it go. If it had been Garrett, the chance had passed. Sadly to have had missed her opportunity to meet him once and for all.

"Hey Tay, could you follow me home, I have a water leak. I'm worried she'll leave me stranded," Toby called from the kitchen, ripping her from her thoughts of Garrett.

"Sure, no problem," pleased for the opportunity to set things right with Toby about her and Jake. Knowing too well how his rationality flew out the window when it came to her, she thought better of making him privy to everything. But, still she wanted to at least clear the air. Long ago she had learned that filtering the particulars kept Toby from getting himself into unnecessary trouble... this would be no exception to the rule.

Driving up to Toby's she rolled her window down.

"Thanks again Tay," Toby said leaning through the window, kissing her cheek.

"You are very welcome," Taylor said resting her head against door. "Hey Tob, I want you to know that Jake is as harmless as a teddy bear. I don't want you to worry about me so much, I'm a big girl."

"Too bad, that's my job. I'm sure he's a great guy, just not for you."

"If you got to know him better you'd really like him, I promise." Doing her best to convince him.

"So what was that about tonight, dropping bottles all over the dining room floor?" He asked eyebrow raised, changing the subject. "Did you see a ghost?"

"Garrett. At least I think it was him, but I can't be sure being that I have no clue what he looks like."

"What? How did I miss that? You should have said something!"

"Hey don't shoot the messenger bud! I didn't even realize it might be him until, well after I dropped the bottles. And then before I knew it, he was gone."

"Wait a minute, so that's what caused the mess?" Toby asked, his curiosity peaking.

"Honestly? I was, um, well… I can't believe I'm going to admit this, even to you! I was captivated, staring at him. Oh I know it sounds stupid, but I was mesmerized and lost myself in the moment. Does that make you happy, knowing how silly your sister is?" Taylor covered her face with the palms of her hands humiliated. "Are you happy knowing that your sister is a complete and utter wreck over the male species?"

"Tay, this is ridiculous, you need a man!" Toby said through laughter. "Bad!" Throwing his head back chuckling even louder.

"I'm pleased that I can so easily tickle you lil' brother," leaning her head against the cool metal frame of the window once again.

"I'm sorry. I don't mean to laugh at your expense, but man Tay you really shouldn't give me so much material to work with here," he said snickering, patting her shoulder in a weak attempt to console her.

Offering Toby a sideways glance, she sighed squeezing her eyes shut, stifling her own laughter. "I know, I know it's ridiculous. So what's new, my life is pathetic. Go ahead and let it all out. Get it out of your system." Taylor sat up turning to Toby. "This is a onetime free laugh at Taylor pass. After this stifle it, okay?" Holding out her pinky finger, "deal?"

Wrapping her pinky in his pinky, Toby smiled, "deal sis."

Waving, she watched Toby in the rearview mirror as she exited his front drive. Making her way home she replayed the night over again in her mind, feeling more defeated as the miles ticked by. Pulling up in front of her house she yawned, pleased to be home after such an insane night. Rolling up the window she stepped from the car. Tilting her face to the Heavens she drew a long cleansing breath of the cool dewy air. Tossing her purse on the lawn she sat down beside it. Cricket song dancing on the evening breeze taking her back to the night shared with Jake under the stars. Rolling onto her elbow smirking, she tugged her purse closer, unzipping it, retrieving her cell phone. Flipping through her contacts list she searched for Jake's number. Pressing the send button she found herself grinning seeing the words typed on the screen. 'Too late?' She lay back on the grass, the sweet scents of the garden tantalizing her senses. Within seconds the cell phone binged with a return text.

"Never. What's up beautiful?"

Taylor messaged him with a quick reply. "Busy?"

The phone sounded again. "Never too busy for you. Change your mind? Want to make out? Or we can simply talk, your choice. LOL."

A wide grin stretched across her face, a giggle bubbling forth as she responded yet again. "Ride?"

Seconds later Jake responded. "When?"

"Tomorrow night, sundown. Meet me at Donna's?" Taylor typed the words, pressing send, butterflies fluttering within. This would fill the bill. Having time on a bike with a handsome man to hold onto that expected nothing, yet desired every inch of her… this would be the perfect distraction.'

"I'll see you there. Don't eat before. My treat. Sweet dreams beauty."

"Can't wait. Sweet dreams beast." Taylor pressed the send button one last time, sighing with pleasure. He wasn't Garrett, but Jake was just what the doctor ordered. Standing from the cool lawn she dusted herself off and headed to the house to pour that long awaited glass of wine, run a steaming hot bath over flowing with silky bubbles and crack the spine of that new novel she'd been waiting for the perfect night to delve into.

Life was good, somehow better than it had been before the wreck. She was enjoying life more than ever. Things were getting back to normal, leaving her with a peace she had nearly forgotten existed. Realizing that before the wreck she had taken most everything for granted, she decided that no longer would such pettiness exist in her life, every moment was important and should be cherished... good, bad, or otherwise.

Chapter Eight

A full day of chores kept Taylor's mind off the night ahead. Vacuuming, cleaning the fridge, dusting the house, along with three huge loads of laundry had her thoroughly preoccupied.

Thoughtfully she searched her closet for the perfect thing to wear. Pulling an ultra-feminine sheer pink three quarter sleeve blouse from the hanger she held it up, glancing at her reflection in the mirror. 'This will do'. Taking a pair of dark jeans from the stack she turned to the dresser. 'Where are those fluffy champagne fingerless gloves, they will be perfect.' Digging through the top two drawers before finally spotting them, she added them to her arm load. Pulling the door closed behind her she lay out her clothes on the chair beside the bed, giving them one last glance of approval before stepping into a long hot shower. Partaking of a much needed catnap before dressing and she was out the door. One brief stop by the car lot at the edge of town to offer her seal of approval on the new SUV her insurance was covering and she was on her way to Donna's.

Steering in the parking lot she quickly slipped the rental car into an open spot off the side of the main entrance so as not to be seen from the front windows. Tonight she would not be guilt tripped into helping. This evening was her night to just be a woman. Her night to take a ride with a friend, simply let her hair down and have a little fun. Tonight, nothing was going to stop her. Tilting her head back against the headrest she closed her eyes lost in thought, when the distant rumble of a bike caught her attention. 'So we're both early, huh?' Taylor thought aloud grinning with excitement. Straightening up she unlatched her seatbelt, leaning into the passenger floorboard to retrieve her handbag. Sitting upright she saw the bike pull into the parking lot in her rear view. The smile on her face quickly fading to confusion and dismay. 'No way! This cannot be,' quickly ducking down so as not to be seen. Peeking into the side mirror, watching him step from the bike, slipping off his helmet, laying it into the side bag. Stunned she watched him tug a baseball cap over the soft wisps of his dark hair. 'This absolutely cannot be happening, ugh!' Taylor's subconscious screamed, face flushed, her head spinning with confusion. It was him! The man with the beautiful black cherry bike she had so lusted over. Watching mesmerized as he unzipped his leather jacket, slowly slipping it from his shoulders, swallowing hard. Guiltily staring at his well-toned body shifting beneath a crisp white Henley he wore so well. How she loved a man built from hours of physical labor. Her over active imagination spurred thoughts, flushing her cheeks to a rosy hue once again. Turning the key over, she pressed the button lowering the window a few inches. Sucking in some much needed air, hoping to steady her nerves Taylor froze. From out of the corner of her mirror she spied the dark stranger staring straight in her direction. Gulping, she sank deeper into the pleather seat praying he couldn't see her. 'Please, please, please just hurry up and go inside.' Taylor silently pleaded. In the distance the familiar purr of Jake's pipes caught her attention. "Timing is everything, ugh, she whispered, covering her eyes, slumping forward over the steering wheel wondering precisely what she had ever done to deserve such torture.

True to form Jake pulled in, stopping just beside the crimson beauty. Taylor held her breath, anxiously waiting to see if Jake and handsome stranger would exchange words. Watching stunned as Jake stepped from his bike admiring the stranger's bike beside him, thankfully seeing that the biker was gone, had vanished in the few seconds that she had looked away.

"Where did he go?" Taylor asked aloud, forgetting that she had the window partially rolled down. The sound of her voice caught Jakes attention and he smiled acknowledging Taylor in the mirror.

"Hey there beautiful!" The smooth confidence of his baritone voice calmed her fragile nerves.

Opening the car door, Taylor smiled brushing off her nervousness. "Jake, you're early."

"Ready to hit the road?" Extending a hand, he helped her from the car.

"More than you know," Taylor blurted, practically leaping from the seat, springing past Jake in a blur leaving him perplexed as he leaned in to lock and close her car door. Without waiting for Jake, Taylor took the liberty of pulling the spare helmet from his saddlebag.

"Wow are we in a rush or what Missy?" He curiously inquired, chuckling beneath his breath.

"Yep, I can't wait to get this show on the road." Pulling her bag over one shoulder, she swung it around behind her, resting her hands on her hips, the toe of her boot impatiently tapping on the pavement.

"Alright then," shaking his head at her oddly anxious disposition. Tugging on his helmet, he threw his leg over. Before he could turn the key Taylor was seated behind him. Stunned he started the bike, pushing it back from the stall. "And we're off."

Pulling from the parking lot onto the roadway sent relief coursing through Taylor. Closing her eyes she sighed. Jake's gloved hand patted her knee in his usual comforting way. Wrapping her hands tightly around him, she pressed her chest firmly against his broad back. Jake opened the throttle and they rocketed up the canyon. The sheer thrill filling Taylor's heart to over flowing.

The sensation of Jake's body pressed tightly to hers drew forth longings that years ago she had so carefully suppressed. Pushing from her mind the disquieting whispers of her sub-conscious, Taylor softly lay her cheek against his back smiling. Temporary respite from reality wasn't illegal. She vowed there and then to take full advantage of such joys as often as possible. Jake was a willing subject, so open to pleasing her with no strings attached. The truth of such freedoms sent a tingling rush racing through her. Allowing herself a little excitement wasn't like indulging in a love affair, as she had so devastatingly done prior. Jake was a safe outlet for pent up fun, nothing more.

Gliding slowly along a long sweeping corner far above town they rode into a tunnel cut from solid granite. Taylor hadn't any memory of such a place. Lost in her thoughts she realized Jake had taken her farther East of town than she had ever ventured. The chiseled rock opened to a panoramic view of the alluring valley below, encircled by the ridge of a brilliant granite summit. Pulling from the road the vast beauty filled their visors.

"It's so spectacular!" Taylor gasped. "I have never seen anything so magnificent!"

"Are you seriously telling me that this is the first time you've been up here?" His eyes bulging at the sight of her shaking her head in agreement. "I did hear you correctly when you said that you were born here, yes?" Amazed by her reaction, he pulled his helmet off, twisting slightly in the saddle. "You look like a kid in a candy store." He said laughing aloud. "I had intended on taking you higher up, but if you want we can stay here."

"It's just so beautiful! Would you mind terribly if we did?"

"Anything you want doll." Jake faced forward, steadying his bike as Taylor climbed off.

"I had no idea. It's as if I've been living beneath a rock," she said, handing Jake her helmet without looking away, mesmerized by the horizon.

"Glad to see you're as impressed as I was the first time I happened upon this place." Jake stepped up beside her, searching the valley below. "This never gets old, no matter how many times I come here."

"So you bring all your lady friends here do you?" Taylor asked teasingly nudging him with her elbow.

Wriggling away from her, a childlike giggle escaped Jake.

"You big beast, you laugh like a girl!"

"No I don't!" Jake said choking on her accusation. "Just so we are clear, you are the first woman I have ever brought here. I come here alone to find peace and to refill."

Seeing Jake's reaction Taylor turned her attention. "Ticklish are we now?" Moving her fingers like crawling spiders in his direction, attempting to skirt the reality of Jake admitting she was special enough for him to share his place of sanctuary.

"Don't do it! Unless you're prepared to see a grown man cry. I beg you to refrain Taylor... please!" Jake strained to speak as he wriggled away.

"Wow, I never would have guessed a big mountain of a man like you to have a weakness of this sort." Taylor threw her head back letting out a belly laugh, a soft snort escaping her. "You made me snarf!"

Explosive cackling poured forth, until Jake held his stomach wincing. "You're killing me here lady!"

"Feeling the burn are you?" Taylor rubbed her stomach refusing to admit she did as well. It had been years since she'd laughed so freely. How nice it was once again to have a friend to spend time with, to laugh with.

Wiping the tears from his reddened cheeks he stepped back to the bike. "What do you say we have a little picnic beautiful?" Jake asked pulling a canvas sack from his saddle bag.

"A real picnic? You are a man after my own heart." Taylor grinned pulling her hair back from her face into a ponytail, twisting until a perfect bun sat at the crown of her head. Tucking the end strands into the silky mound she caught Jake starring. "What are you gawking at?" She asked fighting a smile.

"You women just amaze me. If I tried to do that I would have ended up with something resembling a rat's nest piled on my head." He brushed past her blushing. Taylor wasn't so sure if he was possibly hiding the truth behind his interesting reaction.

Her mind suddenly turned to Garrett. Startled, she pondered how this man that she no more than spoke to could occupy so many of her thoughts? Such a silly idea most certainly that this could be happening, but still she had to face the raw truth. Her heart longed for Garrett, regardless of what a wonderful, funny, interesting hunk of man Jake was. It was Garrett alone that stirred something deeper than physical within her, this there'd be no denying.

Seeing Taylor's eyes glaze over, Jake cleared his throat. "Come on girl, let's eat." Hopeful that his words might bring her back to him from wherever she had drifted off to.

Taylor shook herself back to the moment, pausing to regroup before following him to the cobblestone wall on the edge of the pullout. Watching mesmerized as Jake spread a small blanket below the wall onto a lush patch of wild grass, setting out a plethora of treasures he had painstakingly gathered just for her. Taylor stood transfixed in amazement of his thoughtfulness.

"Join me?" Jake motioned for her to take a seat beside him on the blanket.

"This was all very sweet of you Jake," as she laid the last of her turkey-pesto croissant onto her paper plate, lifting a plump chocolate dipped strawberry to her mouth. A drop of juice trickling down her lip, onto her chin as she closed her teeth on the delicacy. Jake leaned in, softly kissing the juice away. Meeting her eyes he pressed his lips to hers again still holding her gaze, lightly biting her lip.

"Naughty boy." Her words barely a whisper beneath his kiss. "Be good."

Smirking, he pushed their plates aside, scooting in closer beside her. Brushing a stray lock of hair behind her ear, Jake softly nibbled her earlobe.

Tilting her face to the sky Taylor lost sense of all time and space. He had found a weak link in her defenses and now Jake undeniably knew it. Her breath caught in her throat, excitement washing over her.

"I want to please you Taylor. Let me drive you crazy little lady, let go, have some fun with me. Just one night, spend this one night with me. Who knows we may really like one another." His steamy offer tempting Taylor senseless. "It's quite possible that we might even like each other so much we'll want more. We'll never know if we don't try. And just think, when we are old and shriveled we will look back and remember this time together and smile at the memory."

"Jake." His name barely spoken before his lips met hers in a long, deep, feverish kiss. The warmth of his mouth against her lips awakened her senses. Reveling in the heat of his body radiating through her blouse, Taylor moaned.

Lifting her onto his lap, running his hands up her back he pulled her tightly into him. A breathy sigh escaped her as Jake loosed her mane. Gently running his fingers through her hair, taking hold he slowly tilted her head back. Tracing his lips along the ridge of her throat, hearing yet another moan escaped Taylor, her breath quickening.

"Loosen up girl," his words falling warm across her skin, as he slid his hands to her shoulders, rubbing them softly.

Her heart pounded wildly, the heat of desire rushing over her. Primal hunger tugging at her, flooding in, drowning out reality as his mouth found hers again, feasting feverishly. Lifting her from him with one arm, he cradled her head laying her back onto the blanket, pressing his body firmly to hers, passionately kissing her neck again and again. Momentarily shaking herself from his sensual spell, Taylor prayed for an ounce of strength. "Jake," she pleaded, her voice barely a whisper, "Jake we need to stop. I need to stop, please."

As if he hadn't heard, Jake stole her breath again, running his hand along her spine, beneath her hips, cradling her against him in tender exploration.

"Jake, please, I am begging you. I need to slow down, this is all happening much too fast, please," Taylor's voice cracking beneath emotional fervor.

"Hey now, it's alright I won't do anything you aren't comfortable with." Leaning away, Jake saw the glittering of tears pooling in her eyes. Pulling her close, he cuddled her lovingly into his arms again. The warmth of his embrace soothing her frazzled mind.

"Shhh, please don't cry. I'm so sorry. I thought you were into this as much as I am into you," Jake's voice filled with concern.

Wiping the tears from her reddened cheeks she met his gaze. "It's not you at all, you are wonderful Jake. Please understand. Please don't be upset. I really do like you, it's just..." Taylor sucked in a deep breath, pausing. "I..."

"Are you married Taylor, is that what this is all about?" Jake's face paled awaiting her response.

"No, oh no that's not it. I promise you that I'm not married and I've never been."

"Then what is it? Are you dying? What is it cancer?" Jake swallowed hard as if the words were poison in his mouth. "Please just tell me what's wrong, Taylor I beg you." Jake stroked her shoulder trying to comfort her.

"I'm in love with someone else... well at least I think I am. Oh I don't know anymore! I just know that I shouldn't be here with you Jake, spending such intimate time with you when I'm in love with another man!" Taylor admitted, her own words turning her stomach. "I am so very sorry. I never should have accepted the offer to ride with you again, I never should've called you, especially knowing we share such an attraction for one another. This is completely my fault."

"So how long have you known." Jakes asked, fighting back the tidal wave of emotions building within.

"I've known for a while, since before my wreck. Please don't hate me Jake, don't be mad please. I realize we haven't known one another very long but, your friendship is very important to me." Taylor covered her face weeping harder.

"Hey now girl, come on stop those tears. I'm not mad. A little confused and maybe a heavy dose jealous, but I'm not mad." Jake said forcing a smile. "So help me understand this. If you are so 'in love' then precisely why aren't you with him? It's him that's married, is that it?" Jake's face darkened with disapproval.

"No he's not married, at least I don't believe that he is. Oh my gosh, I pray he's not married! I have no idea, this is so stupid!" Taylor wept harder still, gasping for breath.

"Wow Missy, you are a wreck! Breathe darlin' or you're going to pass out." Jake brushed a hank of tear soaked hair from her cheek, tilting her chin up, locking eyes with her. "Look Taylor, you are obviously in no place emotionally to be seeing anybody and you know that I am a diehard bachelor. I told you that from the very beginning. Though I won't deny that if there was anyone I could imagine sharing more with, well, honestly it would be you. I hate to admit it but even though we have only known each other a nanosecond, I've actually considered sweeping you off your feet and hanging up my bachelor boots for good. But I am absolutely at peace with this, do you hear me? So pull it together and tell me about this man that has you so messed up, okay?" Jake snugged her tight against his chest again. "Come on girl talk to me." The depth of his raspy voice stirred her, confusing her once again.

Pressing her face into the steel muscles of his shoulder Taylor felt her stomach flip. The utter thrill Jake drew from the depths of her caught her off guard. Clearing her throat she tried to focus. Her head spun as Jake squeezed her tightly. Pressing her hands against his chest she sat back, drawing a ragged breath. Slowly exhaling she patted her hands on his chest moving onto the blanket in front of him.

Taylor wiped her palms across her tear streaked face again, regrouping before speaking. "We met on the phone by sheer miracle. We talked of everything and before we knew it the night had slipped away. As we were saying goodbye he asked me to meet him; to join him and his friends for a sunset ride. Then as fate would have it I wrecked the day we were to meet, so I obviously didn't show. He probably thinks I was just toying with him, that I was playing games when I agreed to come. The worst is that I have no idea who he is or how to find him!" Exasperation poured from Taylor.

"Wait a minute. So you mean to tell me that you are in love with someone that you haven't even seen?" Jake sat motionless, staring dumbfounded.

"I realize it's stupid, trust me, don't think I haven't thought it all out. I have tried to stop myself from feeling the way that I do, from wanting this stranger. But he's somehow set up residence in my soul. I'm utterly exhausted trying to forget him. He distracts my days and haunts my nights, even as I sleep!" Frustration peaking, Taylor stood pacing about. "That's where you came in. Handsome and tough, all gorgeous and buff." Taylor smiled realizing how silly the words sounded. You come on strong, sweeping me off on romantic rides, kissing me into a trance. It seems that somehow when I am with you, I am temporarily freed of thoughts of him."

"So I am simply a distraction for you? No more than a diversion to keep your mind off of the real feelings you have for a total stranger? A total stranger, mind you… that may have already forgotten you no less?" Pausing Jake smirked, amusement distracting him from his underlying frustration.

"Are you laughing at me?" Taylor stopped in her tracks. "Seriously, you think this is funny? You do! Look, you can barely hold back!"

"I'm not laughing at you, only at the situation. It's just things like this only happen in romance novels and on women's television programming. And somehow I waltzed myself straight into the midst of it. I seem to have a knack for attracting unavailable women." Jake looked to his feet smirking, nervously running his fingers through his hair, standing.

"It's not funny… well it's not that funny. Alright, so I know it's ridiculous!" Letting out a long sigh, tears streaming down her cheeks once again, as she joined in laughing at herself.

"Now you think this is funny too?" Jake asked, cracking a smile before throwing his head back, cackling uncontrollably. "You're seriously going to make me wet my pants girl!"

Minutes passed, the two of them riding waves of laughter. Meeting her eyes, Jake took her hands helping her to her feet, looking to her once again, smiling sweetly he brushed away the last of her tears with the tips of his fingers. "Oh Taylor, you are something else girl, you really are something else. If ever you change your mind please promise that you'll call me?" His kind eyes sparkling in the last light of day.

"You have to know the effect you have on me. It is of dire importance that you believe I wasn't simply passing time with you. I truly love spending time together Jake, more than you will ever understand." Staring into his dreamy eyes, Taylor softly laid her palm on his cheek, taking in the moment. "You are much more than simply a bookmark to me."

"I do know, Missy, I do." He leaned closer still, brushing his lips against hers, neither closing their eyes, soaking in every last detail of the moment. Stepping back Jake offered her his hand. "Let's get you out of here before I try to change your mind about this mystery man, what do you say?" Lifting her hand to his lips, still holding her stare.

"Thanks Jake."

"Honey if I am one thing, it's a gentleman all the way. If I wasn't my mamma would hang me by my toenails! And Momma Nancy isn't a woman to be reckoned with, believe me."

"Not just for that Jake, I mean for being so understanding. You are the best friend a gal could ask for," kissing him on the cheek smiling sweetly.

"I always thought it might be cool to have a girl for a best buddy. See things always work out." Bumping hips with her, he grinned. "Still keep me in mind."

Riding back Taylor soaked in the scents, the sounds, wanting to engrave these precious moments into her memory forever. This being possibly the last time they would spend the evening together in this capacity, the reality a bitter pill to swallow for both of them. Taylor held Jake as tight as she could without cheating his air. Submerging herself in every last detail of the night; his scent, the feel of his chest beneath her palms. He was a quite a catch, if only she hadn't this one little issue of being in love with another man. A single tear escaped her eye as they pulled into the parking lot at Donna's, both sorrowful for the night to be ending.

Jake started to say something as she stepped from the bike, then stopped, seeing a tear trickle down her rosy cheek. "Hey Missy, let's not say goodbye on a sad note. Okay? You have my number and I have yours and we'll keep in touch. That's what buddies do isn't it? Besides I would miss you too much if we didn't," gently tugging at her jacket sleeve, smiling.

"I know your right, it's just sad. You are such a great guy, we get along so well and I really like you Jake."

Drawing her into to him, wrapping her in his strong arms, squeezing her tight, he softly pressed his warm lips to her damp cheek.

From behind Taylor arose the roar of pipes striking up, revving then resting at a low rumble. Her eyes bulged from her head with shock. The black cherry bike! She would know the sexy growl of those pipes anywhere. Frozen she stared at Jake. His eyes met hers, the mirror image of her surprise.

"What? Is that him?" Jake whispered, peering over Taylor's shoulder, then back to her once again. "Nice bike! Is it him?" He asked again, his nose nearly touching hers.

Taylor listened as the bike backed from the stall where it had been parked when they'd left earlier. Could he have been waiting to see if she got back safely? Such a notion played on her emotions, toying with her mind.

Slowly turning from Jake, Taylor peered nonchalantly over her shoulder. There he sat, staring her straight in the eye. Taylor found herself swept away, spellbound by the depth of his olive rimmed hazel eyes. So perplexingly familiar, yet still so mystifying.

Revving the engine, rumblings poured from the pipes filling the air. In the blink of an eye he slid his glasses on, kicking the bike into gear, tearing into the street he sped off, once again leaving her behind. Taylor gasped, struggling to catch her breath.

Jake stared along-side her into the distance, listening until they could no longer hear the bike. "So let me get this straight, you two have never spoken, you have never been so much as introduced... having only a singular phone conversation between you and there's already such tension? You are both in dire trouble my dear." Jake's tone wavered with emotion as he removed his helmet, looping the strap over his grip.

"I'm honestly not positive that it's even him. While I was in rehab a man visited me across the pond in the front of the hospital nearly every day. I couldn't make out the bike, but it was dark. I assumed after several interludes that they might be one in the same, but still I can't be certain."

"Wait a minute!" Jake lifted the helmet from her head, shocked by her words. "So you mean to tell me that this guy, if he is 'one in the same', as you put it, has been watching over you since your wreck? And there's a possibility that this is the same man you were supposed take that ride with? I can't believe after all this time you have still yet to meet one another! Ridiculous is an understatement my dear! This needs to be remedied and soon, before you drive yourself insane." Shaking his head, he lowered the helmet into his saddled bag. "Life is too short Taylor. If this is what it seems, you have found each other against all odds. What if he's your soul mate? Are you willing to keep avoiding him until he simply slips away? You need to clear this up as soon as possible, it is as simple as that. And if he isn't all that you think he might be, well then, you're wasting precious time worrying about nonsense when I could be spending time with you," he interjected bluntly, shrugging his shoulders.

Taylor stood in silence as Jakes words played in slow motion, seeping deep into her core. 'Soul mate... soul mate...

what if he's your soul mate?' An emotional tug of war wrenching within her. Taylor felt her knees waver beneath her, the sky spinning. How could it be that there were two men battling within her heart, after nearly a decade of complete male deprivation? Dizzied by such thoughts, she reached for Jake, steadying herself.

"Whoa! Are you alright girl? Don't go passing out on me now. I'm not trying to stir you up, I am simply saying we need not waste a moment finding out if he's your 'Mr. Right'." Smiling, he touched her chin, tipping her face to his winking. "I didn't mean to sound demanding. I'm sorry if it came across that way. It's just that we could be sharing some incredibly memorable moments by now if it weren't for those pesky feelings you are harboring for this complete stranger." Clearing his throat, Jake closed his eyes, obviously frustrated.

"There is always that, yes." Taylor searched his face, the lean, muscular line of his chiseled jaw, the thick curve of his irresistible lips. The memory of his fiery kisses lingering in her thoughts. Running her fingertip down the bridge of his tanned nose, across the indentation beneath, over the smooth warmth of his mouth she smiled.

Jake tilted his face to the sky. "Well I best head on before I change my mind, throw you on my bike and steal you away." Jake cleared his throat, trying to distance himself from her velvet touch. "Before I just take you so far from here he never gets the chance to meet you," Jake quipped, tugging his helmet on, attempting to disguise how very flustered her touch had made him. "The offer still stands beautiful. I'm merely a phone call away." Blowing her a kiss Jake started his bike. "Anytime." The moment hung between them heavy with unspoken possibilities and ever growing desires.

"Good night Jake, thanks again, for everything."

"Be safe," sweetly winking as he backed away. Offering a quick wave, moving onto the roadway before gunning it.

"Show off!" Taylor yelled in vain, drowned out by the roar of his pipes, smiling to herself as she watched him speed away.

Walking back to her car she reminisced over the night, praying that she was making the right decision. Jake's unnerving words running through her head as she made her way home. "What if we are soul mates?" She asked herself aloud. Her own words seeming even stranger than coming from Jake. Precisely what was a soul mate anyhow? How could it be possible that two people could be made specifically for one another? There was no proof of any such union. The mention of it had been nothing more than a silly notion... or was it? 'Yes, it had to be'. She thought once again, hardly convincing herself of the impossibility.

How dare Jake put such nonsense in her head! And then on top of that throw in that he might be willing to toss in the wild life in order to be with her! How dare he fill her with such confusing ideas. How dare he be so... sweet, so kind, honest and utterly gorgeous! "Ugh!" Taylor's head spun with confusion. The thought of God having created a special someone, a perfect counterpart just for her left her dazed. Jake's words clouded her head, leaving her reeling.

Pulling into her driveway, Taylor's cell phone rang. Peering at the screen she groaned. "Hey little brother, what's up?"

"Are you alright Tay? You sound upset." Toby inquired with concern.

"Just deep in thought about life and the cosmos. What has you calling so late?"

"What do you think about working a few hours for me tomorrow? I kind of have a date. Well maybe not exactly a

114

date, we're only meeting for coffee. Anyway, I just need you to fill in from four to seven thirty. But to be safe let's make it eight. What do you think Tay?" Toby asked as sweetly as he could muster, impatiently awaiting her reply. "You there?" His voice cutting through the silence emanating from the other end of the line.

"What, sure. I mean yes I will cover for you," quickly recovering, struggling to focus on his words. "Do you believe in soul mates Toby?"

"What brought this on?" Perplexed by the question.

"Just answer me please. Do you think it's even remotely possible that soul mates really do exist?"

"I never really thought about it before. But I can't see why not. I've heard of people falling in love as soon as their eyes meet and spending the rest of their lives together. There must be something to it other than simply lust. What is this all about Tay? Please tell me it's not that biker dude you've been hanging out with! Please, not him!"

"No, don't worry little brother, this isn't about Jake. Though he did offer to hang up his desperado single life in exchange for me." Her words leaving Toby stunned to silence. "See you around three thirty." Taylor smirked, reveling in having left him speechless as she hung up the phone.

Pushing the French doors open Taylor stepped out onto the back porch. The soothing glow of garden lights spilling across the brick lined pathway meandering through the yard. Home, there was simply no place like it. This sweet freedom was something that she never wanted to take for granted. Smiling she stepped onto the mossy bricks tilting her face to the open sky, taking in the vast blanket of stars sprinkled across the Heavens she sent up a silent prayer for the answer to her questions.

Chapter Nine

The day breezed by. Taking breakfast on the back patio, a chapter of her newly started novel read in the hammock followed by a load of laundry helped the time slip away. With a quick shower Taylor headed off to Donna's. Her heart sank seeing the parking lot packed as she pulled in, not a single space left for her. Why did she always seem to be suckered into nights like this?

Toby swung the door open, jogging toward her. "Take my spot Tay!" Hurrying to his truck, quickly backing out, leaving her a space near the front door. Beaming with joy he waved, continuing past her out onto the street. Rolling forward she parked, stepping from the car. Rushing inside Taylor was met with the tremendous buzz of the crowd. "Wonderful, what did you get yourself into now Taylor?" Her own words barely audible above the ruckus.

"Well don't just stand there, help! Those bikers at the end need their drinks freshened up and a dozen lemons need slicing before the next wave of drink orders comes in."

Shoving an apron into Taylor's hands, Liz vanished into the kitchen once again.

"Hello sis, yea it's great to see you too," Taylor mocked Liz, shaking her head sighing.

Once the customers at the bar were set with fresh drinks and a bowl of lemon wedges were sliced, Taylor started a batch of popcorn, grabbed the bus cart and headed to the dining area. There before her was all but one table covered in half eaten plates of food, heaps of used napkins, empty beer bottles and dozens of sweat drenched, mostly full water glasses. Tonight she definitely had her work cut out for her. Pondering again the reality that once she had been out in the real world, living in Seattle, working as a successful photojournalist, with a posh flat above her private studio. The haunting reality that once upon a time she'd had time to travel and money to spend. The mere thought of which made her ache for her old life. Pushing out the past, she plowed through each table until she had the dining room whipped into shape. Shaking her head in disgust she tucked the floors whopping three dollars of tips into her apron. Hauling the overloaded cart back behind the counter once again, she stepped to the sink. Scanning the crowd lined up elbow to elbow along the bar as she washed her hands.

"Busy night."

Taylor froze at the sound of his voice. Blinking hard before slowly turning to face him. "Yes." Words escaped her at the sight of him.

"Could I please get a Land Shark when you have a moment?"

Tilting her head, surprised by his request. "Really I would have thought you more a whiskey man," Taylor said teasingly as if she would have had an inkling. Swallowing hard at her failed attempt at humor, she drew a bottle from the cooler below, popping the top, setting it on a paper napkin sliding it toward him. Reaching to take it from her, his hand rested momentarily over hers. Chills shot through her as lightening might on a dry still prairie. Meeting his gaze, time seemed to slow. The knowing warmth and over powering kindness he exuded taking her breath away. Admiring the sensitive strength behind his eyes, the depth of spirit flowing from him had Taylor mesmerized. He was more than she'd imagined in the brief seconds they'd encountered. Who was this mystery man? Was it he that had visited her at the hospital as well? 'Could they truly be one in the same?' Momentarily carried off by her thoughts.

"Hey barmaid, you think you can tear yourself away from pretty boy long enough to get us something to drink down here?" An impatient biker hollered from the far end of the bar. "Anytime now legs!" Yet another rowdy biker called out.

"Excuse me please, I have animals to tend to." Stepping back she held his stare before finally turning away.

"Another round for all of us before we hit the road!" Yet another biker yelled in a booming voice, the drunken crowd around him barbarically erupting.

Taylor found herself hating the obligation to serve such patrons, especially those willing to drive so closely following tossing them back. Shrugging off her personal disapproval, she served the twenty some rambunctious men. Clearing their mess from the bar she watched them stagger to the door, pleased that they were finally on their way. Ringing in the last tab, she slid the cash into the register before turning back to the bar.

His empty bottle sat alone. Searching the room, he was nowhere in sight. Frustration raged inside her for yet another missed opportunity.

The front door swung open abruptly. "Thanks for taking over for a bit Tay! Looks like you had a big night!" Toby said pushing his way past the still heaping bus cart. "I got it from here."

"I wasn't very happy with you leaving me like that, it's been quite a while since I handled a full bar all alone. Thank God my instincts kicked in or those monsters might have eaten me live!" Taylor huffed, untying her apron, tossing it at him as she hurriedly stepped from behind the bar. "Make me something to drink please, I need to cool down. How about one of your secret concoctions? You owe me big time little brother."

"Anything, you name it." Toby smiled, tying the apron around his waist.

"Something sweet and creamy with a splash of coconut, and make it virgin... that's just what I need, to be woozy," taking a seat at the bar.

"I know Tay, I would never offer you anything with alcohol." Toby paused meeting her unrelenting glare with another smile. "Okay then, one creamy coconut surprise coming right up." Toby turned to start on her drink pausing. "I'll be right back, there are secret ingredients needed." Toby gave her an over the shoulder nod winking, then slipped into the kitchen.

Taylor lay her face in her hands replaying the moment that his hand had touched hers. The intense electricity she felt in his presence, the notable change in her heart rate. There was a stirring power about him that no other had brought before.

"So how about that ride?" The depths of his warm voice carried from down the bar, streaming through her.

Lifting her face she turned toward him. "Ride?" She asked, as if she was unsure of his question, silently praying she wasn't dreaming.

"I'm hurt. You stood me up that night, and now you don't even know what I'm talking about? I over estimated you I suppose," a smirk tugging at the corner of his mouth.

"Garrett?" She stared in amazement seeing him smile. It had been him all along. The mysterious visitor, the black cherry bike, they were one in the same. Finally all the pieces fit. "It wasn't like that, I didn't purposely stand you up!" Taylor stiffened, sitting perfectly upright on the stool, startled by the realization she had blurted the words forth louder than intended. Clearing her throat she lowered her voice before continuing on. "I was in an accident..."

"I know, there's no need to explain, I was there. I'm just giving you a hard time." Garrett said interrupting her.

"You were where? What do you mean?" Taylor grasped to conceive what he was saying.

"I saved your hair from sudden death. Do you really not remember me at all?"

"That was you? You seemed so familiar at the wreck, but I was so messed up and we had only spoken." Turning from him, her eyes nervously searching the bar top before her. Taylor's head spun attempting to digest the foreign concept of his words. He had been her hero, the calm amidst the storm, as well the mysterious biker that captivated her, they were one in the same, they were all Garrett. Regrouping she turned to face him once again. "Thank you by the way, for saving my hair. I know it may seem odd, but it really meant a lot that you did something so selflessly without judgment." Taylor wiped her damp palms on her jeans, praying he couldn't see how frazzled she truly was.

"I must admit I had no idea at the time that it was you either. I found out days later when they ran the story of your wreck in the paper. I put two and two together when you hadn't shown that night. They spoke your name and that you owned Donna's Place. I honestly didn't know it was you for sure until the story broke. I thought you simply changed your mind about the ride. Knowing we hadn't exchanged numbers there was no way for you to cancel, so I just assumed…" Nervously running his fingers through his dark hair, he stood moving closer. Pointing to the stool, silently asking permission to take the seat beside her.

Smiling she nodded, "yes, please go ahead," her cheeks flushed with his nearness, her heart pounding frantically.

"So it took forever but I found… it." Toby came around the door way stopping in his tracks. Glancing from Taylor to the man seated next to her confused.

"This is my brother Toby. Toby this is Garrett." Hearing his name pass so freely from her lips felt somehow foreign to her. The near unbelievable truth of the moment having yet to sink in. The fact that here they were here after everything, sitting mere inches apart, exchanging words, breathing the same air seemed more a dream than reality. Taylor sent up a silent prayer of thanks that this moment was sincerely happening, that indeed she hadn't been dreaming.

"It is a pleasure to meet you," Toby smiled, reaching over the bar offering a hand shake.

Taylor watched as their hands met, dazed by the surreal reality unfolding before her. He was real, more real than ever before. Finally Toby knew for certain that she hadn't created this mystery man in the confines of her imagination.

"So you're the dark stranger that Taylor so often speaks of." Toby stopped, instantly realizing what unnecessary truth he'd just offered up.

She held her breath, terrified of what Toby might say next.

"So she's spoken of me has she?" Garrett's eyes sparkled with mischief, knowing he had her squirming beneath their words. Smiling he nudged her foot with the toe of his boot beneath the bar, grinning.

"Toby don't you have dishes to wash in the kitchen?" Bestowing him a threatening glare, imagining the pure joy of launching over the bar, firmly stuffing a towel into his mouth.

"Yes ma'am, you are right, absolutely correct. I do need to get this mess cleaned up, I must get right on that in fact. It was certainly nice to finally meet you Garrett." Toby turned toward the kitchen, catching her eye, smirking before disappearing.

"So have you simply been avoiding the question or have you changed your mind about riding? I believe I have yet to hear an answer from you." Pausing he turned, starring deeply into her eyes, as if searching the confines of her soul.

The sheer essence of him had Taylor reeling. His ruthless charisma, flagrant abuse of charm, tender depth and surprisingly refreshing authenticity had Taylor effortlessly fantasizing about being closer to him. How was it that from a simple phone conversation she had become so much more open and willing than ever before to give of herself, to give her heart? What was it in Garrett that had her so conscious of her own desires? What was it that had her fully taken by him, more than with any other man she'd known before? Sitting so close she yearned to scream out 'take me now, ride with me now!', but still she held back.

"She hasn't been back on her bike since the wreck," Toby blurted out as he rounded the corner, passing by carrying a bag of kernels to the popcorn machine.

"Toby!" Taylor's face flushed with fury.

"But you do ride, as I saw you with your boyfriend, no?" Garrett said looking away, his words smothered in distress.

"Jake's not my boyfriend!" Taylor spewed. "He's just a good friend, nothing more," she continued, gathering her composure once again, taking note of his ability to so easily push her buttons. "He…"

"He wants more, but Taylor is waiting for her soul mate," Toby said before quickly ducking into the kitchen.

Taylor squeezed her eyes closed praying she would soon awaken to find this all having simply been a nightmare. Her heart skipped at the startling feel of his heated breath on her ear.

"Ride with me?" His whisper sent chills racing over her, stirring irrefutable longings within. Standing from the stool, Garrett pulled his wallet from his back pocket tossing ten bucks on the bar, moving toward the door without looking back, silently beckoning her.

Taylor swallowed hard as the door swung open, slowly closing behind him. "What just happened?" She asked aloud. The roar of his bike echoing through the empty dining room.

Peeking his face around the corner. "Is he leaving? What happened Tay? After all this time you finally meet face to face, there's obviously an undeniable connection here and you're just letting him walk away! Get up and stop him!" Toby's flailing arms driving his point poignantly home.

"He's waiting for me. He wants to take me for a ride," she replied quietly, seemingly paralyzed, staring at the bar top still dazed by his invitation. She had awaited this moment for so very long, and now that it was she was weak in the knees, heated with nausea.

"So what are you waiting for sis? Go!" Toby marched around the bar with her leather jacket and purse in hand, shoving them onto her shoulder, uprooting her from the stool.

"Get it together sis! This is it, your chance to finally ride with him. Go, go… go! Call me later and fill me in on all the juicy details!"

Shaking herself from the fog, she slid her arms into her jacket, zipping it up. Trying hard to grasp reality, slowly making her way to the door.

"Don't do anything I wouldn't do sis!" Toby jabbed as he pushed the door opened shoving her through.

Without words Garrett lifted a helmet offering it to her. Taking her purse, he slipped it into his side bag before straddling the bike. Taylor met his stare as she weaved her long hair into a French braid. His unblinking eyes locked on her every move. Twisting a thin strip of hair around the bottom, she tucked it into itself snuggly securing it. His stare penetrating through to her soul. The nervous excitement of butterflies danced within her as she stepped on the peg throwing her leg over. Steeped in the intensely personal way in which he moved her, she marveled at his ability to take her breath simply being in his presence. Wrapping her arms tightly around him Taylor felt her heart melting.

Garrett backed the bike out of the stall, pulling back on the throttle, revving the engine before slipping it into gear driving away. Taylor's pulse coursed in her ears as they moved onto the open road. Garrett reached back pressing her thigh tightly to his. Taylor slid closer to him, indulging in the pure thrill of guiltless pleasure having him so near. They were on a speeding bike after all, it was necessary to hold on tightly so as not to fall off. She thought convincingly, silently admitting that any particular excuse to hold this man would do. Throttling up hard they sped away from civilization. The open road ahead thrilled Taylor more than ever before. Riding seemed somehow more mysterious with Garrett, surprisingly more exciting. Closing her eyes, immersing herself in him, in this moment they alone shared. Knowing this very place in time would never come again, she clung tight to every moment. If he never brought her back Taylor decided it would be perfectly fine with her. She bit her lip thankful that he could not read her thoughts.

Smoothly maneuvering, Garrett took each curve of the mountain road as if they were one with the bike. This seemed somehow more than simply a ride, more an intimate dance of ebb and flow, gliding around each bend of the road in perfect sync. Taylor sighed, savoring every last drop of intense unexpected pleasure.

Something altered within her in these moments shared so close to him. Though she couldn't distinguish what precisely the change was, she simply knew she'd never again be the woman she had been before this night, before this ride… before knowing Garrett.

Slowing he signaled, pulling off the main road, bringing the bike to a stop on the shoulder. Turning to Taylor he flipped up her visor. His sheer confidence taking her by surprise. Never had she known a man with such boldness, yet still harboring such tenderness within. His uncommon dimensions sparked a fierce fire within her, blazing a path to her soul.

"Are you hungry?" Garrett's deep voice revived the chills he'd brought before.

"Sure, I could stand to eat," Taylor spoke softly attempting to hide the building excitement safely disguised beneath her calm exterior. 'Anything to spend more time alone with you.' Taylor froze, saying a prayer she'd merely spoke those words to herself.

Sliding her visor closed, he patted her knee gently before gearing up. Pulling onto the road Taylor squeezed her legs against him, feeling his muscles tense as he shifted once again. He lay his arm against her thigh, affectionately squeezing her knee. Their unspoken language taking her breath away. In return she squeezed her arms tightly against him, holding before slightly loosening her grasp again. Taylor's heart swelled with desire, passion stirring within her as she had never known before. Garrett was arousing intense primal needs, a deep seated gnawing hunger, reviving rich fantasies that she had so carefully tucked away in order to simply survive the lonesome lack luster days of her life.

Taylor had known the desires that come with maturity much earlier than one really should. In realizing that if she continued allowing herself to so recklessly indulge in intimate relationships she might possibly be ruined for life, she made a pact with God to stop such madness and save herself for her one true love. Too many times had she been tempted to give in to the deep desires dwelling within. Too many times she had left herself no choice but to flee the situation so as not to lose control, leaving a trail of broken hearts behind. Sadly, there had come a time when she had gotten herself in too deep and found it necessary to escape her situation rather than being taken against her will. The countless lies she'd been told by her first love had weakened her resolve, allowing for much unnecessary damage. Years ago Taylor had ceased allowing men to take advantage of her, knowing she had already so demoralized herself, nearly losing all hope of any semblance of a healthy relationship.

But this... whatever this was with Garrett, seemed somehow different, she felt it in her core. His nearness lent a calm, a peace that seeped deep into the essence of her being. Beyond the physical realm, more than just that, he touched her soul somehow. The mere reality that another could move her so profoundly frightened and exhilarated her all at once.

Garrett geared down as he turned on Lake Front Drive, quick shifting again forcing Taylor to squeeze him even tighter. The wind buffeted hard against them. Taylor glanced at the speedometer as they swiftly took the straight away. Garrett grabbed a gear once again. Ninety, one hundred, one twenty! Taylor had never been at such speed! Fighting fear she held her breath. The sheer thought of traveling at such velocity sent adrenaline coursing through her. Their bodies pressed hard against one another, Garrett slowly removed his palms from the grips. Taking her hands in his, he laced his fingers through hers slowly lifting their arms out beside them, until they were level with their shoulders. Taylor felt as if she were flying as she lifted inches above the seat. Was she crazy? They could die! But if it happened, what a way to go! Her fingers clamped tighter to his, she watched the road ahead barely breathing. Taylor knew in that moment, allowing another such complete control over her, had unleashed the bondage that she'd been crushed beneath for so long. This ride with Garrett was reinstating new facets of trust. In these moments she had discovered a deeper sense of wholeness somehow. Closing her eyes she basked in the decadence. Slowly Garrett allowed his bike to decelerate. Lowering their hands he pressed her fingers firmly to his chest before taking the grips in his palms once again. Taylor dug her fingers into the supple leather of his jacket before moving one palm to his waist, pressing the other firmly against his chest. Imagining holding him against her skin, blood flushed her cheeks. Ashamed that she'd allowed her thoughts to drift, she shook it off.

The tree line opened to their left exposing the glassy still lake. Taylor watched as a flock of ducks circled and landed on the placid water. The sun sinking low on the horizon, set the sky ablaze. This would go down in her mind as the perfect night, the perfect ride shared with the perfect man.

Turning into the parking lot of South Fork Burgers, Taylor loosed her hold. Once they came to a stop she stepped from the bike. Pulling the helmet from her head, a haze of electrically charged hair stood erect on the crown. Trying desperately to calm it before Garrett noticed, Taylor unsuccessfully smeared her palms across it, only to find it mercilessly rebelling.

Removing his helmet, he opened the side bag handing Taylor her purse. "Here you can borrow this." Without looking her way, he kindly offered her his baseball cap so as not to embarrass her.

Taylor pulled the cap over her wild hair, taking note of his sweet, unselfish gesture. Garrett was proving to be much deeper a soul than she had expected, the reality bringing a smile to her lips. "Thank you."

"How about a burger?" He offered, smoothing his own hair, tapping the bill of the ball cap smiling.

"Sounds good," Taylor answered, pulling the cap down tighter as they started toward the restaurant. The thought of wearing his hat brought back memories of letterman jackets and long kisses behind the gym after games. How she wished they had known one another back then.

Garrett opened the door for her stepping in close behind, quickly motioning to the waitress that they would sit at the counter. Before taking a seat on a stool he turned one offering it to Taylor. She accepted, watching as he took a seat beside her. Having the chance to be seated next to him once again thrilled her beyond words.

The waitress lay menus in front of them. "Can I start you two off with something to drink?"

"Lemonade for me, thank you," Garrett said without pause.

"Sweet tea for me please," Taylor answered, quickly peering into the menu, closing it before laying it on the counter in front of her.

"I can take your order whenever you two are ready."

"Looks like we are," Garrett quipped, laying his menu atop Taylor's watching the waitress retrieve a pen and order pad from her apron.

"Ladies first," he said turning toward Taylor.

"I would like the turkey club please, extra lettuce, no mayo and no pickle."

Garrett smirked giving her a sideways glance. "And I would like the Bass burger with extra lettuce, no mayo, no pickle."

"Any fries or dessert with that?" The waitress asked pausing.

"No thank you." Taylor and Garrett looked to one another with surprise as they spoke in unison. Taylor quickly turned her eyes forward hearing Garrett clear his throat.

"Okay then, I guess that was unanimous," the waitress said, curiously raising an eyebrow, "I will get your order in and be right back with your drinks."

Garrett shook his head at the disconcerting moment before speaking. "So have you been back to work much since you've been home?"

"I just started back on a few short shifts and then I fill in when need be. Doctor's orders are for me to take it easy for a little while longer. I guess the outside heals much quicker than the inside. Too much too soon can set back healing time and that is the last thing I want."

"I was in a pretty bad wreck a few years back myself," Garrett said nervously clearing his throat again.

"Really? You wouldn't know it by looking." Taylor caught herself giving him the head to toe once over, making any excuse to enjoy the view.

"I remember driving home after a late night at work and the next thing I know I am being jolted awake as my truck caught air. I saw the generator I had in the back sliding toward the cab. After that nothing. I had a huge gash in my head, more stiches than I could count. I had my head shaved for a while there until it could all grow back evenly. Other than that, I was thankfully no worse for the wear. There's nothing more sobering than living through something you truly should not have survived." Garrett ran his hand across the side of his head remembering the ordeal. "It takes a while before all your confidences return. I have a sneaking suspicion that you completely understand where I'm coming from." Garrett smiled, his shoulders relaxing again.

"Definitely can alter ones perspective on life." Taylor paused watching as the waitress sat their drinks in front of them. "Thank you," she said, waiting for her to walk away before continuing. "Such an experience makes you want to live better, to be more open to life and all it has to offer. I also found that I am beginning to accept and be thankful for every day, regardless of circumstance, whether it be good or bad. I am much more aware of all that is happening around me as well. I find myself paying more attention to my choices and giving more thought to what I spend my time doing."

"Really, how so?" Garrett turned to her seemingly spellbound by her words.

"Seriously, I care more about what I eat, the music I listen to, I really think about everything more now. Nearly losing your life really puts everything in perspective." Turning to him Taylor paused before continuing. "Like who I spend my time with."

"That is of up most importance," Garrett replied, staring into her eyes, searching them admiringly. "I concur."

"Here you go. Can I get anything else for you two?" The waitress asked as she lay their plates in front of them, realizing she had stepped into an intense moment. "Sorry for interrupting."

"That will do for now, thank you," Garrett said, still peering deeply into Taylor's eyes.

Bashfully Taylor looked away, brushing a loose strand of hair from her cheek. Lifting her glass to her lips, the heated feel his eyes still on her, watching her every move sent chills running up her spine. The idea that he was so interested, so intent on her sent thrill rushing through her. The intensity emanating from him flushing her checks with fervor.

"You up for a little fun later?" Garrett inquired, finally turning to face his plate.

"What kind of fun?" Taylor quipped, giving him a sideways glance fighting a smile, wanting badly to admit that she already was.

"Was that a yes or a no?" Smirking, playfully bumping his knee into hers beneath the counter, he slowly laid his foot over the top of hers. Taylor realized how he wanted so to touch her that he would resolve himself to child's play. The mere thought leaving her twitter pated.

"I'm all yours," Taylor replied, stuffing lettuce into her mouth before she could get anymore of her foot in it. "Tonight, I mean yes." Squeezing her eyes closed with embarrassment, her words muffled by the un-chewed greens. 'Nice Tay, really nice,' she thought, silently scolding herself.

Garrett turned his face away, hiding that he was grinning ear to ear. Her slip of words having secretly thrilled him.

After swallowing she continued, "so you're not giving me even a little hint?"

"Not even an inkling of a hint," he answered chuckling under his breath.

Pushing the plate away Taylor wiped her mouth with her napkin, adding it to the plate. "Thank you for dinner."

"You are very welcome. Thank you for joining me." Garrett replied standing to retrieve his wallet from his back pocket. Laying money on the counter, he lifted his glass to his lips, taking one last swallow. "Thanks again," he said waving to their waitress before heading toward the door. Pulling it open for Taylor, he admired her as she moved past him.

Garrett pushed the bike out of the parking space, angling away from the direction they had arrived. Taylor tugged her helmet in place, climbing on, once again scooting herself snug against his back, wrapping her arms firmly around him as she had before. Smiling at the thrill brewing in her soul that she could get use to this. The sudden feel of his hand over the top of hers made her body tingle. Offering a soft squeeze, before moving it away again. Shifting, Garrett pulled the throttle back hard as they raced away into the hazy light of dusk.

The final minutes of sunlight fading behind the trees sent brilliant orange ribbons dancing on the misty smoke of fresh lit fires around the lake. Savoring the most perfect moment she had ever lived, Taylor memorized every last detail wishing this night would never end. Never before had she understood when others spoke of time stopping, how they had desired to live on forever in one particular moment... until now. Garrett ran his fingers across her knee, tracing along the seam of her jeans. How could the simplest touch from him send her soaring, leave her reeling, yearning for more, much more? Before Garrett, Taylor had truly thought she knew passion, love, desire, and emotional connection. Yet in this moment her eyes were opening to much more than she ever could have imagined.

Further and further away from the lake they road, deep into the mountains beyond, losing touch with time and space. Simply immersing herself in the beauty of the moment, reveling in the sheer euphoria of being with another human so intimately, without typical stigmatic sexual connotations, had Taylor's heart soaring. Knowing that Garrett was somehow so capable of imposing such an effect on her with little time and effort had her revisiting Jake's idea of soul mates. Holding fast to the moment, Taylor kept herself from thinking of tomorrows to come. There was only this night, only this moment before her, nothing more.

Clearing the forest edge Taylor watched as the harvest moon peeked from behind the ridge of rocky crags, casting a soft glow across the rolling hills below. In the distance Taylor spied a giant white barn glowing ghostly in the moonlight. They slowed as Garrett pulled the bike off the side of the road. Pushing open her visor again Garrett pointed to the barn, looking across the seemingly endless lush emerald meadows beyond. "Beautiful isn't it? I always wanted to live here when I was a boy."

"Paradise," the hushed word slipping from her lips barely audible. Stunned that as a child he'd had such vision for a future. Garrett was different from any other man she had met, this was becoming more apparent by the second. The truth of his depth thrilled her so that it frightened her. This man had within his power, in such a brief time of knowing her, to completely spoil her for any other.

Taylor stared amazed as they rode closer and closer to the barn, impressed by his immense sense of knowing, by the soulful depth he had been graced with. The truth was, it mattered none how long she had known him, Taylor was falling hard for a man she barely knew, for this man that in turn barely knew her. 'Soul mates,' a whisper echoing in the back of her mind once again.

Traveling along the winding road they rounded the final curve. Before them stood a majestic white barn set just off the edge of endless lush meadows, seeming to glow in the moonbeams. Grand oak trees dotted the surrounding pasture as if they were guardians standing watch. The swollen ever rising moon now above the tree line spilled eerie shadows across the ground.

Taylor's stomach fluttered at the thought of such a romantic voyage, of such a romantic destination. Her entire life she had dreamed of just such a night.

"So here we are," Garrett announced, turning the bike off, coasting up to the barn doors.

"It's just so beautiful," Taylor gushed softly, admiring the breathtaking surroundings.

The still of the night enveloped them as they stepped from the bike, removing their helmets. Garrett took Taylor's hand in his as they walked in silence to the back of the barn. Vast emerald meadows stretched out before them like an endless plush shag carpet.

"Can you smell the lilac trees and the lupine from the fields below?"

"It's like candy floating in the air," Taylor smiled, closing her eyes inhaling the sweet scents.

Garrett grinned, pleased at her reaction, tilting his face to the glittering velvet sky above, inhaling a long deep breath. "Have you ever seen so many stars? The lights of town hide the true night sky. From here it is as God intended. That's the Milky Way there." Garrett stepped behind her, taking her hand in his, pointing at the thick lay of stars clustered in a mystical shimmering river stretched across the infinite sky.

"It truly makes one feel small, realizing there's so much more out there, more than we even know exists."

Taylor sank into the warmth of his chest, relishing his touch, glancing to the sky then back to Garrett awestruck. He was far different from any other man she had known before. The depth of his thoughts, the passion for the little details life offered up set him apart from most people she knew.

"How did you find this place?" She asked in a hush, drunk with wonder.

"My grandparents lived over that ridge," Garrett pointed to the mountain beyond the oak trees. "I would explore the hills, take make believe journeys, my own little adventures. One day I meandered further than ever before. When I came over that ridge and spotted this old barn and… well my life changed. I still recall standing there for the longest time captivated by this place. I knew in that very moment, right there and then that I wanted to live here one day." Garrett turned her to him. Searching each other's eyes they stood unmoving, serenaded by cricket song floating on the evening breeze. Taylor felt her soul shift beneath his intoxicating gaze. Never before had she known someone so filled with such compassion, creativity, and even more… such soulful depth.

"Come with me, I want to show you something," motioning in the direction in which they came.

In Garrett's presence she felt something she hadn't before. In this moment she knew undeniably that she was falling hard and fast. The energy between them had stirred something deep within her. As if he'd simply beckoned her heart, her soul from a long, deep emotional slumber, Taylor stepped from the woman that had been so alone, so shattered and withdrawn into a new. With this truth, she knew in her heart there would be no turning back.

Standing before the giant doors she watched as he unlatched them, tugging one open just enough for them to slip inside, sliding them closed again. "Follow me," Garrett whispered. Taylor moved in close behind him mirroring his steps, as they ascended the creaking stairs to the hay loft. The narrow steps gradually widening, opening to giant beams angled to the peak of the roof. Massive posts standing stoically in rows along the wide plank floor supporting the beautiful artistry above. The far floor of the loft held stacks of hay bales, old toys scattered about.

"I've never shown anyone this place before, it's my secret hideaway from the world." Stepping across the bales Garrett stopped in front of wooden framed panels, lifting the cross-brace two by four from the steel brackets anchored to the wooden frame. "Would you mind doing the honors?" Garrett smiled, motioning for Taylor to open the doors.

Making her way over the stack of hay Taylor's stomach leaped as he slowly laced his fingers through hers. Looking to their hands she swallowed hard, clearing her throat nervously.

"Don't worry you are safe with me," Garrett winked, smiling as he helped her down from the hay.

Pushing the doors open she gasped, "oh Garrett!"

"I know, breath taking isn't it?" Garrett scanned the horizon as a king admiring the bounty of his kingdom.

"I had no idea it was so, so, there are no words. No wonder you wanted to live here as a child. You'd have to be blind not to see the magic here." Taylor stepped forward lost in the beauty.

Garrett lunged to the doors just in time to pull her safely back from the edge. Staring down to the ground her eyes gaped like saucers at the reality she'd just been spared.

"Thank you!" Taylor gasped, trying to catch her breath. "Someone should really build a deck out there."

Pressing her tightly against the open door, he stepped closer. Swallowed by the shadows they stood nose to nose, motionless. Taylor's head spinning with the heavy dose of adrenaline surging through her veins.

"I'll be right back," Garrett whispered before stepping away, leaving her breathless.

Taylor listened to his boots falling against the hardwood floor as he made his way across the loft, followed by the creaking of something opening and clanking closed again.

"I don't have many amenities here, you'll have to forgive my rough sense of hospitality, but I'm not use to having company." Climbing back over the bales in the dim light he shook out what looked to be an old quilt, spreading it across the hay. Taylor stood frozen in place, still not having fully recovered from the thrill his breath falling upon her skin, now facing unknown expectations.

Pulling a lighter from his pocket Garrett moved to one of the massive posts, removing an old lantern from a curved iron hook, lighting it before returning it to the hook once again. The room came to life before her eyes, bathed in the soft glow of the flickering flame. Walking back to the hay, he took a seat on the edge. Leaning over he picked up a rusted toy tractor and ran it along his thigh. "I use to stay here all day, playing with these old things. Those were great days. Sometimes I would get so lost in this place it felt as if time would simply cease. I so often hoped it would. I never wanted those times to end, then one day I realized I had grown up. I still came as time would afford, but it seems the older I get the less time I actually take to stop and smell the roses." Sitting the toy tractor back on the floor boards by his feet, he met her gaze.

Shyly turning away, she moved back to the doorway, leaning against the frame. Tilting her face to the glowing moon her thoughts running amuck. "I felt guilty while I was in rehab, for not being productive. Silly I know when there are those who can work but refuse to, that I feel guilty for a few months of allowing myself healing. It seems an epidemic with my family, thinking down time is a sin. It saddens me to think of the gap widening between those that push toward to success so hard that they rarely come up for air and those who simply leach off of the system as long as they can. When was it that I was brainwashed into believing that we are only truly successful if we work twenty hours a day and are completely exhausted? Then others wear their unemployment as a badge, thinking it fair that we pay their way. I'm squandering my life away like a worker bee working at Donna's, completely ignoring my love of photojournalism. Here I am taking up time with you talking about work. I'm so sorry, I just see the beauty here and it makes me realize all that I am missing. If I lived here I would definitely not allow my work to keep me away any more than necessary. "

"Let's make a pact," Garrett gently patted the quilt, offering her a seat beside him.

Stepping from the doorway, Taylor fought to refrain from meeting his eyes for fear of losing composure. If only he knew the power he held over her with the simplest of gestures, she would never survive the night, let alone the next few minutes.

"I think we should make a pact right here and now to spend more time doing things that we find joy in, everything that bring smiles to our faces. From this moment forth I swear to make the time to do fun things, to go places that I love and spend time with people that mean something to me."

"Me too, I swear to do all this as well. Pinky swear?" Extending her baby finger to him.

Linking his pinky though hers Garrett leaned in close, his breath falling warm on her cheeks once again. "Sealed with a…" Without finishing his sentence he pressed his warm lips to hers, lingering unmoving.

Taylor's heart pounded against her ribs, her pulse racing. With a sudden rush her skin tingled beneath his touch as he traced his fingers along the line of her jaw, the nape of her neck. Powerless beneath his touch Taylor sank into his arms, their lips melting together with sensual, soft kisses. Gently he lay her back onto the quilt moving over her, seamlessly continuing to kiss her. Running her fingers into the silky layers of his dark hair, along his shoulders. Taylor surprised herself, succumbing to the cravings of her heart, openly expressing her feelings, her desires; moving against him in slow waves. Never before had she so wanted to throw a man back and have her way with him, until now, until Garrett.

From beneath her, Taylor felt waves of peculiar vibrations shuddering between them. Once again, then once more. Confused she ceased kissing him.

"Not now!" Garrett sighed sitting back from her, digging his hand into his pocket retrieving a pager. "Man of all times. I am so sorry Taylor but I have to take this call out. I'm on rotation this week, and unless I am dying there's no acceptable absences." Shoving his pager back into his pocket Garrett pushed himself off the hay, offering her a hand up. Pulling harder than necessary Garrett landed Taylor in his arms once again, pressing his forehead to hers, squeezing her against him smiling. "Just one last hug before we go, and maybe a little kiss?" Flashing a cheesy grin he awaited her response.

His sensual flirting left her shamefully flustered. "Maybe just… one more." Pressing her lips softly to his time seemed to halt. The soulful power of his embrace, the soothing comfort of his warmth had her hungrily craving more.

Lost in one another, moments passed before they came up for air. "You've got to go," Taylor breathlessly whispered against his mouth.

"I do, sadly." Brushing his lips against her once more before stepping back, taking her hands between his. "I'll get the doors and the blanket if you'll turn off the lantern," he said, kissing them before hurrying off.

Back on the road Taylor watched the barn fade in the distance, slowly growing smaller and smaller until vanishing from sight. Pulling herself tightly against Garrett she closed her eyes replaying their moments together in the loft. There had been something so very familiar about his touch, his kiss. Taylor was all but certain that they had been made to fit together. With Jake she had felt the pull of animal attraction, a purely physical hunger. But this was so very different. Though she desired the utmost intimacy with Garrett, she wanted so much more than that. For the first time in her life she wanted a deeper, intense, more intimate connection than merely physical, she craved more than she could even fully admit to herself.

Moonlight flashed on the ebony pavement through the towering pines lining the edge of the road as they sped onward toward town. Leaning into each corner as one, the exhilarating brush of the wind blasting against them, drawing them closer together yet. The lights of town rose on the horizon marking that the night was quickly drawing to a close, savoring every last second as they pulled into Donna's. Stepping from his bike she pulled off the helmet, handing it back to him. "Thank you for tonight Garrett, I had a wonderful time."

Taking the helmet from her hands he turned placing it into the side bag, turning back to her once again. "Thank you for joining me. I could have ridden all night with you. I'm sad that we have to end the night so abruptly." His face lit with the most endearing smile as he searched her eyes.

"If we could have, I would have. I honestly didn't want to come back myself." Smiling, her heart swelled with that sweet unfamiliar rush once again.

"Can I call you when I get off of this fire?"

"I would like that, very much,' Taylor replied, wishing she'd found more eloquent words to truly express the utter joy brought upon her by his asking.

"Since we didn't exchange numbers last time, might I have your number?"

"Of course. That would certainly make it so much easier to communicate." Smirking at her dry humor, she searched her pockets. "If I can just find some paper. Oh my purse, I nearly forgot it."

Garrett reached into the side-case pulling her bag out, offering it to her. Watching as she desperately searched up a pen and paper.

"Got it," quickly scribbling her number before offering the paper to him. Their hands touching, lingering, engrossed once more in the feel of one another. "Thanks again Taylor, tonight meant a lot to me." Nervously clearing his throat before continuing. "Well, as much as I would love to stay, I best be going." Garrett backed the bike out holding Taylor's glance, his eyes speaking volumes more than the simplicity of his words. "We'll talk soon."

Taylor's heart pounded as she stared, watching Garrett pull away, his hand raised in a slow wave. "Yes soon," Taylor said to herself. Her heart skipping a beat at the sight of his eyes in the mirror, fixed on her as he pulled out onto the street speeding away.

Frozen in place she played the evening over in her mind. His touch still lingering on her skin, his kiss on her lips. Smiling she reminisced on the majestic beauty of the land stretching far beyond the old barn, of Garrett's sweet remembrance of the priceless time spent there as a child, and how he had dreamed of one day living there. The endearing way that he'd recounted all those memories had undoubtedly warmed her heart to the core. Taylor knew in that moment she no longer had control over the ways of her heart. She had fallen hard for Garrett, from this moment forward there would be no turning back. Closing her eyes she sent up a prayer for the strength to refrain from letting her feelings be known too soon. Her grandmother's words echoing through time. 'Always let the man express his love first, this way you know he is not saying the words simply because you have.' Her fortuitous words had saved Taylor much embarrassment. 'Be true to yourself, allowing time for you to find the one God intended for you. Most importantly, make sure to play your cards close until he arrives, as a heart may deceive, the soul cannot. Your soul mate will find you my sweet girl, have patience and believe.' Taylor sighed, smiling at the thought that quite possibly she had just spent the evening with the man of her dreams, her soul mate. If so, this would show that dreams really can come true.

Every little girl dreams of her very own prince. Awaiting her whole life for him to come along, sweep her off her feet and ride off into the sunset. Taylor wanted nothing more, yearned for nothing more than to find a man to truly desire her above all else. She so longed for a love that she never had to wonder about, a man she could trust with her whole heart, a partner to share in the joy of the happiest days, as well one to hold her hand through the most difficult. She hungered for a once in a lifetime love that would fill the soul with ardent devotion so abundant that she would never be tempted to stray. She desired the kind of love that makes one complete, her very own man to love that even in times of discord would leave no doubt. Offering the security of a lifelong relationship, one that proved daily to be rock solid, always having one another's back. Taylor wanted the fairytale, no matter the hard work that true devotion required. Regardless of the compromises and the full offering of self-deemed necessary for any relationship to survive the challenges living so close to another brings forth. Still she craved to have that once in a lifetime love she had rarely witnessed.

Driving home Taylor's head overflowed with questions. She couldn't help but wonder if Garrett had any of the same thoughts running through his mind as well. Was it possible he too was seeing pieces of the puzzle fitting as they never had before... was he too feeling such intense emotions, sharing in such desires? Quick as the thought came she dismissed it, knowing he was on a fire and had to be fully concentrating on the dangerous details at hand, he couldn't be thinking of such. Or could he?

She had so longed for a life filled with passion and laughter, shared with a man that unconditionally loved her. Even as a child she had ached for such a sacred spiritual connection with another. Garrett just might be the unbreakable relationship she had always dreamt of. She so craved a man of her very own, a man whom would cherish her, who looked at her with respect and reverence as well as with insatiable passionate hunger, to be his everything and him to be hers as well. Realistically she knew that this all might be too much to ask for. Soul mates were just some silly fantasy, weren't they? Regardless, Taylor wanted to share as much time with Garrett as she possibly could. He filled her soul in ways she had yet to know, leaving her craving more. The rest would be known… only time would tell.

Chapter Ten

The morning sun poured through the sheer curtains, spilling warmth across the room. Taylor stretched her arms, yawning. A smile crept across her lips reminiscing over the night before. Tugging the covers over her head she let out a giggle, feeling more alive than she had in decades. Silently she prayed this feeling would never leave her. Today was the dawning of a new chapter in her life.

The phone rang, startling her from beneath the sheets. Brushing the covers off, she surfaced donning a wild mane, reaching for the receiver. "Hello," the groveled sound of her own voice startling her. Clearing her throat she began once again. "Hello."

"Good morning Taylor." As warm and smooth as it had been that first evening they talked forever on the phone, his familiar voice poured through the phone line.

"Garrett?" Taylor said, attempting to sound calm as she excitedly set her feet onto the rug below, struggling she wrestled to free herself from the wad of tangled sheets.

"Yes, it's me. Sorry my reception may be bad. I'm in the command center, these radio phones aren't the greatest."

"Is everything alright?" Taylor asked with earnest concern.

"Everything is fine, I just... well I wanted to tell you how much I loved spending time with you last night."

"You didn't have to call. I know you must be very busy. Though I must admit, I'm glad that you did. I too had a wonderful evening Garrett." Taylor sank back into the warm blankets, twirling a strand of hair around her finger, the way she had as a small child. Closing her eyes she smiled, once again reminiscing over the moments they had shared, the lingering heat of his sweet kiss, his sensuous touch.

"They called me in prematurely, so I'm being released in four hours. I'm only about a two hour drive out, so I was wondering if you would like to go to dinner."

"Tonight? Won't you be spent?" Taylor answered quickly, hating that she hadn't simply jumped at the invitation, slapping herself on the forehead.

"I don't mind. I just really would love to take you to dinner Taylor. I'm not above groveling if it's necessary." Garrett quipped, laughing under his breath.

"I would love to," she said sitting up once more, quickly recovering.

"Great. So I will pick you up at eight... if that works for you?"

"Perfect. I will text you my address."

"See you then."

"Okay," swallowing hard at her inability to form an entire sentence, "goodbye Garrett." Laying the phone onto the nightstand Taylor threw herself back onto the bed pulling the sheet over her head, grumbling at her inept attempt at relating.

A long steamy shower coupled with a massive dose of caffeine and Taylor was eager to face the day. Pulling the garage door open she smiled at the sight of her bike. "How about a bath old girl?" Rolling it out onto the driveway she heard the house phone ring and rushed to answer it. "Hello."

"Did you already forget about me?" Garrett questioned jokingly.

"What? Oh, I was just getting ready to text you right now," Taylor answered squeezing her eyes closed, her cheeks flushed with embarrassment. "I swear I will send it right now." Wracked with guilt for telling him a little white lie she retrieved her cell phone from the pocket of her jeans, locating his number and began typing as they spoke. "There, I sent it."

"So how is your day going?"

"Good, I was just getting ready to wash my bike actually. And yours?"

"I've been helping with some paperwork until I'm released. I'll actually be heading out a little earlier than I thought when we last spoke. Boss overheard me on the phone, so now he's pushing me to get on the road," Garrett chuckled. "He's pretty excited about me taking a woman to dinner."

"More than you?"

"Impossible."

His words stopped Taylor in her tracks, stunned to silence she swallowed hard.

"Hello… Taylor, did I drop you, are you still there?" He asked concerned.

"Yes… yes I'm here," chills racing across her skin hearing her name pass through his lips.

"Thought I lost you for a moment. There it is, just got your text. Alright, well I need to finish tying up some loose ends so I can get out of here. I will see you tonight."

"See you at eight," Taylor said, thrilled by the thought of the night ahead.

"Until then," Garrett replied in return before hanging up. Stepping outside once again, Taylor turned her face to the glorious heat of the sun. Closing her eyes she said a silent prayer of thanks to the man upstairs. Life was good and moving toward great at a nice clip. The mere thought of peering into those captivating eyes over dinner took her breath away. The way he could move her with a simple thought was beguiling. A man possessing such bewitching power had only before existed in her imagination. This was definitely a first in her life.

Two hours of sweat and she stepped back to admire her glistening bike. How she had always loved the sight of a clean motorcycle and especially chrome so perfectly polished that you could see yourself in its mirrored surface. Rolling it back into the garage she set the kickstand down, securing the bike before moving to close the door. 'What to wear?' Her mind drifted, daydreaming of the night ahead as she made her way through remainder the of the day's chores.

With plenty of time to spare, she headed to her closet to search for the perfect ensemble for the evening ahead. The thrill of being alive, the reality that she wanted to dress beautifully for Garrett excited her beyond words. For the first time in longer than she wished to admit, she cared about the details. The smallest, most minute of details mattered to her once again.

Hanging her final choice onto her changing screen just outside the closet, she held out the soft hem of the shimmery teal chiffon blouse. She had always loved this blouse, the simple line of the gathered waist, the graceful fall of the scalloped sleeves, how the right light accentuated the line of her through the thin fabric.

Moving to the dressing table Taylor sat before the mirror, seeing her mother looking back through her own engaging dark brown eyes. Running the tip of her finger along the pale line of her jaw she remembered helping her mother dress for an evening out. Though she was barely five Taylor had soaked in every second. Still, even now she could smell the fresh scent of her mothers' lemon verbena perfume as she had misted her neck and wrists, playfully squirting Taylor. The graceful way her mother had slowly tapped the fluffy white powder puff on the edge of the pearl adorned talc box, running it along the line of her shoulder, softly dusting behind her knee, trailing the silky vanilla powder across her smooth skin. Taylor closed her eyes hearing the distant echo of her mother's sultry laugh as she touched the puff lightly on the tip of Taylor's nose. The surreal memory playing tricks, she reached to wipe the non-existent powder from her nose. Opening her eyes she returned to present time powder free. Staring into the mirror Taylor smiled, pleased that her mother's eyes stared back. "I miss you momma, I miss you so." A single tear trickled down her cheek, splashing onto the glass tabletop. Brushing away any trace of the emotional moment she shook her head attempting to clear her mind.

The thought of her mother, the way she would transform herself from the hard working woman everyone knew, into such an elegant lady had always so impressed and intrigued her. Taylor longed to be so multi-faceted in her own life. She so longed to be completely comfortable, regardless of where she was or what she was doing, true to the woman she was at her core. A lady so at home in every circumstance that came her way… this was her true desire.

Silently making a pact with herself, the essence of her mother stirring in the room. This day she would vow to move forward with the curiosity and self-confidence to be just such a woman. From here on she would be all she wanted to be, do all she longed to do with the wild abandonment of youth coupled with the wisdom that comes with maturity beyond her years. From here on she would fully be vested in each moment, true to her own heart.

Shaking herself back to reality, she swept the blush brush over the round of her cheekbone. Softly smoothing powder over her face, she reached for the pencil slowly lining her eyes, then brushed on a touch of mascara to enhance her lashes. Running her calendula gloss cover her lips, she pressed them together before admiring the refined transformation of her reflection. Gathering the sides of her long dark softly curled hair up into a crystal barrette, Taylor stood moving to her changing screen. Shrugging off her robe she stepped behind the screen to dress.

Adorned in the silky teal blouse and jet black crepe slacks she emerged from behind the screen again. The beauty of this decorous formality set in place the reality of the night ahead. Standing before her full length mirror, she slipped into her black Mary Jane pumps. Pleased with the final result, she glimpsed at herself head to toe one last time. Startled by the doorbell, Taylor nearly jolted from her skin. "Show time girl, deep breath, relax, no worries," winking at the image in the mirror, trying to convince herself that there was surely nothing to be nervous about.

Hurrying to the front door, Taylor drew in a long deep breath before opening it.

"Your chariot has arrived..." Garrett froze mid-sentence in awe of her beauty. "Wow, please remind me what was I saying?" Smiling, his cheeks flushed with excitement.

"Come on in. I just need to grab a jacket and my purse." Taylor opened the door wider allowing him to pass by her, attempting to remain composed in the wake of his flattery. The tantalizing scent of his aftershave tickling her senses.

"Nice place. Do you live here all alone?" Garrett asked taking in the lay of the house.

"Yes, just me. I threatened to get a dog every few months, but I've still yet to. Have a seat, I'll be right back." Taylor motioned toward the living room as she made her way down the hall, savoring the scrumptious scent of him once again.

Garrett spied a group of framed photos set along the console table. Leaning in close, he smirked at an old Polaroid of a trio of young kids prancing in what appeared to be an Italian water fountain. Next to it was a photo of a lovely woman that reminded him of Taylor only a bit statelier, slightly more pretentious and formal. The lineup continued with several portraits of family, followed by a couple of Taylor with Toby, and yet another one of her walking along the shoreline at sunset with the stately woman.

"That's my mother with me there. That was her last birthday with us," surprising Garrett stepping from the hall.

"You take after her a great deal," smiling he turned to face Taylor. "If I haven't told you yet, you look quite lovely this evening," his eyes admiring her top to bottom as he spoke. "Absolutely lovely."

"Thank you. You clean up very nicely yourself." Taylor met his eyes as he lifted his gaze to hers. Motionless they stood transfixed, staring deeply into one another's souls.

Garrett shifted clearing his throat, turning his gaze to the ground. "We best be heading on." Clearing his throat again, he turned to the door quickly pulling it open.

Taylor shook herself back from what seemed a faraway land, moving to the side table to turn on a lamp. Setting the alarm she stepped to the front door flipping a switch, illuminating the doorway and front steps, pausing to regroup before stepping outside, closing the door behind her.

"I hope you don't mind riding in my truck, the Camaro is in the shop until Monday."

Taylor's heart skipped seeing the creamy white 1968 Ford. "This is your truck?" Swallowing hard at the sight. "Yes it is. Why, is that bad? Would you rather not ride in it?" Garrett held his breath awaiting her answer.

"Oh no, I love your truck. It's just that this is the exact truck my grandfather drove when I was a kid. He'd take me and my little brother fishing off the tailgate at sunset down along Jenson Creek." Taylor starred in awe of the incredible coincidence.

"I bought this from an estate sale the next county over ten years ago. I couldn't resist. It had been garaged its whole life, nearly as pristine as the day it was purchased new." Garrett pulled the handle, opening the passenger door.

Taylor's face paled. "Montgomery Avenue and Elm Street?" Seeing the key ring hanging from the ignition took her breath away. How many times had she played with her Grandfather's keys, held that very embossed leather piece in her hands?

Seeing her expression, Garrett gasped. "You are kidding? I have your Granddad's old Ford?" He stood mesmerized by the chance of such, watching as Taylor climbed in. "What's the probability of that?" Garrett said closing the door, both of them stunned by the unbelievable notion as he made his way around the front of the truck. Climbing in, he pulled the door closed meeting her stare. "Are you as shocked as I am?"

"This is surreal. I loved this old truck. I use to daydream of owning it once I was old enough to drive. He didn't have a will so the estate lawyers sold it along with most everything else to pay off his debts not long after he passed away. I wasn't told until it was too late," Taylor sighed. "I am very pleased to know that you have it now. You take very good care of her it seems. Grandpa would be thrilled to know that she's in such good hands." Taylor turned her eyes to the side window swallowing hard, attempting to hide her emotions.

"I use to ride with my grandfather on Saturdays to get produce at your grandpa's market stand. He let me sit right here and pretend that she was mine one afternoon. I remember the first time that I saw her, seems like just yesterday, it was love at first sight. So when I heard about the estate sale I made sure I was the first to arrive. I remember the look on the lady's face when I said I wanted the truck. She asked if I wanted to see under the cover before I decided for certain. You could have knocked her over with a feather when I handed her the envelope of cash and drove it away. It is such an honor that I have his truck. I tell you what... I promise that I will never sell her without telling you first. Though I love her so, they'll probably have to pry the keys from my cold dead paws." Garrett patted Taylor's hand resting on the seat, giving it a soft squeeze. Turning her palm to his she opened her hand accepting his fingers, as he laced them slowly together.

"Thank you," her words falling softly, feeling her heart rate speed at the prompting of his touch.

Driving along hand in hand in silence, sunlight danced on the glossy paint of the hood. Taylor drifted, entranced by the intensity of the moment, lost in a daze. Memories of afternoon rides with her grandpa to visit their favorite fishing hole played on her mind. A smile crept over her lips as she closed her eyes reminiscing.

"Penny for your thoughts?" Garrett's deep voice lulling her back to the moment at hand.

"Oh, sorry. I was just remembering fishing trips in this ole' girl." Taylor brushed a stray hair back from her face embarrassed by her momentary displacement.

"Good memories should never be apologized for. I was a bit envious actually, I wish I could evoke such a smile from those lips." Garrett squeezed her hand smirking.

"The night has just begun," Taylor quickly responded, secretly stunned at her precociousness.

"Touché!" He said, laughing aloud. "I take that as a challenge my dear lady."

Taylor blushed three shades of red, laughing aloud at the raw truth of her own words. Something within her was altered in his presence. The walls of inhibition seem to be crashing down, dissolving more with every passing moment shared. Long ago she had hidden away her deepest, most intimate self. Yet somehow this man was reawakening that long lost woman. Being near him made Taylor feel more alive, more open to feel, free to speak and even more so to laugh. Spending time with Garrett was simply opening countless doors she had tightly guarded for so long. Deep inside of her something stirred that she had never before experienced, the raw excitement of such peaking her curiosity.

As the truck came to a stop, Taylor felt Garrett's hand slip from hers and immediately she longed to have it back.

"Here we are," pushing the shifter into park. Turning the key off, Garrett leaped from the truck hurrying to Taylor's door, opening it he offered her a hand.

"Thank you," smiling as she stepped from the truck, suddenly stopping in her tracks. "Oh Garrett, its spectacular!" Taylor's eyes scanned the tall slender panes of leaded glass tucked between panels of thick sheeted redwood. The angled line of the decorative metal railing along each side of the wide slate steps drew the eye to a massive set of French doors. Continuing along the pathway to the ornate outdoor slate stack stone fireplace surrounded by elegantly rustic, curvy iron chairs. The emerald blanket of the forest surrounding them left Taylor awestruck. Garrett placed his palm on the small of her back, gently ushering her on. Stepping through the ten foot tall iron laden double doors, her eyes widened at the beauty of the magnificently vaulted open beam ceiling. Dozens of two foot thick support beams spanned above, handsomely adorned by massive rusty patina steel plates and large steel railroad washers and bolts. Such distinctive beauty had her spellbound.

"Two for dinner?" The hostess inquired quietly.

"Actually we have reservations," Garrett replied.

Taylor turned away mesmerized, peering across the gleaming wood plank floor, seeing the magic of each table perfectly set with crisp white linens and sparkling clear glass vases filled with white peonies... her favorite. In the midst of the dining room her eyes caught sight of a glossy black Baby Grand piano, above it hung the most spectacular glistening Swarovski crystal chandelier, its lights dimmed romantically.

"Right this way," the hostess motioned toward the dining hall, briskly brushing past them.

"Follow her," he whispered, pressing his hand lightly to Taylor's back once again. "Thank you," Garrett said to the hostess, as he pulled a chair out for Taylor, then moved to take the seat across from her.

"Your server will be Paolo this evening. He will be with you shortly." Laying a menu before each of them she turned walking away before either could speak.

Garrett leaned in running his fingertips along Taylor's fingers. "Thank you for joining me tonight."

"Thank you for having me," Taylor responded, meeting his intense stare. Her stomach a flutter gazing into his entrancing eyes.

"The salmon is supposed to be out of this world," Garrett said opening his menu, trying to hide the blush Taylor's touch afforded, spreading like wildfire across his cheeks. "They fly them in alive, coming all the way from Alaska in tanks within the bellies of planes. Can't get much fresher than that."

"That sounds wonderful. Salmon happens to be my very favorite," closing her menu, laying it before her, watching Garrett follow suit.

"Good evening, my name is Paolo and I will be serving you this beautiful evening. May I bring you something to drink, possibly our award winning Pinot Noir or a chilled glass of Chardonnay, and might we start you off with one of our five star appetizers?" The waiter inquired through a thick Italian accent.

"I would like an ice tea please. Taylor, would you like something to drink?" Lightly touching her elbow seeing that she hadn't heard the question for still taking in the beauty of their surroundings.

"Water, no ice with lemon please." Taylor smiled, attempting to pull herself together after finding that she was reeling at the scrumptious feeling his touch once again.

"Lovely, were we ready to order?" Paolo asked, slipping the menus under his arm, looking from Garrett to Taylor.

"Please go ahead, ladies first," Garrett motioned to her.

"I would like the pan roasted Herbs de Provence salmon please. I hear it's the talk of the town." Taylor paused, meeting his eyes before continuing. "With the toasted almond wild rice medley and an heirloom tomato butter lettuce salad with house dressing on the side please." Giving Garrett a sideways glance she smirked, hopeful that she had impressed him with her decisive order.

"And you sir?" Paolo inquired politely.

"I would like the herb encrusted filet minion, medium rare, accompanied by a butter and chive baked potato and the walnut feta spinach salad with creamy raspberry balsamic please. Thank you," Garrett smiled holding Taylor's stare, nodding in return.

"I will get your order in immediately, thank you." Their odd demeanor left the waiter unsure if they were dueling or ordering dinner, as he stepped away leaving them alone once again.

"So how is your bike?" Garrett diverted the conversation.

"Perfectly fine, why do you ask?"

"No reason in particular, I just can't wait to see you ride."

Attempting to turn the spotlight off herself, she quickly changed the subject. "So tell me more about those childhood daydreams of yours for the barn."

"What more would you like to know?" Goading her to continue on.

"Stories, dreams, memories, anything… everything."

"Well let's see, did I mention that I fell in love at first sight. I've only done that twice before in my life, but I somehow knew that was to be my home one day from the very moment I set eyes on that barn. Once I was standing within the walls I could envision everything from the sheer curtains to the dark stain on the floorboards. I knew in an instant where the master bedroom would be, even how the gourmet kitchen would open to the living room. I'd never before seen anything that sent my imagination into such a frenzy, my mind just kept filling with endless ideas. From the white wash pickling of the wood walls to the wide skylights allowing sunlight to spill in across the floors. It was all there somehow, like a picture awaiting to be painted. I knew I wanted a garden with countless flowers and vegetables, and a huge greenhouse to grow lemons and special plants that couldn't grow in the diverse weather we get. I knew that one day I'd like to have roses that flooded the yard with fragrant scents in the heat of the day just like my grandmother had. I imagined moss covered rocks scattered through the garden, tulips, and daffodils popping up here and there. The doors would be giant wood paned glass that opened onto a fire pit set at the center of a slate patio, as my grandfather had off of his study. I always loved old metal lanterns, so I knew they would light the paths, hang alongside the doors, and all around the patios in varied sizes." Garrett's eyes widened as he poured out his childhood visions before her.

"Wow... that is a lot for a little boy to imagine, so very beautiful though." Taylor spoke in hushed tones, trying to contain her hearts' desire to cry out with joy. Never had she heard a man so interested in having such a place of his own, of dreaming so vividly. Most men she had known would be perfectly happy in a tent as long as the T.V. was large enough. To her amazement Taylor realized Garrett had not mentioned even one stereotypical male past time, not one!

"Have you ever felt something so strong you just know that you know? I somehow believed beyond a shadow of doubt. My dreams were just as real as the air I was breathing. I simply knew that I would one day own that old barn, restore it and build my life within those walls. As crazy as it might sound, I just knew."

Paolo arrived back at their table just as Taylor realized she felt this for him, she just somehow knew Garrett was the one. Setting their drinks down, along with a basket of fresh baked leaf shaped dinner rolls and a miniature silver tray of burgundy pats of butter formed in the shape of blooming roses, he cleared his throat realizing he'd interrupted them.

"Beet juice. That's their secret," he whispered, proud to have such an interesting tidbit of knowledge. "They spare no details here. That is one of my favorite things about this restaurant, there is nothing left to ordinary," Garrett admitted seeing her admiring the beautiful creations, offering the bread basket to her.

"They are lovely, but no thank you. I want to save room for that salmon." Taylor swallowed hard for her deceit, deciding it best he not know her stomach was in knots. "So when did you know you wanted to fight fire for a living?" She asked hoping to further the conversation.

"One evening, I think I might have been four at the time, I was staying overnight with my grandparents, just past three there was this loud explosion. It literally shook the windows of their ranch house. Within minutes we were all watching from the porch as lightening fingered across the sky striking trees all around. The thunder was so loud we could barely hear one another screaming. The sky lit up like it was broad daylight suddenly and the biggest lightning bolt I've ever seen struck their barn. In that moment the roof was blasted open, unbridled flames speedily sweeping through the stalls. The horses went ballistic thrashing about so much that they wound up knocking out the back wall to save themselves. When the fire trucks arrived it was like watching magic. They worked together as if they could hear one another's thoughts, putting the fire out in a blink. Seeing those men in action made me want more than anything to learn that unspoken language. And that was all she wrote, I knew I had to be a fireman." Garrett's face glowed with the rush of recalling the experience. "So what about you? What did you do before coming here to help run Donna's?"

"I studied photojournalism at Brook's, then worked as an assistant for a local event photographer in Seattle. Once I'd saved enough to purchase my equipment, I opened my own studio. I was just beginning a coffee table book on the U.S. Hotshots before my mother passed away. I also wrote a travel column in the local paper where I lived." Taylor tried to sound positive, struggling to hide the looming sadness for her life lost, feeling the tug on her heart simply speaking of it.

"You should do the same here. I saw that sunset photo framed above your fireplace. That was yours wasn't it?" Garrett said intently interested, seeing Taylor shake her head in acknowledgment. "You really have an eye. The way the light was falling across that open field in the clearing below, shimmering on the pond water, how it danced on the dragonfly's wings as they hovered above the grassy shore. You should be living your dream. We all should, life is too short not to, don't you agree? If we know our gift we should live to unleash it, to share it. I think we owe it to the man upstairs for engraving us each with such a blessing."

"That would be a dream come true, but with the restaurant, I can't see my sister allowing me any freedoms. She's not above guilt tripping me for having to take a bathroom break while on shift. Besides, she gave up her gourmet catering business for Donna's, so that wouldn't be fair to her if I abandoned ship to chase my dreams. It's certainly nice to daydream though." Taylor unfolded her napkin laying it on her lap to refrain from looking into his eyes, fearing she might lose her composure. To once again have her own life, that sincerely would be a fantasy come true.

"Your salmon miss," Paolo said, setting the beautifully displayed plate before her, then moving to Garrett. "Medium rare steak sir. Is there anything else I can get for the two of you?"

"A bottle of steak sauce." Garrett held Paolo's stare doing his best not to laugh aloud. "I'm just kidding! I would never massacre such a beauty."

Paolo let out a long sigh. "Thank goodness! I thought that Chef would lose his mind hearing such a request.

160

"That's all, everything looks perfect, thank you," Garrett said smiling. "That poor man nearly had a heart attack," he whispered watching as Paolo walked toward the swinging kitchen doors, wiping the back of his hand across his reddened forehead.

"You had me fooled, I must admit," Taylor laughed sipping her water, thankful the tension was breaking.

"Good evening guests, I hope that your dining experience has been exceptional thus far," a handsomely tall, sleek, impeccably dressed man said pausing as the room erupted with applause. Bowing his head gracefully in acceptance of the guest's approval, he continued. "We are honored to have the magnificent Mr. Monroe Bantergard tickling the ivories tonight. Please help me welcome him." Placing the mic under his elbow, he began clapping, turning toward the cocktail lounge doorway.

The crowd erupted once more as a short, stocky, dark haired man made his way to the piano. Silence fell over the room as he stepped in front of the bench, lifting his tuxedo tails over the back, taking a seat before the piano. Laying his hands to the keys he took a momentary pause, closing his eyes. As his fingers began gracefully flowing across the keyboard, the dining hall filled with the loveliest melody Taylor's ears had ever heard. She recognized the tune from somewhere in her youth, but couldn't quite recall.

"What a perfect night," Garrett said softly, his eyes glued to Taylor's every move. "Have I told you how beautiful you are tonight?"

Bashfully smiling sweetly, "yes, but thank you."

"How is the salmon?" Attempting to lighten the intense mood building in the room.

"It's delicious... and your steak?"

"Wonderful, probably the best cut that I've ever had, besides that chicken fried one that I had at Donna's. If only I hadn't been interrupted by the crashing of beer bottles hitting the floor," grinning, Garrett winked. Realizing that he was embarrassing her he quickly changed the subject again. "My great grandfather built this place. It was the county saw mill for the first one hundred fifty years of its existence. When they planned to tear it down he rallied a group of local builders, gathered funds and saved it. Pops would be proud to see all they've done here." Garrett cut into his juicy steak savoring a bite… savoring the moment.

Through remainder of the meal the conversation flowed, enabling them both get to know one another much better. Taylor began to relax and enjoy herself, in turn giving Garrett the confidence to ask her something he had been thinking about all night. Standing from the table he extended a hand to her. "Dance with me?"

Swallowing hard, dabbing her lips with the linen napkin, she lay it beside her plate then stood from her chair. Slipping her hand into Garrett's, they both stared at the sensual union of their fingers. The feel of his skin shooting electrically charged tingles surging through her. Dizzied by his touch, she followed as he led her through the tables to the open area circling the piano. Turning to her, speaking not a word, he stepped in close sliding his hand to the back of her waist, confidently pressing his body firmly against hers. Taking her palm in his, Garrett raised their hands together. The dance had already ensued though their feet had yet to move. Each touch between them made for intense waves of shared longing, nearly consumed by overwhelming rushes of hunger. Every moment in his arms left her with deepening desires for more.

"Trust me?" His heated whisper falling softly upon her hair, sending chills racing down her neck as he spoke, his lips nearly grazing her ear.

"Yes." She bit her tongue before speaking the rest of the words that had come to mind. Never had she craved another as she found herself with Garrett, so impassioned in his arms. Never before had she cherished the feel of another's warmth, their flesh, as she had found herself with him. Such longings brought thoughts of deeper intimacy, commitment and of a possible shared future even more than she would admit to herself. Those before had left an emptiness greater than she had known until this moment with Garrett. He was soon becoming her true North, the mere thought she welcomed open heartedly.

Floating across the glossy wood floor Taylor felt her heart melting; her composure weakening with every step. Garrett drew her across the panels, seamlessly weaving between countless other couples that seemed to be simply rocking in mini circles. Taylor closed her eyes immersing herself in the moment. Before she knew what was happening, Garrett danced them past the piano, across the dining room and out the double doors onto the patio. The cool air pulling her from the moment, back to reality.

Opening her eyes she glanced over his shoulder admiring the grand rock fireplace, roaring with a crackling fire. The fresh scent of pine filling the air, sizzling sap bubbling in streaks along the logs, the frantic flames dancing wildly. The blaze splashing brilliant light across the rock hearth and onto the slate patio beneath them. Taylor stepped back, her gaze fixed on Garrett. Searching one another they stood unmoving beneath the starry sky. Garrett shifted closer taking her firmly around the waist, running his hands up her back pressing her tightly to him once again. Eye to eye, breathing the same air, they stood mesmerized by one on another.

Unable to hold back a second more, she pressed her lips to his, moaning softly. Garrett took from her, giving even more in return. Tasting one another feverishly, then slowing savoring, before once again feasting. Taylor's cheeks flushed with heat, her whole being taken with desire for him.

A sudden snap... pop echoed from the fireplace as the wood settled into the grate, shaking them from the limerent splendor of the euphoric moment. Their bulging eyes shot to the fireplace, then back to one another. The realization of their overreaction making them laugh aloud.

Running his hand over his hair Garrett grinned. "Give me a moment, I'll be right back," kissing her hand. Turning away before she could reply, he stepped through the doors.

Watching as he returned to their table, speaking briefly to Paolo then retrieving his wallet to settle their tab, taking in his every move, Taylor found herself wishing they were back at her place. Moving to the hearth she smiled at the thought of him knowing her true thoughts, so very grateful that he couldn't read her mind, she took a seat before the fire. Blushing, she imagined the trouble she might be in if he truly knew the desires of her heart.

"How about something warm and chocolaty?" Garrett extended a steaming porcelain mug of swirled sweet cream topped hot cocoa to her, seating himself beside her on the hearth. "This has got to be one of the most amazing places. Or maybe it's more about the company?" Grinning as he took a sip, searching the forest line.

"I agree with both," Taylor replied in a voice that somehow sounded foreign to her. Sultry had never worked for her before, she always found it to feel cheap and dishonest, but within his presence it came naturally. There were more than simplistic waves of lust moving through her, this was something she had yet to experience with any other. Closing her eyes she inhaled a deep breath of the refreshing night air, praying the evening would never end.

"I am not one to gush over another, but you are really something. The way you move, the feel of you in my arms... I've never had such a reaction to a woman before." Garrett moved his eyes to the moonlight playing on her dark hair, to the line of her cheek, the curve of her lips. Sitting his mug down beside him he leaned in close, slowly pressing his lips against hers once again. Such sweet lingerings held them captivated, unmoving, entranced in what felt like dream.

Parting, Taylor gasped softly. "What are you doing to me?" Balancing in a dizzied stupor.

"I'm not sure, but it's effecting me as well." Garrett joked, unable to muster a smile for the profound trance he found himself dawdling in. "Go somewhere with me?"

"Yes," Taylor replied without a thought, setting her cocoa onto the hearth she stood, taking Garrett's outreached hand. Moving in step silently across the patio, through the parking lot. Garrett walked her to the passenger door of his truck, opening it, offering her a hand up. Taylor felt his eyes on her as she climbed in, her skin fevered in knowing.

Once on the road Garrett reached to flip on the radio. Taylor was thankful for the distraction, something to break the emotional roar of the hush hanging between them.

Garrett signaled, turning from the main road into the forest line, swerving aggressively back and forth navigating the narrow, bath tub sized pothole laden logging road. Taylor winced hearing the painful screeching of branches raking their way along the trucks sides. Garrett slowed none, as if he hadn't heard the trees gouging his perfect paint, he forged onward. They climbed and climbed, bumping along the ever narrowing trek with more need of throttle with each passing mile. 'Maybe this wasn't such a great idea after all.' Taylor thought, her stomach queasy over the thought of the damage done to her grandfather's truck. The salmon dinner seeming to swim within her belly.

"Here we are."

"Where precisely is here?" Taylor leaned forward in the seat, mesmerized by the seemingly endless horizon of countless stars blanketing the night sky. The harvest moon hanging flawlessly over the sea of multicolored lights that would be their little town. "It's magical from up here. I've never been this far up the mountain before." Taylor peered out in awe. "My friends and I use to drive up to the helicopter pad to hang out and watch the sun set. But you couldn't see half of this view from down there."

Garrett turned off the truck and lights, staring into the distance alongside Taylor. A few moments passed before he pushed his way from the truck, closing the door behind him without a word. Seconds later Taylor's door opened startling her. Raising his arms to her, she lay her hands on his shoulders as he took her by the waist, sliding her down his body, holding her stare in the moonlight. There beneath the vast night sky they stood, unmoving amidst the serenade of the cricket song floating on the cool evening breeze.

Taylor shivered as Garrett ran his fingers deep into her hair, tilting her face to his. Moaning, she welcomed his lips to hers. Pressing closer into him, tightly wrapping her arms around his back, their bodies moving as one, urgency sweeping over them as they hungrily feasted on one another. In a whirlwind of passionate kisses, her nails clawing at his shirt, Taylor found herself lost in waves of dangerous fervor for Garrett. Starving for more she tilted her face to the cool night sky praying for strength.

Leaning back he smiled, shaking his head in disbelief. "Taylor, Taylor, Taylor." Her name slipping from his lips like warm honey, leaving her desiring even more still.

Taking her hand he lured her to the rear of the truck. Pressing her back tight to the fender as Garrett moved in snug against her, his thigh between hers, kissing her ear, her neck, nibbling ever lower. His eyes sparkling mischievously he paused meeting her wanton glance, before taking her in yet another long heated kiss.

Taylor's head spun. The intense dizziness reminding her of those first steps just after exiting a Tilt a Whirl. Without a moment's notice he moved away leaving her stunned. Opening the tailgate, jumping into the back of his truck he offered her a hand up. Laying her hand in his palm she felt her feet leave the ground quickly finding the tailgate beneath her. Stepping in close beside him she turned her face to the sky once again. "Look at all these stars!" Marveling at such a vast clearing. The few extra feet of the truck height allowing for an unbelievable three hundred and sixty degree view of the horizon. Trillions of stars glittered across the black velvet sky.

"This has to be my second favorite place on Earth," Garrett spoke in a hush, brushing her hair away from her face, grazing his moist lips sensuously across her ear.

"Your favorite being…" pausing at the heat of his breath falling upon her bare shoulder.

"The barn," speaking in unison they chuckled.

Smiling, Garrett turned her to him, taking her hand in his. Kneeling into the back of the truck, he sat Indian style summoning her down to his lap, wrapping her in a warm embrace. Tilting her face to his, Taylor smirked. "What are you up to?"

"That obvious, huh?" Garrett whispered, softly nibbling her earlobe, along the line of her neck. Slipping her blouse slowly off her shoulder, drawing her into a trance.

A large crunch echoed from just outside the clearing they were parked within. "Did you hear that?" Garrett spewed the words in a hushed tone, his eyes bulging.

"What was that?" Taylor uttered gulping.

"I'm not sure, but whatever it is it must be pretty big to make that loud of a noise."

Taylor leaned closer into his chest. A wave of shivers racked her body as her wild imagination played an imaginary scene of Sasquatch feasting on their remains after dragging them kicking and screaming back to its' cave. 'I have got to stop watching scary movies.

"You mind if we get out of here… now?" Garrett pushed her back to standing, joining her much faster than seemed humanly possible. Jumping from the tailgate he turned to help Taylor from the back of the truck. Seeing her instead quickly climb over the opposite edge of the truck bed onto the tire, hurrying to the cab pulling the door closed. Slamming the tailgate Garrett all but ran back to the cab, frantically climbing in. Rolling his window up, he started the truck and locked the door in one harried move. Seeing that Taylor had already safely locked and safety belted herself in he grinned slipping the shifter into gear.

"What do you think that was?" Taylor asked once they were safely on their way.

"Not really sure, but I wasn't about to wait around to find out, that's for certain," hurriedly maneuvering the truck out of the forest.

Riding in silence, Garrett reached to turn the radio up a notch louder. "What would you like to hear?" He asked, pausing before choosing a station.

"Anything really, other than Rap and island music I really like all music." She smiled, watching as he tuned the local oldies rock on, thankful that he chose her favorite without knowing.

"Would you like to do anything special? The night is still young, as they say." His sweet tone giving away his desire to prolong their goodbye.

"Do you play chess?"

"I try, I even have a board and all. My mother felt it would make me more... worldly, so she gave me my grandfathers. Why, do you play?"

"No, though I always wanted to... I was just curious. So I guess you can take me home."

"Oh... alright." Garrett sank in his seat digesting her words, exceedingly confused and saddened.

Pulling into her driveway Taylor unbuckled her seatbelt, quickly exiting the truck before Garrett could move an inch. He watched her walk through the headlights to his side of the truck, her shadow playing on the garage door as he rolled down his window.

"I had a great night tonight."

"Me too. Except for the forest scare I thought it was an exceptional evening. I really enjoy our time together Taylor.

"You do huh?" Smirking, she watched amused as he squirmed in his seat.

"Yes I do... and I hope you feel the same," swallowing hard, he nervously cleared his throat.

"Garrett..." Taylor whispered leaning into his window, her steamy breath tickling his ear. "If you would like... and you promise to behave, you can come in for a while."

Garrett turned the key off, pausing to roll the window back up, looking to her shaking his head. "Taylor, you are trouble." Opening the door he stepped from the truck grinning at her.

Hearing him following her up the steps Taylor smiled to herself, fully relishing the moment. Never before had she felt safe enough with a man to have such unabashed fun, to flirt and tease without worrying that he would take it as an open invitation to do as he pleased. This was an absolute first for her, inviting a man into her home, but Garrett was not just any man.

"Would you like something to drink?" Taylor asked as they made their way inside. "I have hot tea, plain and sparkling water, ginger beer or how about hot cocoa, since we never finished ours earlier?"

"That sounds perfect."

"Can I ask a favor Garrett?" The sound of his name rolling off her tongue thrilling her ever more.

"Anything," Garrett answered in a playful sultry voice.

"Light us a fire please," she continued, offering him a smoldering glance before disappearing into the kitchen.

A perfectly built fire blazed, filling the room with an entrancing amber hue when Taylor returned. Sitting the tray with their steaming mugs onto the hearth, she lifted two giant pillows from beneath the coffee table, along with a silky soft cashmere throw from the arm chair. "Come join me?" Motioning to the area rug beneath the hearth, she watched as Garrett sat down next her, accepting a mug as she offered it to him. "Mini marshmallows?"

"You read my mind woman." Taking a scoop of them into the spoon, sprinkling them over his steamy cocoa. "Would you like some?" He offered dipping the spoon into the bowl of mini sugary pillows, filling it again.

"Now who's reading minds?" Taylor held her mug out allowing him to top hers as well. "Perfect, thank you." Taking a sip she spied Garrett watching her.

"Let me help you with that." Leaning in close Garrett ran his finger along the edge of her top lip. Taking a line of melted marshmallow onto his finger slowly slipping it into his mouth, locking eyes with her.

Taylor sat her mug back onto the tray, then reached for Garrett's, placing it beside hers. Turning back to him she held his stare, her heart beating so that she knew he had to be able to hear it being mere inches away. Without pause she lay herself over top of him, pressing her lips firmly to his, taking his lower lip between her. Their bodies melting together as one, hungrily moving against one another atop the soft mound of down pillows. Time slipping past without notice.

"Taylor…" Garrett gasped for breath.

Sitting back she sighed in frustration, laying her head back onto the pillow beside him. "I know, I know… we need to slow down."

"We're getting ahead of ourselves here." I just don't want to rush and ruin this."

"I know, but you are so… I want to make love to you Garrett," drawing in a long ragged breath, she continued, "but I know, not now… not this early, not here like this. Thank you Garrett," Taylor breathlessly whispered, her eyes stinging with raw unchained emotions.

"I care about you Taylor, more than I thought I could. I simply don't want anything to mess this up. I want so badly to see where this takes us, without relying on our obviously ferocious sexual attraction. We already know we have that in spades, wouldn't you agree?" Holding back laughter.

171

"I'm sorry, I know that we need to slow down, it's just that I've never felt so safe with another before. I have to admit these feelings are outside of my understanding."

Snuggling his face into the long silken waves of hair pooled along her neck, squeezing her tight. "I swear to you here and now this was not a ploy to get you in bed Taylor. This relationship means so much more than that to me. To have met someone that I care so much for and feel so close to, so drawn to in such a short time... I cannot just ignore such truth. Spending time with you, that's all I want right now. I promise that I won't stop calling if we don't... Let's really get to know one another, just let this take us where it will." Garrett lay his head upon her shoulder, sliding his palm against hers, watching their fingers slowly lace together.

"I feel the same. I'm just a little scared. I don't want to blow this."

"Don't be, please trust in this, in us... trust in me. Know that I'm more than a one track, shallow excuse for a man. If we are truly feeling all we believe to be real, then in good time we will have it all, but only when and if the time is right." Searching Taylor's eyes for a sign of acceptance, hopeful for a chance to prove himself to her, he smiled.

"I do trust you. Sometimes I just need to regroup and put the past behind me. I too want to get to know you better, spend more time together and not rush things. Just let this carry us wherever it will." Squeezing his hand she smiled back sweetly. "Besides there's that barn. I really want to see what happens with that barn," biting her lip, bashfully batting her eyes.

"Oh I see, that's it, you only want to hang out to see what happens with the barn. I knew this was too good to be true," leaning in quickly to steal yet another kiss. Pulling her tightly to him, he turned over smoothly maneuvering her on top of him. "Why Mizz Taylor, what do you mean by renderin' me so utterly helpless?" Garrett joked in his best Scarlett O'Hara drawl.

Taylor threw her head back cackling. "I'm like that, you best just get use to me throwing you on your back and mauling you at any given moment." Passionately pressing her lips to his again Taylor savored him, reveling in his warmth. "You are addictive," her whispered words falling hot against his mouth as they continued kissing.

Taylor awoke to find Garrett asleep next to her, his rhythmic breathing somehow comforting her. Glancing to the clock she squinted attempting to clearly see the time. Three forty-five A.M…. how time flies. Sitting up onto her elbow she admired the muscular line of his jaw, the curve of his tanned cheek, the dark mantle of lashes reminding her of a sleeping child. The upturned corner of his lips convinced her that as he was most likely dreaming of their night as she had just been.

With nothing beyond embers remaining in the fireplace, the room came under a slight chill. Standing to retrieve another throw, Taylor saw Garrett stir.

"Where are you off to?" He asked rubbing his eyes. "What time is it?"

"Late, early, it could go either way at this point." Taylor grinned, enjoying the site of him sprawled on her living room floor amidst a heap of pillows. "I was just heading to the hall closet to get another blanket. Without the fire it's a bit chilly."

Garrett stood, folding the throw, laying it across the back of the arm chair that it had come from. Taking note of his considerate move, this man was truly set apart from others. This more apparent with each precious moment spent in his presence.

"What's that little smirk about?" Garrett asked, pushing the large pillows back beneath the coffee table, running his hands through his hair. "Never mind, I don't even want to know. I hate to say it but I should be heading out. Thank you for the wonderful evening. It was the nicest I've had in... well, the best ever I believe. I'm not sure that I should've even admitted that to you though."

"With the exception of the Sasquatch encounter, I concur. One of those grandchildren stories I suppose. You know, sitting around the campfire telling scary stories," his eyes sparkling at the thought.

"Grandchildren huh? So I guess that means you want little ones someday?" Taylor raised an eyebrow, having previously avoided the present topic of conversation.

"I think maybe ten or so will do. I always wanted my parents to adopt more kids. I thought what a fantastic thing to do for another human. To take their life from disastrous loss to having a home, a family, and a future. "They found they already had enough on their plate, so I figure why not me." Searching her face, he awaited a reply, unsure of the odd expression. "You alright?"

"Yes... yes, I'm perfectly fine."

"I'm just kidding. Gotcha! One or two would be perfect," offering a cheesy grin, proud for his handy work.

"Not funny," Taylor exclaimed, fully relieved.

Walking to the door Garrett turned in the entrance way meeting her eyes again. "I know you have a bad taste in your mouth with past experiences... of men being less than gentlemanly. I pray you will give this long enough to see that I am different. To prove that I'm not one of those men. Our relationship will never hinge on sex and the like." Taking her hand in his softly pressing it to his lips, leaning in closer kissing her on the forehead before turning to open the door.

Laying her hand onto his shoulder just before he stepped onto the threshold, turning him into her arms, firmly pressing his back against the wall, kissing him passionately one last time, leaving him spellbound. "Thank you again. Good night, drive safely," she called out watching him walk dazed toward his truck, her heart soaring with sheer delight for the effect she had on him.

Running a steaming hot bubble bath, she lit several vanilla lavender candles and slipped into the luxurious water. Garrett had left her wound much too tight for sleep. A warm relaxing sabbatical seeming the perfect ending to a perfect evening.

Barely fifteen minutes passed when she heard the phone ring and the machine pick up. "Leave a message after the tone, thanks!" She closed her eyes praying it was Garrett.

"Tay, pick up! It's Toby… Liz cut herself on the slicer. We're headed to emergency now. Taylor come on, pick up! She really wants us both there. Come as soon as you get this!"

The click of the call ending had Taylor leaping from the tub. Turning to pull the plug, she reached for a towel, rushing around to blow out the candles. Hurrying down the hallway pulled out a pair of jeans tossing them onto her bed. Rummaging through her drawers she retrieved under clothes and a long sleeve t-shirt. Throwing on her clothes she pulled her button up sweater from the dressing table chair and slipped her boots on. Grabbing her purse she took one last glance around the room before flipping off the light. Hurrying down the hallway to the entrance, she set the alarm. Pulling the front door closed behind her she ran to the SUV shoving the key into the ignition, not even allowing it to warm before peeling out of the driveway. Ignoring her speed she hurried through street light after street light, moving through town on auto pilot, instinct alone carrying her safely from point A to point B.

Rushing through the one hour lot to the long term parking, Taylor steered into an empty spot. Stepping from the SUV she slammed the door, sprinting to the double automatic doors beneath the glowing red emergency sign, speed walking through the hall to the security station. "Excuse me, can you please tell…"

"Taylor!" Jake's voice stopping her in her tracks.

"What are you doing here? Are you alright?" Taylor's face wracked with utter confusion.

"I came with your sister. I was the last to leave the bar and heard her let out a blood curdling scream. I ran into the kitchen with Toby to find her covered in blood. She's pretty bad Taylor. Follow me." Jake took Taylor's hand rushing her toward the emergency room, her feet barely touching the floor.

"Tay, am I glad to see you! Liz has been asking for you repeatedly!" Toby cried out, wrapping her tightly in his arms. "She's in a bad way Tay, be prepared. They're bringing in a plastic surgeon to consult on the plan to repair the damages as best they can, to try and save her hand," he whispered, leading her around a partition wall.

Taylor froze at the site of Liz laying on the gurney covered head to toe in dry caked blood.

"I know, it's harsh, but she really needs you," Toby whispered again, ushering her on.

Composing herself, she slowly stepped to her side. Liz looked up, tears pooling in her eyes, streaking down her blood spattered cheeks. "Taylor!" Liz wept, sucking for air between sobs.

"Hey now try and relax sis, I'm here and I am not going anywhere. I promise I will be here until you say I should go, okay?" Carefully kissing Liz on the forehead.

"Hello, I am Dr. Westfall," a tall thin grey haired man announced, stepping around the curtain. "I will need a few moments alone with Elizabeth," looking to Taylor he offered a stern smile before turning his eyes back to Liz. "Looks like you did a pretty good job on yourself, didn't you?" The surgeon jabbed.

Taylor stepped back behind the partition once again, wanting to slap the doctor silly for treating her sister like a five year old.

"She must be elated to see you, she hasn't let up since we arrived, asking for you over and over," Jake said moving closer, speaking barely above a whisper.

"Thanks again for helping get her here. If you hadn't been there I am not sure she would have made it," Toby stepped up behind them extending a hand, offering Jake a hearty shake to further show his new found respect.

"I did what any decent man would, that's all."

"How did you get blood all over you Jake, are you cut? You have just as much blood on you as Liz does it seems."

Toby interjected before Jake could speak. "He held Liz's arteries so she wouldn't bleed out Tay. He held her in his arms while I drove. He's the real hero here," patting Jake on the back.

"Oh Jake, that's…" Taylor's words vanishing beneath her emotions. Wrapping her arms around his thickly muscled neck she sucked in a ragged breath. "Thank you," Taylor whispered in his ear before turning away again. "I'll be right back," hurriedly pushing past Toby, rushing to the restrooms as fast as her feet would carry her. Pushing through the door she pressed her back against the inside forcing it closed faster than the door was built to allow. Taylor let out a low moan as waves of unstoppable emotions began exploding from her. Tears pouring down her cheeks dripped onto the collar of her shirt, soaking it through. Hurrying to the sink she turned on the cold water repeatedly splashing her heated face. Peering into the mirror she was horrified at the sight of her red, swollen eyes. "Pull it together Tay, Liz needs you more now than ever." Ripping off a sheet from the hand towel dispenser she lightly dabbed her tender eyes. Retrieving a compact from her purse she patted it over her face, rolling gloss over her lips she gave herself one last look and rushed out of the bathroom before yet another wave of emotions could arise.

"Taylor! Hurry, they're taking Liz to surgery!" Toby exclaimed, quickly herding her down the hallway toward the elevators.

"Tay, I was afraid I wouldn't get to say goodbye!" Liz's voice cracked with fear.

"Hey sis, this isn't goodbye." Taylor offered her best sweet smile amidst the chaos brewing within. "We will be here when you wake. You just relax and have a great nap and before you know it you'll be on your way to recovery with us spoiling you rotten. Okay?"

"Tay, I know now that I wasn't there for you as I should have been… I'm so very sorry. I love you." Liz squeezed her eyes closed weeping.

Taylor kissed Liz's bloody cheek. "I know that you were there in spirit. Don't worry about any of that just focus on getting better." Taylor blew her a kiss as Liz was rolled into the surgery elevator.

"I love you guys," Liz said weakly.

"We love you!" Toby and Taylor said in unison as the elevator doors slid closed.

Taylor turned to Toby throwing her arms around his neck. "She can't die… she just can't!" Weeping between words she continued. "Who's going to be ticked at me all the time if she's gone? She can't die!" Taylor blubbered, burying her face in his shoulder.

"God won't take her yet, she has work still to do here on this crazy planet, truly I believe she's going to make it. You need to trust God isn't going to do that to us Tay!" Squeezing her hard, they stood unmoving, sharing their pain, silently sending up prayers.

Chapter Eleven

Taylor's prayers had been answered. Liz had come through surgery in perfect shape. The blades had missed nerves and all important soft tissue. In a few weeks she would be able to return to work, and life would be back as they'd known it before Liz had tangled with the slicer.

Taylor's schedule had been insane. Trying to keep up with her own hours along with sharing half of Liz's shifts with Toby there hadn't been much time left to vacuum her house, let alone do anything enjoyable. Thankfully Garrett had been patient with her, taking time out of his busy life to visit her at Donna's. He had even jumped in a few times helping wash dishes when they were in dire straits often clearing tables so that she and Toby could take much needed siesta. Some nights waiting for hours so they could share a meal together. Though they hadn't much time he was eager to share what little he could steal, this warmed Taylor's heart.

The dinner crowd had cleared and the dishwasher had things under control in the kitchen. Toby had nearly cleaned the entire inventory of glassware and the bar top was gleaming in the lights, when the phone oddly rang for the third time in thirty minutes. Toby once again rushed to pick it up before anyone else could make an effort. "Donna's Place. Yes sir, I think I can handle that. Thank you," Toby said turning to Taylor. "Why don't you take a break sis, I've got this. Go take a walk in mom's herb garden off the veranda and get some fresh air."

Though Toby was acting most peculiar, the sound of such a lovely moment away had her smiling. "Thanks for the thought little brother, I really could use a breather." Untying her apron, she pulled the ribbon from her hair letting it fall across her shoulders. Taking a long deep breath she pushed the back patio door open stopping in her tracks. Strands of tiny sparkling fairy lights swaged across the cedar arbor in a glistening web above her. Hundreds of white candles lit the perimeter of the patio with the soft glow of flickering flames. In the midst of the terraced cobblestone dozens more were set inches apart, encircling a round table beautifully decorated in all shades of purple. A stunning bouquet of fresh lilac set in a large tapered crystalline vase graced the crisp white linen tablecloth atop a table romantically set for two. Lavender rose petals and iridescent flat marbles lay sprinkled around a dozen matching candles set in frosted glass votives around the flowers. Taylor gasped at the magnificent beauty before her, staring in disbelief, struggling to catch her breath.

"So, I decided if you can't come to me, I will come to you. I hope it meets with your approval. I know you love white peonies best, but a little birdie told me lilacs are a close second." Garrett stepped from the shadows of the arbor post, moving slowly toward her.

"I have never, I mean, I …" The perfect words escaped Taylor, tears filling her tired eyes.

Stepping to her, Garrett wrapped her in a warm embrace, kissing her neck as he held her. "You are killing me here. Are these tears of sorrow or joy?"

Pulling back from him, Taylor smiled. "Joy Garrett, these are tears of great joy. No one has ever been so kind to do something this grand, this beautiful for me. I am not sure how to feel, honestly I am a bit overwhelmed. What is all this for?" Taylor asked, wiping her tear stained cheeks.

"For you silly, there need not be a specific reason to have a romantic evening together. You have been going nonstop since Liz's mishap. I figured this was a perfect way to get you to stop and smell the... lilacs," grinning at his own words.

"You are too sweet Garrett. Thank you, its breath taking!" Taking him in her arms once again, giving him a tight squeeze, she softly kissed his cheek.

"Your dinner is served peoples," Toby called out, stepping through the doors behind them carrying a large serving tray loaded with delicious looking dishes. Making his way to the table he opened a service stand, setting the tray on top. "Please be seated," Toby said in a poor attempt at a British accent.

Garrett extended a hand and Taylor lay her palm on top as he led her to the gorgeous spread before them. Pausing as Garrett pulled her chair out from the table offering it to her. Taylor took a seat, scooting closer to the table.

"Thank you," glancing over her shoulder to him smiling.

"You are very welcome."

"Okay no making goo-goo eyes at one another until after I'm gone." Toby smirked as he placed a silver trimmed porcelain plate before Taylor, setting another in front of Garrett."

"Toby did you do all this food yourself?"

"Oh heck no, Garrett arranged all this. I'm just here as part of the ambiance. How am I doing so far?" Toby asked jokingly, nudging her lightly with an elbow.

"Great, just hurry it up I'd like a few moments alone with her before she has to get back to work," whispering loudly, smiling at Taylor as if she couldn't hear his words.

"Oh no, the remainder of the evening she is all yours. I have things covered out front." Toby set a small plate of pansy topped salad in front of each of them, a basket of piping hot rolls accompanied by mini burgundy blooming rose shaped pats of butter.

"You didn't! From the restaurant where we had our first date?" Taylor covered her mouth in sheer surprise.

"Only the best," Garrett admitted winking at her.

"Well kids my job here is done," topping off their goblets of ice water, moving quickly toward the door. "Don't do anything I wouldn't do," disappearing inside before they could reply, Toby peeked back through the window.

Taylor sat in awe of the lavish table before them. "This is so lovely Garrett. I cannot believe you did all this... for me. I feel like a princess."

"You haven't had a break in quite a while. I figured a night of relaxation might do you good. I knew you would never agree to leave Toby to deal with this place alone, so with his help, wah-la!" Garrett's excitement filled her with renewed energy. "Oh... wait just a moment." Winking, he pushed his seat back rushing to the corner of the patio. With the flick of a switch Madeleine Peyroux singing 'La Vie en Rose' filled the air. "We can't have a perfect evening without some of your favorite music." As Garrett moved toward her, his eyes spoke volumes to the desires of his heart. "Dance?" Offering her his hand he bowed as if she was royalty.

Standing she accepted his outstretched hand, recalling their first dance. Sliding her arms around Garrett's neck pressing her lips to his with more passion than she realized harbored within her. Running her fingers into the silky layers of his dark hair, Taylor felt the walls of inhibitions for loving him fall away, desiring to tell him all she held inside. She ached to say those three sweet words, longing for him to truly know her heart.

Garrett kissed her with equal fervor, pulling away he peered deeply into her eyes. "Taylor, I need you to know how I am feeling. I know it's early in our relationship, and I certainly don't want to scare you away, but if I don't get this out I may explode." Garrett closed his eyes sighing, then looked to her once again. "I'm falling for you Taylor. I wasn't sure how very much until tonight. I thought quite possibly that it was no more than deep seeded desire. Only fools fall in love so hastily, right?" Garrett left no time for Taylor to answer before continuing on. "I can't, I won't hold back any longer. You have to know... I love you."

Taylor's eyes stung with raw emotion. Unsure how to respond, she stood unmoving replaying his words over again attempting to convince herself that he had sincerely said that he loved her.

"I shouldn't have said anything, I had no right to spew all this and ruin a perfect night. I'm sorry. I am so very sorry if I've upset you."

Seeing him turning away, she grabbed his hand before he slipped away, pulling him firmly to her. Searching his eyes she smiled. "Garrett you silly man you haven't upset me, I love you too."

"What, you...?" Garrett stood before her unmoving, stunned speechless.

"I have from the very moment we first spoke on the phone. I wanted to tell you but our relationship is so new, I was afraid I might run you off." Taylor wrapped her arms around his neck once again, whispering in his ear. "Kiss me."

Garrett took her tightly against him, kissing her dizzy. With that applause erupted from the other side of the patio door. Parting they looked to see what was happening inside. Peering out through the windows, Toby and the kitchen staff were lined up watching them. Wolf whistles and hoots of celebration rang out as Toby pushed the intercom button on the wall. "Hey guys, you must have switched on the P.A. system as well as the music out there. That was very romantic you two. Congratulations you love birds." More cheers of joyous celebration followed.

"What did I do?" Garrett ran to check the levers he had turned on.

"Wow, this is one of those moments that we may never hear the last of." Taylor sighed, taking a seat at the table shaking her head at the humor of it all. The most romantic moment of her life, the very moment she had prayed for since she was a little girl and it had been broadcasted through the entire restaurant via loudspeaker.

Garrett returned to the table sitting across from her. "I am so sorry. I had no idea I had switched that on too. It's off now I promise." Garrett's face shone thirty shades of utter embarrassment.

"I will forgive you if you kiss me," she purred leaning across to him, elated as he met her half way. Their admittance of love ignited a passion that set their hearts afire, their souls soaring, their desires for one another a blaze.

Finishing the impossibly delectable meal, they danced the night away lost in one another's embrace. Taylor had never been kissed so passionately, so lovingly. She wanted nothing more than for time to stop in the beauty of this moment, in the midst of their perfect evening. Falling in love, truly finding such a soul connection had proven to be more than she had ever expected. In that moment Taylor knew she wanted for Garrett to know all about her. For him to know every dark secret of her past, all the unforgettable moments that altered her, shaped her. And even more she longed to know about his life, his family and all he dreamed of. For the first time in her life she ached to build a future with a man. She desired a life with Garrett. A life with such depth and understanding she'd finally feel complete.

How many times had she seen couples gazing into one another's eyes, as if they merely saw each other? Never had she understood all the fuss that people made over their partner. Never, until now had she felt there was anything to all the hype. Being in Garrett's arms gave her a new perspective to what love was truly all about and for this she was grateful. If she died that very second she knew her life was all but perfect, still she prayed she wouldn't wake to find this all but a dream.

Watching him as he spoke, Taylor felt something shift within her, knowing that she had been forever changed in these moments with him. Garrett had found the key to open her heart.

Chapter Twelve

With Liz back to work Taylor found more time for her own life once again, grateful for the end of eighteen hour shifts, for her renewed freedom. Garrett made the most of every opportunity to spend time with her outside of Donna's. Countless sunset picnics, rides on his bike with no particular destination, late nights floating on the pond beneath the stars in his rowboat and slow dancing in the loft of the barn had Taylor's heart overflowing. This was the beginning of the rest of her life, for such blessing she could be no more grateful.

Though she had never favored the early shift being such a night owl, she had agreed to switch shifts with Liz to accommodate her physical therapy appointment. Donna's had never served a booming morning mob. Following the late night crowd the previous shift, she welcomed the quiet. Wiping the bar top down, thoughts of Garrett circled in her mind. The time they had shared since the surprise on the patio had drawn them even closer than she could have fathomed. Hearing him speak those beautiful words had meant the world to her, but feeling his love was more than she could have ever envisioned. This freedom she had yet to experience in any other relationship washed through her, leaving her filled with such joy she'd only read of in fictional novels. There was something so peaceful and reassuring about Garrett. The sense of security in knowing that he wasn't going to do anything to sabotage this love they shared solidified her feelings for him even more. Knowing for certain that he wasn't the cheating type and above all the way he unabashedly loved her proved this time and time again. This time she had truly found the one. Garrett was hers forever. With the grace of God she had found her way to him, she had sincerely found her soul mate.

The ringing of the phone jolted her back to present time. "Donna's Place, Taylor speaking," forcing one of the perkiest morning tones that she could muster, still lingering amidst thoughts of Garrett.

"Good morning beautiful. Are you busy this evening?" The smooth depth of his voice never ceased to send chills of sheer ecstasy pouring over her.

"I am now." Smiling at her own remark, she bit her lip, anxiously awaiting his reply.

"I have something to show you."

"You do huh, and just what might that be big boy?" She drawled in her best sultry Mae West.

Garrett laughed aloud. "Young lady behave yourself. Can you meet me at the barn around seven?"

"Should I bring anything?"

"Just your beautiful self. So I will see you then. I love you Taylor."

"I love you Garrett," she said slowly closing her eyes, languishing in the sweet sound of his voice long after hearing the line go dead.

"Um hello, can I get a coffee please. Geez what does a man have to do to get service in a hole like this?"

Taylor's eye sprung open. "Jake?" Turning she hung the phone up searching the room for him. "Look what the cat drug in! How have you been?" Taylor hurried to the end of the bar to greet him properly. Throwing her arms around his massive neck she squeezed him hard, feeling her feet lift from the floor momentarily.

"You're looking mighty fine these days Miss Taylor," Jake took her hand spinning her around so he could take in the full view, "mighty fine indeed girl," grinning ear to ear, winking at her.

"Never fails that you can make me blush harder every time I see you Jake, you naughty boy," bashfully brushing her hair back from her reddened cheeks.

"Get rid of that biker boy and I will show you blush."

"Behave yourself Jake. You're a bad influence on me!" Laughing as she playfully punched him in the arm.

"Oh no sweetheart, the naughty is already there, I just bring it out in you." Throwing his head back Jake let out a bellowing laugh.

"Thank goodness there's no customers in here, we would have rumors flying all across town."

"I welcome rumors with you darlin', they might even help my reputation."

"Ah come on your reputation doesn't need any shining… well maybe only a little," batting her eyes at him sweetly.

"Hey I hate to hurry off, but I'm here for the breakfast burrito I called in, then I'll need to be on my way. I have customers meeting me out at the shop in a bit. I need to set their gates up outside so they can give their final approval before delivery. You should come by sometime Tay. It's the old red barn out off of Bridge Creek. In fact, if you have any extra time this Sunday, I'm hosting a painting party bright and early. Since this place isn't open until noon on Sundays that leaves you five hours to play in the paint with me. You should bring those siblings of yours as well. Oh and I guess that guy that you're seeing is invited too." Jake tossed ten bucks on the counter as Taylor handed him the brown paper wrapped burrito. "Just no lip locking in front of me alright? I'm still getting use to this whole Garrett thing."

"Hey now, that isn't fair."

Jake smiled, inhaling the enticing scent of his burrito. "Smells delicious as always." I hope to see all of you on Sunday!" Jake called turning for the door, blowing her a kiss.

"I will be there, and I'll do my best with the rest of them. We all owe you after what you did for Liz. Have a great day Jake!" Untying her apron as she watched him step through the door. Hearing the truck start she stared through the window as his grey 79' flatbed Ford pulled away. Taylor felt a pang in her heart knowing now how wonderful of a man he genuinely was behind all the tough guy, Norwegian God personification. Jake was truly a keeper.

Setting the tip jar to the tray she dumped it out and began dividing the day's earnings. The sound of someone hurriedly pulling into the parking lot drew her eyes toward the door.

"Man am I late? I'm so sorry! I hate it when the next shift is late!" Toby exclaimed, bursting through the doors with such might Taylor jolted.

"Relax, it isn't as if I have a hot date. Well not until later any way," Taylor offered her cheesiest proverbial Cheshire grin, freeing her hair from a French twist.

"Still I hate it, I didn't mean to be late but I stopped by the produce stand to grab some duck eggs for a venison quiche I was going to bake for a dinner special tonight and wow, there she was." Toby stared off in space as if she stood before him.

190

"There who was?" Taylor asked, stuffing her tips into her pant pocket, wrinkling her forehead at the sound of him being so overly excited about a female.

"My dream girl. Tay it was as if everything was moving in slow motion, just like they show in the movies. I have never felt so much just being in a woman's presence before. Now I get it, I totally get it! That weird drunken love trance you have been walking around in lately, I actually think I experienced it today! She is all I ever could want. She's intelligent, quick witted, funny and oh those eyes!" Toby excitedly cooed like a love sick school boy.

"So did you get her number?"

"Yes... well I already had it actually, and I didn't even know it. She's the duck egg lady, the one that owns 'Tail Feathers'. I had just never seen her in person before. I always pick our eggs up at the produce stand off Mayfield Lane and head on in, but today the little old lady that runs the place used every excuse in the book to get me to stay and talk. I was finally getting ready to leave and there she was."

"This is so unlike you Tob, gushing over a girl."

"She's a woman, not a girl!" Toby snapped.

"Sorry, I meant woman." Taylor snickered under her breath, finding much humor in Toby's emotional reaction. "You're cute when you're in lust little brother," smirking at him.

"I really want to call her, but what do I say?"

"Hello, want to grab a coffee some time," shrugging her shoulders as if it was just so easy.

"Hello... coffee, that's it? That can't be all there is too it. If it's so easy then why do people make such big deals about dates?" Toby's forehead wrinkled with confusion.

"All a lady really wants to do is hang out and get to know a guy at first. You can't talk at the movies and dancing only tells you if there is physical attraction, and realistically there is almost always some animal magnetism. Dinner with a total stranger can bring pressure to bare much too soon. But to sit face to face in a safe comfortable setting and really take the time to learn about one another, that's a perfect date to a lady. Unless she's out for money or to get... well, a piece, and if that is the case run like your hair is on fire. A coffee and a couple hours can tell you a lot about another person."

Toby sat staring at Taylor as if she had told him he had won the lottery. Throwing his arms around her neck he squeezed her, kissing her cheek as he let go. "Thanks Tay! You are the best!"

"So, since I helped you... what are you up to this Sunday?" Taylor asked smirking.

"Oh great, what did I just volunteer for now?" Toby pushed his hair off his forehead with worry.

"Painting party at Jake's place. He bought that old red barn just up the way to run his welding shop out of. She needs a new coat of paint, so we're all invited to join in the fun."

"I guess that could be arranged. You think that I could bring a friend? I mean if the coffee date works out and all."

"The more the merrier. Best get that duck lady on the phone ASAP if you're going to squeeze in a coffee date before Sunday though," winking at him as she pushed open the door heading to her car. "See you tomorrow Tob!" She hollered as she stepped outside.

"Have a great night Tay!" Toby answered back just before the door closed.

Driving home Taylor wondered what Garrett had up his sleeve. The excitement of simply being with him was enough for her, but who was she to stop him from doing something special for her, right? Grinning ear to ear she made the decision that this would be the night... she would ride tonight.

Following a power nap, quick shower, and touch of makeup, she put on her jacket and headed out. Pushing her bike from the garage, she lit it up, sliding the door down, latching it. Throwing her leg over, she pulled her goggles and helmet into place, slipping into her gloves then headed out. One last stop for fuel, bottled water, and cinnamon gum and she was on her way.

The evening had cooled more than she'd expected, sending chills rushing through her as she made her way along the curving road. The looming sky darkening with eerily oppressive thunderheads gathering along the ridge. The brisk air lending an unexpected nip against her bare cheeks as she distanced herself from town. Thunder boomed across the canyon, wicked lightning striking shortly after... shooting electrically charged fingers all around. Taylor's teeth now chattering, the bite of freezing sleet pelting her face. Again the sky flared, illuminating the now darkening road ahead. Beneath her Taylor felt her bike jolt hard, sputtering, then violently jolting once more. Glancing to her speedometer she watched in horror as the slowed to 40...30...20. In an instant the sky opened up, shooting spears of electrifying brilliance across the pavement striking a giant oak just off the roadway. Fiery sparks lit up the rain soaked road, causing Taylor to swerve. Settling the bike she came to rest near the shoulder of the road just as the engine died. Looking to the horizon, Taylor spied the barn just around the final corner. Dismounting, she pushed with all her might, barely budging the six hundred pounds of sheer steel. 'Tonight of all nights... seriously!' Taylor said to herself shaking her head at the thought. Struggling to hold the bike upright she set the kickstand. Wiping the water from her goggles doing her best to ignore the rain seeping through her jeans, running off her helmet, making its way down her collar trickling down her back. Wanting to cry out in frustration, a flash along the road caught her eye, flickering again and again. Light streaming through the pouring rain from the direction of the barn, shifting and shaking as it grew closer still. Taylor watched with relief as Garrett made his way on foot to her side.

"Congratulations Taylor, you're back on your bike!" Garrett's hollering barely audible above the roaring thunder.

"Not such a brilliant decision tonight it seems, but I'm excited nonetheless," Taylor's screams barely heard above the storm. Shrugging at her own predicament, she gritted her teeth, fighting off waves of chills building within her.

"Let's get you out of this," Garrett yelled through the pouring rain, motioning toward the barn. Taking her bike by the grips he quickly flipped the kickstand.

Trudging their way back toward the barn, Taylor watched as Garrett maneuvered her bike across the stretch of quickly flooding roadway, intrigued by his sheer strength and tenacity. Nearing the barn, he motioned for her to open the doors. Taylor tugged hard on the handle, heaving with all her strength. As the doors slid open Garrett pushed her bike inside next to his, helping to pull the water logged wooden slider closed again. Throwing themselves against the doors panting, they looked to one another through dripping strands of rain soaked hair, laughing.

"Well aren't we just lovely," Garrett joked, throwing his head back cackling.

Taylor spewed a dripping chunk of hair from her mouth, rolling her eyes before joining in again.

"I would have called to warn you when I saw the storm brewing, but I had no idea you were going to ride," wiping his hands over his rain soaked hair, shaking the water off.

"I just got on and came. I still can't believe I did it. Will she be alright?" Motioning toward her bike. "She just died on me."

"She'll be fine, just give her a chance to dry out."

"Thank you, by the way. This really seems to be your knack...helping people." Taylor glanced to Garrett standing beside her, their backs still pressed against the wood.

"I have a thing for this one particular damsel..." Garrett said meeting her eyes. Turning to her, gently wiping his fingers across her forehead brushing back a strand of dripping hair. Stepping to her, face to face, he stood searching her eyes. "You're so very lovely Taylor." Her name slipping like melted honey from his lips, just as he pressed them to hers in a long, slow, profoundly passionate kiss.

Taylor steamed from within, entranced by his touch. The fierce unencumbered way he moved his hands over her hips, along her sides, pressing her back firmly against the hard wood leaving her mesmerized. Lightening crashed just above the barn, startling them from the moment.

"Wow, that was close," Garrett said between heavy breaths, nearly grazing his lips with hers as he spoke.

Tilting her head back Taylor sighed with pleasure as he unzipped her jacket slipping it off her shoulders, hanging it onto a horseshoe hook mounted just beside the door frame. "You need to get dried off before you catch a chill." His intoxicating gaze taking in every inch of her as he slid his hands down her arms lacing his fingers through hers. "Come with me," his eyes sparkling with mischief.

Taylor smirked raising an eyebrow, excited for anything Garrett had to show her. Turning to the staircase he loosed her hand, slipping from his rain soaked leathers, draping them across the banister. Meeting her eyes again he slid his fingers along hers, lacing them together once more. Their palms firmly matched as he led her up the stairs. Glancing upward Taylor caught sight of tiny beams of light sparkling through the loft floorboards above. Reaching the top step he turned to her, running his fingers deep into her still soaked hair. Gently tilting her head back, pressing his lips to the front of her throat, tracing along to just below her ear, softly nibbling on her earlobe, sighing. His heated breath tickling her ear, driving Taylor to utter distraction. Stepping away, Garrett left her standing alone, cloaked in the dim wavering light, reeling in the wake of his touch. Peering across the candle lit room, Taylor watched as Garrett climbed over the haystack, making his way to the loft doors.

"The thunder strikes are farther apart now, the storm must have shifted." With a slow heave Garrett pushed open the doors exposing the loft to outlying flashes of light, thunder rumbling in the distance. "Join me." Garret beckoned, motioning with his eyes toward the hay stack.

Stepping over the bales Taylor gasped, feasting her eyes on the beautiful spread he had awaiting her on the other side. His quilt lay across several bales set beside a romantic spread. Moving closer Taylor spied a low rimmed glass bowl graced with a solitary flawless white peony surrounded by tiny ivory floating candles. Crackers and cheese were splayed on a fancy paper plate circling a cluster of plump crimson grapes. Individually wrapped Sliders, layered with romaine lettuce and thick slices of bright red tomatoes peaked from the brown paper sheaths. A bottle of bubbly sat chilling in an ice filled stainless steel bucket. Taking a seat on the quilt Garrett offered Taylor to take a seat beside him.

Garrett munched on a few grapes pulling a slider from its wrapper. Offering Taylor a plate he stopped, realizing something was distracting her. "Taylor?"

"Yes?"

"Are you alright? You haven't said a word since we sat down. If you don't like dinner I can run back to town and get something different."

"No my sweet man, everything is perfect… simply perfect. I was just lost in thought." Leaning in close, kissing him softly she smiled.

"About?" Garrett asked in a hush, his lips still grazing hers.

"You, us, how unbelievably wonderful being with you is. I just can't believe this is my life. It honestly seems too good to be true, like one day I will just wake up and find it was no more than a dream."

"That's not going to happen. I promise you this is real Taylor. Though I must admit I'm as surprised as you are. Believe me, I never thought when I picked up that phone at Donna's that this would have come from it. That I would meet the woman on the other end of the line and fall head over heels in those first moments. You must know that I care for you more than I thought I ever could. I can't imagine life without you Taylor. I hope that I never have to try. It's overwhelming really, loving another the way I love you. I realize now how very lonesome my life was before I met you. Having grown so close to you has awakened my very soul. I hear myself speak of you to others and it seems so surreal that I have been given this chance, blessed with this profound love. I'm not going anywhere, please believe me."

Intensity building, exchanging wanton glances, as Garrett slipped a warm grape between her lips. Clearing her throat, Taylor swallowed hard, getting to her feet. Making her way across the hay, she stepped to the loft doors, gazing out across the dramatic horizon. Breathing in the cool night air she sighed, attempting to calm the emotionally charged yearnings stirring within. Luminous swollen storm clouds crowding the steely gray skyline above. Brilliant flashes of electricity radiantly pulsing beneath the cloud line.

Garrett sat watching from the haystacks, silently admiring the line of her silhouette; pewter shadows shifting in the changing light. Flashing flares of distant lightening dancing on her hair as it swayed in the dewy breeze. A brief parting of clouds cast moon glow across the barn floor, falling like diamond dust over her in the ever dimming light.

Standing, Garrett made his way across the loft to her. Pausing just behind her, sweeping his hand across her cheek, brushing loose strands of hair from her neck, softly kissing just below her ear, along the line of her jaw. Taylor turned her face to his, their lips meeting again with burning desire. Garrett's hands roaming, grazing her ribs, lingering along the curve of her bosom. Her breath catching at the overwhelming sensation. His blissful touch igniting lascivious desires across her skin. Turning to him she ran her fingers deep into the silky layers of his dark damp hair, hungrily kissing him again.

Searching one another, they stood face to face unmoving, ardently absorbed in their shared longings. Garrett ran his hands along the curve of her spine firmly taking her to him, their hearts beating in unison. Tilting her head back, gasping at the sensation of Garrett's warm wet tongue traveling the nape of her neck, voraciously kissing his way to her ear once again. Lightening flashed, the thunderous rumble shaking the loft, startling them from the heated moment.

"That was even closer," Taylor whispered, eyes bulging.

Sweeping her off her feet, Garrett carried her back to the haystacks tenderly laying her onto the quilt, snuggling in beside her. Intertwining their legs, pressing himself firmly against her, running his hand beneath the waist of her blouse, moaning at the feel of her supple skin. Feathering his fingertips across the soft swell of her ribs, he smiled hearing

Taylor moan with unfathomable pleasure, her body quivering beneath his sensuous touch. Sliding his thigh between hers, he shifted his weight, rolling her over on top of him. She gasped in ecstasy as their mouths met once more with fierce intensity. Opening her lips, she languished in the warm sensation of his tongue exploring hers, the heat of his body enveloping her. Parting, they stared intently into one another's eyes, wind whistling through the holey barn wood walls, their hearts pounding wildly.

"In all my life, I've never known another woman to have such profound effects on me. You drive me to distraction woman, make me ache as no other before. I long to feel you skin on skin, our bodies becoming one." Garrett whispered breathlessly running his hands through the length of her dark damp hair, softly grasping it, tilting her head back as he ravaged her neck once more. "I wish I could stop time here and now," feverishly kissing below her collarbone.

Taylor sat stunned by his words. Never before had a man evoked such a plethora of solicitous feelings from her. Her heart swelled with such immense passions she struggled to keep them contained. "Garrett make love to me. I want to be as close to you as possible, I want to show you the love I have for you as well. Take me now, make love to me Garrett," running her palms over the firmness of his chest.

Sucking in a deep breath Garrett sighed heavy. "There's nothing in this world that I would rather do than to make love to you Taylor. But here, tonight, this isn't the way I want something so very special between us to happen. I need you to trust me on this, please. Regardless of how we are feeling now I know we would regret it later. You deserve more than a quick roll in the hay. And I want to give that to you, when the time is right." Moving closer once again he leaned in to kiss her, abruptly stopped by the feel of Taylor's hand pressed firmly to his chest.

"So basically you are saying that you love me, but you don't want me? I have never felt so rejected in all my life! How can you feed me all those lines about how you feel so much for me and then so easily deny my love? You think I'm going to just take only what you are willing to give?" Taylor stood brushing his hand from her arm as he reached to try and stop her from leaving. "Please don't! You have made it perfectly clear, all those words were just meant to buy you time to see how you really feel. I'm not blind Garrett, I now see the truth, you need not say any more." Shaking her head she stood, starting for the stairs. Quickly turning to him again before descending the steps. "If I were you I would stop making alterations to this barn, the real owners might not appreciate that you are messing with their property."

Making her way to her bike, refusing to look back as Garrett called from above, she tugged her jacket and helmet on, continuing to ignore Garrett's desperate pleas to stop… to stay, to not run away. Lighting her bike off, hearing it sputter then clear, she shoved open the door. Hearing his feet on the stairs she hurriedly climbed onto her bike, tearing from the barn into the yard, onto the paved road leading back to town. 'What a fool you are Taylor! Why did you even trust a man again? Look where it got you last time, now here you are again. Why can't you simply leave well enough alone and accept that you are destined to be single?' Arguing with herself, Taylor's heart tugging her in opposite directions, as she rocketed down the road.

Having loved and lost, surviving horrendous heartache, she knew too well the pain that loving another could bring. Yet here she was, alone again after devoting nearly a year of her life to Garrett.

The misty glow of town came into view from over the horizon, snapping her from the trance that she had somehow safely traveled home in. As she rounded the last long corner Taylor struggled with heading home. At the last second she took a right onto Bridge Creek Drive. In the distance the new metal roof of Jake's barn shone brightly in the hazy light of the moon.

Pulling up in front of the doors, Taylor sank back in her seat seeing them closed tight for the night. Rubbing her hands over her eyes she pulled in the clutch shifting, rolling her bike back over the muddy ground, angling her front tire toward the road. Something moving behind her caught her eye in the rearview mirror. Focusing her eyes she watched Jake roll one of the doors open.

"Taylor!" Jake called out above the rumble of her pipes. "Hey girl, I'm here!" Raising his hand in a quick wave seeing her look his way.

Rolling her bike back she turned the key, stepping off.

"To what do I owe this pleasant surprise? It's an awfully stormy night for such a pretty lady to be out gallivanting all alone."

"I just wanted to stop by and see the place. When I didn't see your truck I just figured that I was too late." Taylor smiled, hating that she was lying through her teeth, especially to Jake.

"Well, come on in and I will show you around." Jake motioned for her to enter, sliding the massive door closed once she was inside. "I was just welding on my flatbed before I grab a bite to eat, but that can wait until tomorrow. Are you hungry little lady?"

Smiling at the humor of the question, reminded of how she had just missed a perfect meal with Garrett all because he

201

didn't want her. "Hungry? Yes Jake, actually I believe I am." She answered.

"Great, then I will whip us something up, just give me a minute to turn off my tanks. Go ahead and look around if you would like. The office will be just inside that smaller door to the side of my sliders and the attic is nearly converted into my loft already. I've always dreamed of owning a place where I could both live and work. I have big plans for this old barn. A new coat of paint and some T.L.C. and she will be just perfect for this old boy," Jake said disappearing behind his truck.

"I had no idea you were living here too. This will be real nice. I'm happy for you, you deserve this." Taylor took in a long deep breath trying to regroup and clear her mind of the troubles of the night. Refocusing her attentions she glanced across the massive barn envisioning all the possibilities.

"Thank you beautiful. I just figured why not put the rent money into this place instead of lining some landlord's pockets. Plus I don't have all the neighbors being nosey when pretty girls stop by late at night." Jake smirked stepping from behind the truck winking at her. "That could certainly lead to some juicy rumors sweetheart… we wouldn't want that would we?" Grinning he moved behind the truck again.

Turning away she squeezed her eyes tightly closed at the confusion stirring within her.

"You seem a bit uptight tonight, are you sure everything is alright?" Jake asked, suddenly stepping up behind Taylor, startling her. "Like I was saying… you are wound up tight as a drum. Would you like to talk about it? You can tell ole Jake anything."

"I'm great Jake, no worries. So how about that food? I am much hungrier than I thought." Her words deceiving her own feelings.

"Right this way girl. Would you like mac and cheese, a grilled chicken salad or would you rather have turkey melts? Sorry there isn't a better selection, I haven't invested in that Viking yet, so I'm a little tight on space." Jake walked toward the iron stairs angled along the wall, leading her from the corner next to the space he had claimed for the office up to the attic.

"Grill cheese sounds great Jake, thanks," following him through a spectacular dark solid wood framed leaded glass door, taken by its beauty.

"You like? I bought it at auction in Daysberry, it's a Frank Lloyd Wright original. I knew the moment I saw it that I had to have it. I thought it would be the perfect mix of art and home.

"It's exquisite, absolutely perfect," though Taylor stood in awe of much more than the artistry.

Pushing the door open, Jake stepped aside for Taylor to enter before following, closing the door behind them. "Stay here, give me a second," making his way across the dark attic flipping a switch. Light beamed from an emerald glass tiffany lamp set on a long narrow table just below a picture window. The still life mountain scene of the window brought to life in stained glass, took Taylor's breath, reminding her of the special place where Jake had once taken her. Light shining through the multi colored masterpiece set in the midst of a dividing wall sent color streaming across the floor.

"You recognize that view?" Watching her, anxiously awaiting her answer.

"I thought it looked familiar," smiling at the thought as she scanned the room. Her eyes falling upon a grand spans of polished wood plank floorboards handsomely set beneath sizeable brick red and golden sunflower yellow woven rugs. A low slung, deep pocket dark mahogany brown leather sectional served to separate the entrance way, living room and dining areas.

Jake stepped into the shadows at the back of the space flipping another light switch on. The kitchen sprung to life under a row of large clear glass pendant lights hanging from a sturdy dark walnut four by four slab of wood. Long lengths of thick oiled rope strung and knotted through holes at the corners added a rustic touch. Taylor's eyes followed the ropes held parallel with heavy wire couplings suspending the lights, to the vaulted support beam above. Gazing at the open beams fixed overhead she admired the huge antique block and tackle affixed to a beam with a chunky length of rusty chain.

"Jake this place is spectacular! Have you done all of this work yourself?" Taylor's eyes feasted on the warm elegant masculinity of the loft.

"You bet, and I'm loving every minute of it. If I ever tire of welding and iron work this is what I am going to do for a living. There is just something so magical about peeling back the layers of old to reveal the true beauty. To take something thought of as garbage, old and spent and ready for the trash heap and turn it into something beautiful, such a simple pleasure."

"I must admit, your insight and creativity is quite impressive," admiring the integrated frame work of support beams, windows and walls, the care in every detail. "Did you restore all these beams as well?"

"That there was a challenge for certain. I had to rent a scaffolding and sand all the old grunge off, mostly while laying on my back with one of those electric sanders. Then I laid on my back for three weeks staining, only to start all over once more with sealer. I learned the hard way that it is best to completely cover every inch of your body when you use that sealer. That nasty goop took days to wash out of my hair. Like with anything, you learn as you go," Jake chuckled at the memory. "The satisfaction of seeing your face was worth it though." Judging by your reaction, I take it that it meets with your approval?"

"Are you kidding, it's like you stepped into a magazine." Taylor's eyes glistening in the lights.

"You are truly beautiful, aren't you? Jake spoke softly staring at her admiringly as he offered her a glass of ice cold milk across the bar.

"I… I don't know how to respond to that. You always seem to know just how to render me speechless," blushing like a school girl.

"Apple?" He asked, slicing a juicy Braeburn, playing it cool.

"Sure," she smiled, equally pleased that the conversation was moving on.

"Take a seat and relax. You can watch me craft some tasty morsels." Motioning toward the six tall wrought iron stools lined up against the bar side of the kitchen island.

Pulling out a stool she smoothed her hand over the ornate marrying of wood and iron before taking a seat. "These are beautiful, are they your handy work too?" Taylor sat across the island, admiring his smooth skills with a paring knife as he removed the peal of an apple in one single piece, watching him slice it into perfect, seed free wedges.

"Yes, they are actually. They were a special order for the barbershop renovation in town last year."

"For Mr. Baker? Didn't he pass away?"

"Yes ma'am and that is precisely why I still have them. I think that they work pretty well here anyway. They would have brought a pretty penny, but since he hadn't paid for them, what was the use in telling the family. I couldn't burden Mrs. Baker with any more debt than she was already under.

What with the contractors and lumber yard calling in his accounts the day after he passed, she was up to her ears in too many bills already. So here they are," smiling he offered her a plate. Turning off the burner, he slid his plate beside hers making his way to the other side to join her.

"Look at you all fancy. I have never seen an apple laid out in a fan before, and triangle cut sandwiches… you are seriously trying to show off."

"All for you girl." Jake's tanned cheeks crinkled as he smiled at her. "So how late do I get to keep you? Or will your man be upset if you don't eat and run?" Taking a bite of the crispy golden grill cheese.

"I'm all yours," wincing at her own words, suddenly realizing she really wasn't sure where she and Garrett stood, seeing that he had refused her.

"Lucky me," winking as he sank his teeth deep into his sandwich again.

Clearing their dishes Jake pointed toward the living room. "Find us some tunes while I take a quick shower."

"In the mood for anything special?" Getting to her feet, pushing her stool back to counter.

"Ladies choice," setting their plates into the stainless bibbed farm sink. Wiping down the last of the coffee brown sealed concrete countertop, tossing the wad of soiled paper towels into the trash can he turned, heading down the hallway, flipping on the light as he walked away.

Taylor watched him disappear down the hall, illuminated by bubbled antique glass sconces. The shimmering burnished gold of the hand trowel plastered walls made her smile. Amazed by such care taken even in the smallest details of Jake's home, never had she expected to find such an interesting man hiding behind the tough biker he portrayed outwardly. Jake had surprising depth; impeccable taste and style. Behind the gorgeous bad boy façade was a tasteful man with a heart of gold, the soul of true giver and a pretty fine cook as well. Taylor wondered if she had mistakenly picked the wrong man to fall for after all.

Perusing Jake's music collection took her on a trip down memory lane. The site of such diverse covers had Taylor's heart thumping. Artists from Zeppelin to Foreigner; Super Tramp, Marvin Gaye, Fleetwood Mac, Lynyrd Skynyrd and Steve Miller graced the shelves. The likes of Cat Stevens, Joplin, The C.C. Revival, Eagles and Hall and Oats. As well, Foghat, Joe Walsh, Kansas and Paul Simon rounded out the collection. Between the vast collective of vinyl, dozens of eight tracks and shelves of CD's she could listen to anything her heart desired. Jazz, blues, oldies rock, hair bands. Everything she had grown up loving was at her fingertips. Her eyes caught site of one of her favorites. Pulling it from the shelf she ran her palm over the still perfect cover. Slipping the record from its sleeve, she lay it on the turn table. Switching the knob, gently setting the needle on the edge of the spinning black disc.

'The words had all been spoken...
And, somehow the feeling still wasn't right...

Jake sang along entering the room, dimming the lights as he passed by the switch. "Jackson huh? I never would have figured you for a Browne fan Missy." Jake said, stopping momentarily to light a three wick candle on the coffee table. "You never cease to surprise me," slowly making his way to her in the romantic glow.

"Funny that was my precise thought about you Jake. That collection of yours is something. There is so much more to you than meets the eye. More to you than the ladies' man façade you put out there. This place, the cooking and now seeing this utterly diverse selection of music has opened my eyes. There's a whole other dimension hidden behind the masquerade, a side that you never allowed me to see before."

"I plead the fifth. So can I get you anything to drink?" Switching gears in the blink of an eye, he changed the subject.

"I'm great, though I drank more milk than I do in a year tonight."

"You should have told me, you weren't obligated to drink it. Now I feel bad. Forcing food on you that you don't like, what a great host I am. Not off to a good start, being my first guest and all," slowly running his hand through his damp hair embarrassed.

"You are a wonderful host Jake. I shouldn't have said anything. So tell me, where was it that you procured such discriminating tastes?"

"Wow, okay, I have never thought of it like that before. Let's see, my mother loved jazz and played rock and roll in the car and dad was hooked on 60's and 70's regardless of the genre. I have this need for substance, especially when it comes to women, cuisine, and my music. I find myself buying music for the lyrics, the instruments and the depth, then listening to the melody after. Backwards to most people I suppose. Food as well has to resonate interestingly on the palate, yet still be tantalizing to the eyes… much like you my dear. Presentation is sincerely half of the entire experience. Some things look better than they taste, which in turn sets one up for disappointment. So it must be the whole package for me to truly enjoy it. That's a pet peeve of mine, things that look better than they really are. That was one of the things I liked most about you girl. You have no pretense. With each time I spend with you I see more beauty, more intuitiveness, depth, passion, heart and soul. You're not just another pretty face that I find less attractive with each passing moment. I truly enjoy the current that flows through you, not simply the structure of your architecture. Though I must admit the view is awfully enjoyable from here," moving in closer, taking her hand in his, leading her to the couch. Sitting, he pulled her gently to his lap. Meeting her eyes he kissed her softly. "I must admit I have missed those lips my dear," his whisper falling with heated breath on her mouth. Closing his eyes he kissed her again, more deeply… hungrily.

Taylor moaned with sheer delight, spurring him on. Lifting her, he faced her toward him on his lap. His lips lingering on her neck, his touch moving over her. Taylor ran her hands along the ridge of his shoulders, lightly digging her fingers into his muscles.

"Jake… Jake, hold on, just wait… slow down," Taylor gasped between heaving breaths.

"Taylor, I want…"

"No, I can't do this! It's awful for me to even be here, I'm ashamed to have led you on this way," getting to her feet, she turned away.

"Talk to me Tay. Why did you come here tonight if you don't want to spend time with me? Please tell me." Standing, he laid his hand on her shoulder slowly turning her to face him again. "Tay I am begging you, tell me please what this is all about," searching her eyes more intently. "This night, this unannounced visit wasn't about us at all, was it?" Jake's forehead wrinkled with heart wrenching confusion. "Taylor you must tell me the truth, we can't keep going on like this."

"I'm so sorry Jake, I feel just awful," the truth slowly surfacing, reality bubbling forth, "I shouldn't have brought you into any of this. I just needed to hideaway from my reality for a little while."

The room grew eerily quiet. Taking a deep breath Jake sighed, bracing himself. "Please continue."

"I was with Garrett tonight, we had a misunderstanding and I left in a huff. I came here looking to escape, if only for a little while. I knew that with you I would find solace. Being with you I always feel so at home, so at peace... so loved. I'm sorry, I know it was wrong of me. Please don't be mad, please Jake!" Taylor covered her face disgraced. "I truly wasn't scheming. You are so much more to me than merely a sexy distraction," she spewed, quickly correcting herself, stranded on an island of twisted emotions. "Say something Jake, please!" Looking to him, her eyes meeting his painful gaze.

"I wish you had been more forthcoming with me earlier this evening," sitting back into the couch, resting his elbows just above his knees. Folding his hands, he squeezed his fingers together hard enough that his knuckles paled from the lack of blood flow. "I am trying my best to not be outraged, crushed even Taylor. Initially I tried to withstand my predictable response to your irresistible charms. Seldom do I allow women to infiltrate my emotions the way that you can. I try to merely celebrate the moment then quickly move on so as not to get too attached," Jake drew a ragged breath, continuing on. "You are correct in thinking that there is so much more to me than the strong, fearless, powerful tower of a man that you see before you! I am not that cocky, self-assured man that propositioned you on that first night. Tay, can't you see that all you have to do is pass me by and I am helpless in your staggering beauty?"

The masterful blending of your timeless sophistication and intricate authenticity captures my heart. With you I immediately allow my imagination to run amuck, losing all realistic interpretation of what is sincerely before me. The enchanting way about you rivals all I've known before. Taylor… simply being near you leaves me wandering mindlessly about. I do my best to keep my distance, then you effortlessly breeze in with your windswept beauty, as fine as any brushstroke on a canvas and all my resolve melts away. Then once again you drift off leaving me riveted, helplessly hungering for more."

Rubbing his hand over his mouth he breathed in a deep cleansing breath. "It's outrageous the delicious images set forth within the confines of my mind simply being in your presence. The distinctive qualities about you, the unmatched splendor of your spirit… I'm thrilled to simply bask in your charming delight, why can't you see this?" Running his hands through his hair once again, Jake squeezed his eyes closed, sighing. "You've unhinged me woman!" His words spewing forth with the fierce power of a heart broken scorned man.

"Please, please believe me, I wasn't trying to be clever, or charming! Jake I absolutely never wanted any of this," her reddened eyes pooling with tears.

"Taylor don't you see how distinctively exquisite you are?" Jake's words stifling her. "Your unobtrusive ways, the air of unpredictable vibrancy that erupts from that delightful heart of yours. I am stunned by the undeniable summoning of long-forgotten emotions you awaken in me. My life has been more a cautionary tale of abandonment and self-preservation than a joy ride of abundant love. If I could cash in on the intense labor that I have invested years, no make that decades of sweat equity in attempting to be illusive, with the real me hiding deep within, I could retire! Then here you are illuminating the darkened pathway with generous proportions of soulful vibrancy! You linger on my mind long after your perfume has faded. If I close my eyes I can still feel your touch hours after we've parted. This isn't easy on a man, it's a bitter pill to swallow, knowing that you have feelings for another Taylor! I may put on the outward armor of such resilience and strength, but that is just a veneer of the real man that lies beneath. Coveting my true thoughts and feelings allows me to separate myself from the substantial danger of falling for a woman, of losing my grasp on reality, of facing the inevitable corrosion of this life of mine as I know it!" An overwhelming emotional eruption of words spewed forth from Jake with volcanic fervor. "I have tortured myself to be accommodating to this new relationship you are exploring, for what? To simply be your fallback guy?" His emotional intensity unwavering. "Staying in the space of friends with you has become a full time job!"

Taylor's eyes glazed over, basking in the breathtaking symphony of words emanating from Jake. Unnerved by the magnificent bouquet of syllables had flowed from this remarkable man, and yet the harsh reality was irreversible. He cared so for her, and still here she was using him as a backup plan.

"I never imagined that you would automatically assume... well anything in me coming here Jake! Your friendship is invaluable to me, you have to know that! I pray it can withstand my selfish ignorance. Once again I have twisted everything into a mess!" Taylor threw herself to her knees before him. "There was no itinerary with you Jake, I promise I'm not that brilliant! I'm just a girl tangling in relationships that I have never experienced before! In the midst of discovering that love is more than the traditional imagery we are raised to expect, I'm trying to keep my head up and my mind clear as I maneuver through the mine fields!"

Jake rubbed his palms over his stinging eyes, sucking in another deep breath, trying to regroup. "It's essential for me to do anything and everything necessary within my power to make you fully understand what I am saying here Taylor." Speaking softly, taking her into his arms, placing his fingers beneath her chin, turning her face to his. "When two souls are interwoven Tay, that bond is forever, their relationship can never be refashioned. Lovers don't ever return from where they have ventured unscathed, this much I know is true. We cannot return to where we began once a relationship reaches a certain level. Even if we try, there are unspoken emotions that are eternal," Jake's heated breath fell across her damp tear streaked cheeks. "Things get confusing, messy and hearts get broken." Trailing the tip of his finger across the gentle curve of her pale face Jake brushed away a stream of tears. His voice just above a soft whisper, meticulously punctuating his every word, he continued. "This… that I feel for you, I am not equipped to deal with. There is a dimension of myself I have always refused to delve into, but now I clearly see that accommodating you when things are off with Garrett isn't enough for me. I know you long for love and stability. I fully appreciate the need you have to feel secure, you certainly deserve this and so much more. You deserve an eternal love with no boundaries, a life rich with elements of exceptional distinction. I have fought to be discreet with all I feel for you, to conceal the sweltering passion burning within me. Yet in all honesty I find this endless battle to temper my desire to be with you… not simply horizontally, mimics a slow painful death. This revolving door has to stop Tay, you are breaking my heart. I want you exclusively, rather than being an alternative to him. I want you all to myself, I know that now. I need to be… deserve to be much more than a distraction for anyone. You know it as well as I do. I may not be as precise or meticulous as you might prefer, but overall I offer untold abundance. With you I find myself exceptionally protective, willing to go to great lengths. I want to be that man in your life, to stand against the world in your honor. In each moment we spend together I am truly realizing the potential in us. My feelings for you are unwavering Tay, there's no graceful way to put it, I want you. I simply can't endure much more of this life suspending, untamed kaleidoscope of indistinguishable emotions masterfully disguised as friendship." Cradling her tightly against his chest he fought to restrain the tidal wave of mixed emotions building within.

Sitting back Taylor tried to find the words. Looking away sighing, she closed her eyes. "You are more than I could ever deserve Jake. I hate myself for leading you on," turning back to him, she continued, "above all else, I regret that it is not you that my heart has been lost to. I wish it wasn't so, but I have no longer a heart to offer you, as Garrett has stolen it. You are such an incredible man, even much greater than simply that. I care more for you, so much more than you will ever know. But I cannot, will not lie to you. I can't look you in the eyes and tell you that I can and will be yours, though this pains me deeply. You above all don't deserve to be hurt. I'm admittedly quite ashamed for bringing you even a single ounce of pain. You are the sweetest, kindest, most genuine man beneath that muscle bound tough guy pretense that I have ever known. I can't imagine you not being a part of my life anymore Jake! Please don't push me out over this, I'm begging you! I wish I could change things, but I realize that I simply can't!" Taylor's eyes brimmed again with heated tears, now spilling forth onto her reddened cheeks. "Please say that we can still be friends, please Jake!" Her lips quivering with raw emotion. "I realize this is a lot to ask, and even more that my actions don't warrant you giving me the time of day, but please say yes."

Pulling her tight against him again, he sighed. Holding one another for the longest time. Drowning in the somber reality, they sat silently digesting the sobering truth of the heart wrenching moment before them.

Sitting back once again, Jake took her face in his hands, staring into the depths of her eyes, searching for an answer... searching for words. "Oh girl, you are so very dear to me, I couldn't ever think of ending our friendship. I wouldn't think of never speaking with you again just because you can't offer me your heart. I just have to get things straight in my head... and even more so straight in my heart. Putting this into perspective is precisely what we have needed for quite some time. Though the unsettling reality that it will be Garrett that holds you, that tastes your deliciously sweet kisses from here out rather than I... I must admit that this is a bitter pill to swallow. I am a tough guy though. I will survive. I care so for you that I could never, would never expect that you do anything that your heart doesn't feel. But if he ever breaks your heart, he best leave town before I find him. I will not be held responsible for the damages unleashed." Kissing her forehead, his eyes falling intently upon hers.

Blinking slowly, Taylor sighed with relief. "Thank you for being so very wonderful Jake. Thank you for all your gracious understanding. I know that all of this can't be easy. You're a very precious, precious man." Kissing him lightly on the cheek, Taylor smiled through tears. "I should get going before I change..." stopping herself before she could say something that she knew well that she shouldn't.

"You were going to say something more?" Jake asked, holding her so she couldn't move away from him.

"Before it gets any later, that's all I was going to say," quickly looking away, fearful that he might press on, forcing her to speak the truth of the words she'd refrained from saying. Smoothing her blouse, biting her lip trying to hold her composure, "this is not easy for me by any means either Jake.

I need you to understand that. You have touched my heart like no other man. If it weren't for..."

"I know Tay, I really do understand... I thank you for your honesty." Jake stood, helping her to her feet. Taking her tear streaked face in the palm of his hands, he slowly kissed each reddened eye, touching his forehead to hers, softly pressing his lips to hers, indulging in one last lingering taste. Parting from her he smiled sweetly. "He's a lucky, lucky man... I surely hope that he realizes it," Jake's whisper hot against her cheek, tenderly kissing it before finally turning away.

Unlatching the rolling doors, Jake reluctantly pulled one back, watching in silence as she moved past him stepping into the night. "So, will I see you Sunday?" Shoving his hands into his pockets in a weak attempt to control the ever growing urge to stop her from walking away for good.

"Wouldn't miss it for the world," smiling as she threw her leg over her bike. "Besides I have to get pictures of Liz actually doing something outside of Donna's. I need proof that she can do more than work." Laughing aloud at the idea as she slipped her helmet over her hair.

"Really... she's actually going to help? How did you manage to convince her of that?" Amused, he leaned against the doorway, crossing his arms over his chest.

"Toby is planning on coming too, so he put on a little guilt trip pressure. It was really rather comical," smiling as she slipped her hand into a glove.

"Wow, so I have the whole gang coming huh? Well little lady, I feel quite privileged. All right, I will see you then Missy. Ride safe." Winking, he stepped back through the door, slowly sliding it closed once more.

Relieved that this crazy night was coming to a close, and more that they had salvaged their friendship, she started her bike, steering onto the road heading toward home. Pondering the stress of the evening, she welcomed a good night's sleep in the cozy warmth of her own bed.

Making her way back to town, she replayed the drama of the night over in her mind, amazed that life could change so drastically in the space of an evening. With a stream of words spoken, her future could have taken such a distinguishingly different path. In the short span of time she'd shared with Jake that evening, the entire outcome might have been completely altered with even the simplest gesture. Taylor marveled at the actuality of how very easily one could create any number of outcomes and scenarios from one singular moment. Sending up a silent prayer, she hoped that such decisiveness wouldn't prove to be a horribly regrettable mistake. Walking away from Jake hadn't been easy, but somehow she knew deep in her core, her very soul, that she had made the right choice. Garrett truly encompassed her whole heart, that truth she could no more deny than the entrancing hazel of his eyes, than the stirring feel of his mesmerizing touch.

Driving along she pondered precisely how she might possibly find her way back to him. Just how was she to explain her erratic reaction and make him fully comprehend her painful past? This was the harsh reality she now faced. The heart wrenchingly painful reality that she hadn't been prepared for after having grown so close to him since that very first ride, that first night they had shared at the barn. What would come of them if her past was too much for him to accept? If the haunting days behind her were known, would he think she didn't deserve a second chance? Worrisome fear of precisely this had gripped her thus far, but now she had opened herself to the full admittance of her reluctance to give of her heart once more. In the relinquishing of Jake, Taylor knew that there would be no turning back. Garrett would have to know everything, no holds barred… as soon as possible.

The lights of Donna's cast a soft mystical glow across the distant sky. Making the final corner, Taylor drove past the parking lot, peering curiously through the crowded stalls. In an instant, her heart flipped. The shocking sight of Garrett's bike parked just outside, and she nearly veered off of the pavement.

Frustrated, she pulled from the road, bantering with herself as to what she should do. 'If I go in I'll have to face him. Then what if he asks where I have been? If I tell him I was with Jake, he might assume that I was there for all the wrong reasons. If I lie and he finds out…it's most likely over. Don't do it Taylor! Drive on, go home and let the dust settle before you face him. You are completely spent. You'll say something wrong and ruin any future that you might have together. Drive on!' Looking over her shoulder she checked for oncoming traffic, heeding her own warnings, speeding toward home. 'Don't look back, just drive on and don't look back.' Knowing the timing in all this would be critical to the desired outcome, she headed on.

Thankfully making it home safely, Taylor pulled into the driveway, leaving her bike idling as she stepped off, opening the garage door. Parking, she closed the door before making her way inside. Pressing her code into the alarm pad, Taylor flipped on the kitchen pendant above the sink. The flashing light of her answering machine caught her eye. Pressing the play button she bent to unzip her boots.

"Hey Taylor," his voice echoing through the room.

The hair stood erect on the back of her neck hearing him call her by her full name. With Toby, this was generally a sign of trouble.

"Uh, I um… I saw Garrett tonight. He's… well he's actually still here. He's not alone Taylor. I really don't want to get in the middle of your personal life, but well, they're getting pretty cozy. Walked in holding hands, sharing plenty of laughter. She keeps putting her arm around his shoulder. I'm not sure if I should even be telling this to you, but I love you sis. Don't shoot the messenger!" The phone clicked off, instantaneously shaking her back to reality.

Taylor sat onto her stool, stunned by Toby's devastating words, ever thankful that she hadn't stopped at Donna's after all. Imagining the reaction she might have had in seeing Garrett with another woman; having to witness her hanging all over him. Her blood boiled at the mere thought of such a scene.

"I just gave up a fantastic man for you, and this is what I get in return?" Her voice raising with each word passing her lips. Stomping through the house, making her way to her room, she slipped from her clothes, crawling into bed crying herself to sleep.

Toby's words had her tossing and thrashing through the night, awakening more exhausted than she had been before she lay her head on the pillow. Shoving the heap of twisted bedding off of her, she made her way to the bathroom. Shocked, she stared at the monster reflecting back at her from the mirror. Dark halos encircling her eyes, the whites riddled with red roadmaps. Thankful for a distraction she turned, making her way to the ringing telephone.

"Hello? Tay, are you there?" Toby asked confused by the silence hanging on Taylor's end.

"What? Oh, hello," shaking her head, attempting to focus on his words.

"You all right?"

Taylor rubbed her face yawning. "Yes... no, I don't know!" Her eyes stinging with the harsh confusing reality the night before had unveiled. "Everything is such a mess Toby." Her eyes brimming with tears, she sniffled.

"Hey sis, don't cry. I am so sorry about leaving that message on your phone. I should have talked to you in person."

"That's not it. I'm glad that you have my back. A lot happened last night, more than you even know."

"Would you like some company?"

"Sure, that would be really nice Tob. Then you think we could ride to work together?"

"Anything you want sis. I'll see you in a bit."

Hanging up the phone Taylor headed off to shower and dress, pleased to have such a wonderful friend in Toby.

The day blew by, sharing the details of her predicament. Toby had always known precisely how to calm Taylor's frazzled soul. Knowing just the right words to make her feel completely capable of surviving, and more thriving through everything she faced. Simply having him with her she felt the fog lift.

"You are an incredible man Toby. I love you more than you can imagine." Taylor moved around the table, wrapping him in a tight hug.

"I meant what I said. Just let the dust settle, don't jump to any conclusions. Not everything is as it seems," sweetly kissing her on the cheek, "now get yourself put together. We have a busy night ahead of us."

"I will be ready in a flash," hurrying down the hall. Pulling her military pressed white embroidered blouse and black jeans from her closet, she rushed through her routine. Drawing her hair back into a loose ponytail, making one last check in the entry way mirror. Tugging her boots on, she grabbed her bag and jacket and they headed to work.

"Am I glad to see you two. It's been non-stop since four. Taylor can you get the bar caught up before the next rush of orders?" Liz herded Toby into the back room before Taylor could reply.

"Sure thing sis," smirking at the lack of communication skills her sister operated her life with. Taking to washing the bar sink full of beer mugs and shot glasses, Taylor drifted away, lost in thought when the phone rang. Wiping her hands on a towel, she pressed the receiver to her ear. "Donna's." Taylor waited for a response, confused when no one spoke. "Hello. Is there anyone there? You'll need to call back, there seems to be a problem with the connection, sorry." The line hung in silence. Taylor waited for them to end the call before laying the phone back into its cradle.

"You alright Tay?" Toby asked, seeing her stare at the phone as he stepped through the kitchen door carrying a freshly washed stack of bar towels.

"What? Oh, ya, I just had the strangest call. They just sat there, even after I said there's a problem with the line. Weird huh?"

"Well, not really. Maybe someone is uh, missing you?" Toby elbowed her in the ribs as he passed by stacking the bar towels into a basket below the bar.

"Sure Tob, that's it," she quipped. Turning slowly to him, her expression melting into a frown. "You are kidding me, right? He wouldn't do that... would he?"

"If you were mine and we had been in an argument, I would do anything to get back to you." Toby shrugged trying to dodge her slugging him in the arm. "Ouch! Hey, I'm on your side here!" Rubbing the frog her fist had left behind, he managed a smile. "I'm just telling you the truth," he offered, turning toward the kitchen again. "He really has you hooked, this Garrett guy." Disappearing through the door once more before she could reply.

Taylor struggled with Toby's remarks through the remainder of her shift, never receiving another call. The possibility driving home his theory that Garrett had just wanted to hear that she was still out there.

Turning the open sign off, she swept the floor then tended to the remaining clean up.

"You ready?" Toby asked, laying her jacket and purse on the bar in front of her.

"Yup, I'm ready. Liz, you all done back there?" Taylor leaned into the back room. Tapping Liz on the shoulder when she didn't reply. "We are all set, you ready?"

Pulling her ear phones off, Liz impatiently turned to Taylor. "What?"

"We're ready to call it a night. Are you close to being done?"

"Give me five," plugging her headset back into her ears, abruptly turning back to the counter.

"She's going to be a few," Taylor sighed, taking a seat at the bar.

"So… what are you going to do about all these man troubles?" Taking a seat next to her, teasingly bumping elbows with her, Toby smirked raising an eyebrow.

"I have no idea, but I am so glad that I didn't invite Garrett to join me tomorrow," Taylor answered rolling her eyes.

"That definitely would have been interesting," smirking at the mere thought of the possible drama.

"Understatement of the year little brother," laughing, covering her face with her hands, shaking her head.

"All right, I'm ready. What are you two laughing about now?" Liz growled, flipping a switch, turning off the last of the dining room lights.

"Boy troubles," Toby said hoping Liz wouldn't inquire further. Knowing too well her talent for making Taylor feel worse about such situations.

"Are we riding together tomorrow?" Taylor inquired, standing to pull her jacket on.

"Tomorrow? What is happening tomorrow?" Attitude oozing from Liz with her every word.

"Paint party at Jakes new place!" Toby exclaimed, as perky as he could muster, egging her on. "We are 'Team Donna's', remember?" Knowing that she had completely forgotten truly tickled him.

"I totally forgot. Is it really necessary that I be there? I'm sure you two could do enough painting to make up for me if I couldn't make it." Liz hung her head hoping to make her point.

"Nope, you are needed. We said three… that means you too. Jake bought waters, brushes, and food for all three of us. We can't let him down. We have to show, we are a team. C'mon Liz, you never do anything outside of this place, plus it will be nice for the three of us to be together away from work. It will be fun to spend some quality time." Toby stood moving closer to her. "Besides, those sexy legs of yours haven't seen sunlight in years. It will be a great day to catch some rays," landing a quick kiss on her cheek, just as Liz began frantically swatting him away.

"Then you are driving me," Liz insisted as she unlocked the front door, pushing her way outside trying to hide a sneaky smile.

Watching the door close, Toby looked to Taylor wide eyed. "Was that a yes? Did I actually convince her to join us?" Toby asked just above a whisper, jokingly slapping his face, seriously shocked at his crafty maneuvering. "Man I need to work it more often. I am getting good at buttering her up." Toby froze seeing Taylor's expression. "She's right behind me, isn't she?" Squeezing his eyes closed, he shrugged his shoulders.

"Yes she is, and she heard every word!" Liz snapped bluntly, pinching his ear between her fingers, jokingly dragging him outside.

Chapter Thirteen

Morning came with renewed energy. 'Today there shall be no time for anything except Jake', Taylor thought, slipping into her holey work jeans and comfy white t-shirt. This reality calmed her nerves as she stepped into her tennis shoes. The time would arise in which she must face Garrett and get to the bottom of why she had reacted so erratically, but today was not that time. Focusing on Jake and his business was a much needed distraction.

Twisting her hair into a loose French twist, she sleepily made her way to the coffee pot, thankful for the invention of its timer. Pouring herself a steaming mug she heard a knock at the door.

"Coming!" Guzzling down a few gulps she moved to the sink. Rinsing her mug out, she laid it into the basin, snagging her purse on her way to the front door. "Good morning Tob! Ready to paint the biggest barn in town bright red?" Offering him the most genuine smile she could muster, as she pulled the door closed behind her.

"You sleep well? You certainly do look a lot better than you did yesterday," nudging her as they walked toward the truck.

"Much better, thank you. I just really want to enjoy the day helping Jake and try not to let my mind wonder. Focus, that's the plan."

"We'll certainly do our best to help, won't we Liz?" Toby chimed as he climbed into the driver's seat.

"What? Sorry I was going over emails," looking up from her phone perplexed.

"Just say yes Liz," Toby sighed, shaking his head.

"Whatever, I have no idea what I am agreeing to but, yes," Liz sighed with disgust.

Pulling into the parking lot Taylor spied Jake unloading crates of paint cans from the shop, waving as he looked up seeing them park. Stepping from the truck, Taylor smiled waving back.

"Hey, good morning guys! Thanks for coming. You're my first crew to arrive," Jake's face lit up as he spoke.

"Brushes, trays, and rags are on the back of the flatbed there. Grab a can and we will hit it." Jake stooped lifting two cans. "Tay why don't you join me on the scaffolding and you guys start over there on the left corner and we will meet in the middle." Jake stepped onto the ladder not waiting for her response.

Taylor watched as he climbed the rungs making his way toward the top. Stepping onto the platform, he turned waving her on from above.

"Wow this is higher than I thought it was!" Taylor nervously exclaimed as she stepped in close beside him grabbing a hold of his arm, eyes bulging as she looked down to where her siblings stood.

"Steady girl, I've got you," moving Taylor in front of him. "Don't look down, that is of dire importance to staying upright. Not much on heights I see. You might have mentioned that whilst we were still on the ground my dear."

"Ya, heights are not really my thing," swallowing hard trying her best not to look down once again.

"Here, take this," Jake smiled handing her a brush. Popping off a can lid he poured the brilliant red paint into the tray sitting on the edge of the scaffolding. Stepping away, he leaned over setting the paint down by their feet. "I'm glad we got things straightened out the other night, I can't imagine not having this relationship," meeting her gaze he smiled.

Turning to him she wrapped her arms around his neck taking him tightly against her. "You are the best man I know. I can't imagine it either," her voice suddenly stifled by the familiar sound of pipes on the street below. Squeezing her eyes closed, silently praying that the bike stopped just off the road wasn't that of Garrett's. Stepping back Taylor's eye's caught site of the gleaming black cherry bike.

Garrett sat unmoving, staring in their direction. Slowly slipping his glasses from his face, he met Taylor's stare. Looking down he paused, then slowly slid his glasses back on, kicking the bike into gear. Checking for traffic before pulling onto the road once again, quick shifting, he sped away.

"Not good!" Toby's words loudly echoing up from the ground below.

"You can say that again," Jake grunted under his breath, nervously rubbing his forehead.

Taylor covered her face sighing, "this just cannot be happening to me."

"What just happened?" Liz asked, utterly confused by their reactions.

Before anyone could answer a car pulled in next to Toby's truck, parking.

"I will fill you in later sis, my date has just arrived." Toby sat his brush on the side of the paint can excitedly hurrying away.

"Date?" Liz's state of confusion ever increasing. "Where have I been, living on another planet?" Wiping the sweat from her cheek she sighed, turning back to the task at hand. "It's like I'm a stranger to my own life." Shaking her head she dipped the brush into the paint again, stroking the weathered boards.

"Everybody, this is my friend Gretchen. Gretchen this is our friend Jake, my sister Taylor, and this beauty is my sister Liz." Touching her shoulder Toby smiled as if he was showing her off, his introduction evoking varied greetings. "Come with me, I will get you set up." Toby's eyes spoke volumes of his excitement for the company of his new lady friend.

"What is this, mass infection of cupid's potion?" Liz spewed, rolling her eyes.

"Well look at that, she actually showed up. I admit I would never have thought this the appropriate scene for a first date. But I suppose a woman that owns a duck farm named Tail Feathers wouldn't be so very particular." Taylor smirked, continuing to paint.

"She is a great gal. And not a pretentious bone in her body," Jake retorted just above a hush. "That pinhead brother of yours would be lucky to share the same air with her." Jake shoved his brush roughly into the tray sending droplets freckling Taylor's face and hair.

"Oh might we have dated her at one time in the past, Mr. Protective?" Taylor flipped her brush defensively in Jake's direction.

"This is a battle you will lose my lady!" Jake sassed, reloading his brush, feathering his finger across the dripping bristles.

Astonished by the gall, Taylor gasped reloading her brush as well. Dancing back and forth along the length of the scaffolding they flung paint over nearly every inch of one another.

"No!" Taylor screamed as her elbow smacked the loaded paint tray sending it sailing over the edge. As if the world was moving in slow motion they stood bug eyed watching as a curtain of paint whirled downward toward the ground.

"Liz! Look out!" Taylor's words seemed to drag as they gushed forth.

Still ruminating over her sheer ignorance of her siblings' personal lives, Liz slowly glanced up hearing Taylor scream. Splat! Liz stood unmoving as the contents of the tray covered her in a wave of crimson slime. "Taylor!" Liz cried out with fierce fury. "This is not my idea of an enjoyable day of bonding!" Liz huffed, smearing her eyes clear of the gooey red paint.

"Let me tend to her, you keep painting. You're safer here than down there, trust me." Jake smirked, wiping his nose.

Laughing aloud Taylor motioned that he had painted himself a red mustache below his nose.

"Hey now, I wouldn't throw stones if I were you!" Jake laughed, giving Taylor a once over as he started down the ladder.

Liz glared at Taylor as she followed Jake to the hose bib still fuming.

"Sorry sis!" Her voice carrying down to Liz, a wave of dismissal her only response.

Watching as Jake helped Liz clean up, it hit Taylor how much she genuinely missed Garrett. 'He should be here, right now', she thought to herself, 'sharing these moments'. Sliding the brush along the sanded wood her mind replayed Toby's words over and over again. 'Why, if he cares so much does he let another woman hang all over him just hours before... and of all places in our restaurant?' Frustration distracting her momentarily, she drifted off in thought.

Laughter flowing from below snapped her back to reality. Peering back over the edge once again, Taylor stood astonished at the sight of Liz spraying Jake with the hose, giggling as he squealed like a little girl. Liz's laughter took her back in time. A time when the five of them would sit around the dinner table sharing the events of their day. Life had so embodied the essence of all Taylor loved in those precious days spent together as a family. How she longed for the stability and comfort of continuity in her life once again. The undying love of a man to call her own. To be cherished, treasured by another human, this was what dreams were made of. Struggling to understand the rumpled remnants of a love she had just days before been so sure of. Those moments with Garrett that had been infused with refreshing hope for a future forged from not one, but two complicated lives. Now, the seedlings of possibility to obtain even a crumb of a storybook ending seemed more a fairytale than a reality. She had so intended on being transparent this time... as Garrett had warranted such open honesty. Knowing the importance in each step of the journey with regard to recycled hearts, she had concealed the deepest part of her being and in turn potentially squelched her chances of true happiness. Though traveling an uncommon journey with Garrett, she had truly felt progressive confidence for their future together. Yearning for the privilege to fully experience the extraordinary possibilities that sharing your life with another allotted had inspired Taylor. Though incorporating two lives was never an easy undertaking, remaining in the shallow, stagnant, solitary life that she simply existed in wasn't acceptable any longer. Alone on this island of profound awakenings she realized how incredibly fortunate her parents had been in sharing such an uncomplicated union. Their endless capacity to completely surrender all to one another; demonstrating immeasurable helpings of extraordinary patience to meet each new day hand in hand, was nothing short of miraculous.

Stumbling along the tight rope of unexpected, ever multiplying challenges landed most couples in divorce court, but not her folks. They had harnessed true peace ever more when the winds of change blew in. Her father's words still resonating...

'Your mother is a bright angel sent by God himself to brighten my darkened world'. Taylor so desperately longed for a man to see her with such delightful perspective. The mere thought of looking into another's eyes and seeing such winsome, sacred treasure reflecting back left her reeling. Then and there she knew it was irrefutably imperative to her sanity, to any semblance of balance and bliss, to set things right with Garrett. A renewed energy ignited deep within her as she made her way down the ladder.

There is no time like the present...

Chapter Fourteen

Taylor opened the door, rolling her bike from the garage. Smiling, she pulled the door closed again, thankful that Jake had offered to run her home on his way to drop Liz off at her house. Turning the key, her bike lit up. Revving the engine, she tugged her helmet on before pulling onto the street. Rehearsing the words she would soon divulge over and over as she traveled along. The layers of possibilities unveiling themselves within overflowing potential with each mile ticking by. Soon Garrett would know how he had set free an emotional avalanche within her; encouraging monumental transformation. How could he have known why she had reacted so irrationally, since she hadn't been completely forthright? Today she would set things straight so that they could recapture all that they had found in those first weeks spent together. Taylor pushed on, her imagination running wild with the tantalizing blend of their shared moments; swells of sacred intimacy and arousing passion, basking in the prospects of their future, the days ahead that they would share loving one another, exploring life side by side. Maneuvering along the road in a state of drunken wanderlust, she lost track of where she was. Rounding the corner she quickly backed off the throttle as the barn came into view.

Vulnerability reawakened at the sight of Garrett leaning against an unfamiliar car, engaged in a rousing conversation with a lanky dark haired woman. Pulling from the road Taylor quickly turned the key, killing the engine. Fury rose from the depths of her anguish consumed soul, fear washing over her. Watching as Garrett tossed his head back with care-free laughter, the sight of which turned Taylor's stomach, butchering any remote aspirations she had arrived with. With each smile, each touch Garrett treaded further into dangerous territory, leaving Taylor teetering on the edge of permanent disconnect. Seeing him with another woman was the furthest thing from her mind. Reality of their situation awakening her to the realizations that he had not meant all those sweet words he had showered her with. Those same words now only tormented her fragile heart.

Not even the demented plotting of an evil-genius's creative handiwork could bring forth such inconceivable destruction as Garrett was in this very moment. She wasn't built to withstand such a ruthless demonstration as this nightmare playing out before her presented.

Watching stunned as Garrett motioned for the woman to join him inside, Taylor's heart sank. Why had he teased her with such intensely relentless illusions, if only to unceremoniously disconnect? Her mind stirred, ruminating her prior thoughts. Why had he spoken so valiantly of their 'soul connection' time and time again if only to shower her with raucous calamity? How could she respectfully allow such a lowdown charmer to begin healing a lifetime of calluses; altering her viewpoint, only to crush her spirit so carelessly?

Smothered by the reality revealing itself before her eyes, Taylor wept into her gloved hands. Glancing to the barn once again she watched mortified as Garrett casually wrapped his arm around the woman's thin shoulder, moving her along as they made their way across the dirt lot. Tilting her head to Garrett the woman returned the gesture. Leaning into him as he kissed the top of her head they disappeared through the barn doors.

Paralyzed, Taylor starred at the barn praying to see Garrett materialize in the doors once again. Desperately she stared, hopeful that the mystery woman would get in her car and drive away leaving them to sort things out. With every moment ticking past she felt more and more dejected, and still no sign of Garrett.

Smearing her tears away she turned the key, sparking the engine to life. Rolling her bike back, she glanced one last time toward the barn before pulling onto the road. This had been a huge mistake. Coming here had been an oversight that she would forever regret. Garrett had lead her on, as he most likely was repeating with his next victim this very moment. The raw depth of the realization that she had lost both Jake and Garrett in one fell swoop felt like a punch to the gut. Tears streamed down her heated cheeks as she crossed the double lined lanes of the pavement speeding away. Taylor's mind perused the memories of the past few months as she made her way back to town.

It was beginning to seem that love simply wasn't in the cards for her. Life wasn't always what we hope for, she realized as she snaked around the final corner just outside of town. The reality a sad discovery indeed. Though she knew too well how attempting to over plan your life makes for inevitable disappointments, Taylor ignored this daily, setting herself up for certain heart break. Clearing her mind, in this moment she accepted the truth that she may never find her knight in shining armor after all. In that very moment she made a promise to herself to never again allow another man access to her heart.

Pulling into Donna's, Taylor parked, sucking in along deep breath before heading into work.

"There she is! Hello beautiful! So great to have the gang all together tonight." Toby's warm greeting evoking a forced smile. "She's being weird tonight, not on her usual ranting rampage," Toby mouthed under his breath, pointing toward Liz working in the backroom.

"Wonder what's up?" Tying her apron around her waist, she leaned in close to the mirror across the back of the bar, checking her face for traces of tears.

"You alright Tay? You seem a bit out of sorts. What happened? I thought you were doing great?" Toby asked with a furrowed brow seeing her rolling her eyes at him. "Oh right, Garrett, I nearly forgot. So did you explain that Jake was just a friend and the hug wasn't what it seemed, just bad timing? Tell me you did please. The two of you are perfect for one another," raising an eyebrow.

"Nope, I never had the chance," Taylor snipped, "he's already got another woman. I'm guessing that she's the same one that you saw him with here the other night. I actually watched him take her into the barn with my own two eyes." Taylor snarled through gritted teeth at the cruel reality she faced, wiping the counter down, pretending to be busy so as not to unleash the anger driven water works mounting within.

"Wow, so I was right about that dark haired chick he brought here huh? That's too bad Tay, I really liked the guy. The way he spoke of you I thought for sure you two…"

"Well if I have learned anything lil' brother it's that not everything looks as it seems or seems as it looks. He smoke

235

screened me and put on a real good show! I guess if I would have put out maybe things might have lasted a little longer, but how glad I am that I didn't. I hate that I offered so much of my heart to some guy that I obviously know so little about. Look where trusting him has gotten me thus far!" Taylor fumed, her voice raised with more and more fury.

"I'm so glad that you didn't go there. That would have just opened you to more hurt, more heartache, trust me. Looking back you will be pleased that you two didn't let things go too far. You've done that before, and look where it got you." Toby bit his lip knowing he had ventured far beyond the borders of acceptability.

"Too far Toby. You of all people know that my past is off limits, period!" Glaring at him.

"Sorry Tay, I know better. I didn't mean to bring that up. I am just so hurt for you. Above all, you deserve to have happiness. I'm sad for you, that's all I'm getting at."

"It's alright, I am just really overwhelmed with the reality that I fell so hard for yet another two faced liar, and so easily too! I should be banned from men permanently!" Taylor screamed, throwing the bar towel into the sink, thankful that the restaurant was empty.

"Not all men are slandering pigs sis. Some of us are a fabulous combination of bold zest and radiant confidence, infused with steely handsomeness." Toby flashed a cheesy grin hoping to lighten the mood.

"Don't get snarky with me! This isn't funny! It took me a lot of courage to dive in again with my whole heart. Do you know how challenging it is to allow yourself to delve blindly into such meaningful experiences? Do you know what it is like to meet someone so deliciously divine, to be utterly blinded by their irresistibly stunning, distinctive essence? Can you understand the pain of finally finding your hearts delight after nearly giving up and then in the blink of an eye having to watch it all slip away?" Taylor's cheeks flushed, her words blurting out in rushed heaps. "Soul mate my eye!"

"Whoa Tay, down girl! I get it, believe me!" Toby took by the shoulders, attempting to settle her nerves. "Breathe, just breathe."

A bike pulled into the parking lot just as Taylor started to respond. Her eyes nearly bulging from their sockets at the distinguishable thunder of Garrett's motorcycle. "You have got to be kidding! I can't deal with this right now. Just pretend that I'm not here!" Taylor gasped, diving beneath the bar, shoving milk crates of empty beer bottles aside to make room for herself on the shelf. Crouching she covered her face with her hands.

"What! You have got to... Hey Garrett! How have you been buddy? Where's Tay, I thought you two would be hooked at the hip." Toby flinched trying not to scream aloud in pain as Taylor yanked on his pant leg ripping out a hank of hair. Kicking at her, he leaned his elbows on the bar top forcing a smile.

"I saw her bike in the stall out front, thought I might have a word with her." Garrett spoke frankly, searching the room for her. "Where is she? Is she here?"

"Well..." feeling Taylor kick him in shin, "not exactly. But I can leave a message for her if you would like." Toby cleared his throat hopeful that he wouldn't press on.

Smoothing his hand over his hair Garrett sighed looking to his feet. "Ya sure, um... just let her know I stopped by if you would," shoving his hands into his pockets, turning to leave. "Thanks Toby," waving as he pushed his way through the door again.

The bike roared to life, quickly pulling from the parking lot. Taylor crawled out from under the bar, peaking over before she stood. "What did you say 'not exactly' for? He knew that you were lying! He isn't stupid you know!" Frustrated, Taylor briskly brushed past, roughly knocking elbows with Toby.

"I didn't want to flat out lie to his face! Do your own dirty work next time if you don't like the way I handled it!"

The evening had been most uneventful making for a ridiculously long, boring shift. Except for witnessing Liz's altered state of mind; her suddenly perky disposition and strangely likeable personality, the night had been a complete waste of time. Taylor and Toby having spoken merely when necessary. Sheer boredom coupled with a total lacking of communication had always driven her crazy. "I'm out of here," tossing her apron into the hamper, "don't forget I have a checkup appointment at the hospital tomorrow. Melody is filling in for me."

"We'll see you next week then. Love you sis," he called out waving, as he watched her pass through the doors without replying.

Driving home Taylor let the wind carry her. Keeping herself from ruminating on the Garrett issue, she pondered new adventures she had awaiting her. With the next few days off she thought of possibly taking a drive to the coast, or making the long awaited journey to the lake. Getting away was precisely what she needed. Going someplace where she could clear her mind of all this nonsense and simply relax was just the ticket to pull herself together. 'The beach, that's where I will go.' Thinking to herself she smiled imagining the feel of the sand beneath her feet, the sun on her skin, the salty breeze tossing her hair here and there. Just the thought and she was already beginning to relax.

Pulling her bike into the garage she glanced to the front yard. The Honeysuckle blooms appeared to glow in the moonlight, their sweet fragrance dancing on the air calmed her heart. Admiring the sparkling droplets of water shimmering across the sidewalk, the calm of evening soothed her weary soul. The sheer beauty of her little yard spoke volumes, bringing great comfort. Although winter months take their toll, the summer arrives again. There would be a spring for her once more. Her heart would heal. This would not be a permanent state of existence for her, it couldn't be. Life was going to be okay, her garden seemed to whisper, 'everything is going to work out for the best.'

Showering she let the waters wash away the day. Toweling off she said a silent prayer to God for a much needed peaceful night's rest. Climbing into the soft linen sheets of her bed, slipping off to sleep, Taylor dreamed of crystalline waves crashing upon the seashore.

Chapter Fifteen

Starring into space, Taylor was lost in day dreaming of getting away to a sun drenched beach, when the sound of the receptionist calling her name snapped her back to reality. Offering a quick wave of acknowledgment, she stood following an unsociable nurse through a confusing maze of hallways to a tiny, austere exam room.

After nearly an hour of patiently waiting she was herded impersonally through the process of post treatment exams as mechanically as cattle might be. A quick stop by the scheduling desk and she was freed from the confines of the dreaded medical system until her next one year check-up.

Wandering about the labyrinth of corridors Taylor struggled to find her way back to the waiting room that she had started in. Seeing a desk set across the hall she made her way to it only to find it abandoned. Frustrated she followed red arrows along countless benign corridors, until she reached two sets of double doors. Seeing 'Emergency Room' plastered across one set, she sighed with relief. Knowing the exit led to the same parking area in which she had left her

SUV, Taylor pressed the large button stepping back as the doors swung open. Moving through them she felt her stomach sink. Before her sat the dark haired woman she had seen at the barn, Garrett kneeling before her. Holding a bloodied hand in front of her, the woman's voice barely audible.

"I am so sorry Garrett. I'm such a klutz. You don't have to stay with me. I know you have so many other things much more important to attend to."

Taylor swallowed hard watching Garrett tenderly brush a tear away from the woman's dark mantle of eyelashes, softly kissing her cheek.

"You can't get rid of me that easy. I love you and I wouldn't leave you alone here for anything. Besides you wouldn't be here if it wasn't for me, so in actuality this is all my fault anyway." He stood pulling a chair to him, sitting beside her. "You could be here for hours, you'll need some sort of entertainment."

The woman smiled through her pain. "I love you too. Thanks for being here with me. I've always had a love hate relationship with hospitals." Her words solidifying Taylor's worst fear for the truth of their relationship.

"I know, that is yet another reason as to why I am staying by your side, period," Garrett said winking. Smiling they shared a quiet moment.

Taylor felt the room shift, the lights seeming to spin, her stomach suddenly twisting in knots. Needing air, she tore through the waiting room, rushing through the automatic doors that opened to the circular drive. Stepping out onto the sidewalk that lead back to her SUV, Taylor sucked in a gulp of air. Dragging her dizzied body along the concrete path toward the parking lot Taylor felt her stomach flip, pushing her way behind the rose hedge she lost her lunch in the flowerbed. Pulling a tissue from her handbag she wiped her mouth, tears of frustration streaming down her cold gray cheeks. The realization that he had forgotten all those beautiful moments they shared and how they had made such an imprint on one another was simply too much to bear.

How could she have so fearlessly dove in head over heels, ignoring the skeptical mindset she had rested so comfortably in all the years before? Embarrassment flooded in, filling her with morbid humiliation. Overwhelming fury simmering beneath her calm exterior beckoned her to turn around and face him, to call him out there and then and put this regretful disaster behind her.

The weight of his caveman mentality left her reeling. Heartache fueled by his cruelty stirred within the confines of her soul. Faced with the harsh reality of knowing with great clarity what needed to be done, Taylor's stomach lurched again. Admitting to herself that she had believed in such a morally wounded soul disguised as a vibrant and distinctive man was somehow physically painful. How foolish to have believed that he could be the one to forever silence the nightmares of her past once and for all, only now to be generously offering well played sequels of his own to his next helpless prey.

It had been so much safer living vicariously through her customers love affairs; reaping the joy yet not having to endure the pains. The repulsive reality that he had so quickly spun a new web, somehow repackaged himself, and was so brilliantly masquerading as the perfect match to yet another unsuspecting audience twisted her heart.

So badly she wanted to run back through those doors and expose the pain that Garrett was setting his next victim up for. Such inside information could prove to be invaluable to a misinformed heart sick fool, provided that she didn't know the truth already. The reality hitting suddenly that this mystery woman could quite possibly be his wife, like a two by four to the gut.

Pressing her hand over her mouth fearful of purging once again, Taylor heard his voice calling out from behind her.

"Taylor!"

Her eyes nearly popped from their sockets at the sound of his steps falling on the sidewalk just behind her.

"Taylor stop please, I would like to speak to you for a moment."

Speeding her gate to a near sprint she raced to open her car door, quickly climbing inside. Trying to shove the key into the ignition, her shaky hand fumbled. Watching the keys tumble to the floorboard, Taylor screamed aloud in utter frustration. Retrieving the keys she refocused, placing the key in the slot quickly turning it over. The SUV sparked up and without looking behind her she was pulling from the stall. A horn honked jarring her from the trance she was lost in. Waving them on, she pulled forward to allow the other car to continue on their way. Once clear she pulled out again, racing toward the exit. Peering into the rear view mirror she saw him running, arms waving frantically above his head. Unable to compose herself any longer she burst into tears. Driving from the parking lot she quickly veered into an empty alley way. Slipping the gear shift into park she slumped over the steering wheel sobbing.

Taylor had been crying so hard she adopted a serious case of the hiccups. Weaving and bobbing with each spasm as she made her way home, fearing being mistaken for a drunken driver. Opening the door she slid her feet to the pavement below relieved to be home. Jamming her key into the front door, alarm code punched, making her way to her room. Kicking off her shoes she stepped to the bed slipping between the cool sheets fully dressed, falling into a deep sleep.

The ringing of the phone jolted her awake "Hello," she answered in a groveled rasp, dazed by the voice on the other end.

"Tay? Is that you? Man you sound like you partied a little too hard last night. Listen, I hate to ask but we forgot to get ice cream for the Davie's party tonight. Do you think maybe you might be able to help out?" Toby's words veiled in despair.

"What time?" She groaned.

"Party starts at seven. Can you please? I hate to leave them without a bartender," his desperation surfacing more with every word.

"What time is it?" Taylor tried sitting on the side of the bed, only to fall back onto her pillows once again.

"Three forty two."

"What? Three... you have got to be kidding me! What day is this?" Taylor sat straight up, stunned that she had slept through the night and half the next day. "I will be there at five thirty Tob," hanging the phone up without a word more. "What is happening to me? I never sleep the day away. This has to stop!" She huffed under her breath, repulsed that she had once again allowed a man, (if he deserved to be considered such), to drag her into the depths of depression.

A long hot shower followed by a pot of extra strong coffee and Taylor felt human once again. Trying to push out from the cloud of negative circumstances, she dressed in her favorite jeans, sheer champagne blouse, and espresso brown square toe cowboy boots. Staring at herself in the vanity mirror she silently pondered how her choices had come with expensive consequences. Knowing the only remedy to such an ailment was simply to become completely inaccessible to any future advancements. Running her hands through her wavy hair she swallowed hard at the thought, curious as to why after all the pain, she still found the concept so difficult to grasp. Being alone had never seemed right... possibly never would.

Sweeping her long locks into a loose bun she focused her mind on the strengths her parents had instilled in her; on the perfect blend of refined grace and universal strength. Pushing aside her propensity for foolish behavior, Taylor smiled at her reflection attempting to end her critical self-analysis. Knowing that though controversial, she embodied an entire subculture of adults her very age reluctant to accept any more rejection... anymore agony for the supposed priceless exchange of emotional ties. These folktales of supposedly cherished gifts of generosity offered between two humans, (that most gave without a thought), often led to painful destinations. The absolute truth being that typically relationships transcend beyond identifying worthy qualities and defining attributes were an absolute rarity. Further examination would show many complex factors would have to align to create this rare perfect storm.

Taylor resolved that if Garrett was not in the cards she would no longer even entertain the possibility of future experiences with love. Such ludicrous rejection she struggled so to define. Repeated loss had caused an irreversible shift within the cosmos of her heart, Garrett being the final blow. Focusing on the challenge set before her now; the redefining of domesticated bliss and true mutual submission, she sucked in a long cleansing breath. These had taken most of her adult life to establish following the heartbreak forced upon her younger self. This journey of repurposing the salvaged treasures of her heart was her new sentimental journey.

Tucking her blouse into her jeans she gave herself one last look before heading to the store. Stepping from the car door she pressed the button watching the hatch slowly open.

Wrapping her fingers around the plastic bags she lifted the tubs of ice cream from the back.

"Hey Tay, need any help?" Toby called, rolling the dolly back from the recycling bin.

"Hi Tob. Would you press the button and close my door please," forcing a smile as she made her way to the front entrance of Donna's.

"You are the best girl, I can't thank you enough!" Liz swooped in freeing the bags from Taylor's hands just as she reached the kitchen door.

Taylor stood frozen with wonder. Liz had spoken words that might be considered happy, kind even.

"That look on your face might suggest you have met our new and improved sister Elizabeth, as she calls herself now," Toby whispered in her ear as he stepped past her, making his way behind the bar.

"Who is she and what has she done with Liz?" Taylor whispered back, looking to Toby in amazement.

"Not really sure I can answer that. She just showed up the other day and surprisingly stayed." Toby shrugged, smiling. "I don't care about the details, I am just praying that she is here for good. It's a welcome change from the two headed beast we've grown accustom to since mom died. Don't you agree?"

"Definitely, it's just so very strange," Taylor snickered, shaking her head.

"So what are you up to tonight?"

Shrugging her shoulders, "no plans as of yet."

"Stay and hang out with me? This party is just starting and they'll be here most of the evening. Teenage parties always make for a slow night. Come on, it will be nice to spend some time together, I miss you." Toby batted his eyelashes at her pouting his lips.

"Sure I will hang out for a bit, if you will make me that pucker strength frozen lemonade you covet the recipe of."

"Anything to have you stay here with me dear." Winking he took her hand in his leading her to a stool at the far end of the bar. "This is more private." Returning to the bar he poured an elaborate mix of ingredients into the blender. Tossing in a whole frozen lemon he gave her a cheesy grin. "Cerise sur le gateau!" His eyes sparkling with creative juices. "The icing on the cake!" He offered, winking as he puckered his lips.

Intrigued by his passion for distinctive potions, Taylor watched admiring his creative expression while working his magic.

"So tell me what you think." Slipping a cerulean straw into the icy butter yellow concoction, he slid it to her across the polished wood.

Holding his gaze she sipped showing no sign of reaction, allowing a few seconds of anticipation to hang in the air. Toby stood transfixed upon her face anxiously awaiting her opinion.

Taylor's face twisted in horror. "What is this? Charcoal with a dose of seaside trash thrown in?" Her lips contorting as she spoke.

Toby's eyebrows arched high in disbelief. "What?"

"Just kidding Tob, it's divine. It's bouquet lingers sweetly on the pallet, reminiscent of a cool summer day." Taylor jabbed, giggling at herself.

"Man you had me there for a minute!" Toby exclaimed, clutching his chest, feigning a heart attack.

"Hey do you think the party would mind if I played some tunes?"

"Heck no. Just keep away from that head banging stuff you so like."

247

"No problem," Taylor jumped from the stool, making her way through the crowd to the jukebox. Scanning the 70's rock, she made several selections before returning to her place at the bar.

The music flowed, calming her weary mind. Stirring memories of her parents walking hand in hand along the lakeshore, the three of them just ahead as the sky exploded in the brilliant amber of dusk. Flying kites on the soccer field at her grade school, lazy days spent lounging on the patio, dad tending the BBQ, her mother swaying in the hammock book in hand, memories taking her back. How a song remembers when...

"Pssst, Tay!" Toby called in a forced whisper trying to alert her of the coming shock. "Taylor, hello!" Sighing he learned against the counter, folding his arms over his chest. "Too late now," he said shaking his head.

The door swung opened and in stepped Garrett. Taking a seat on the first barstool he stared down the counter toward Taylor. Sipping her drink she remained clueless. Tapping her fingers on side of the glass she smiled as another familiar song sprang from the jukebox.

"What can I get for you Garrett?" Toby asked louder than necessary, looking back over his shoulder as he made his way to him.

Swallowing hard hearing his name, she squeezed her eyes closed she sucked in a deep breath. Turning her stool away she stepped down. 'More music, we need more music,' she thought, trying to remove herself from the inevitable moment at hand. 'Just play it cool and he will get what he came for and leave.' Exhaling, she stared into the jukebox attempting to still her frazzled nerves.

"Taylor," Garrett spoke her name through wavering nerves. "Please don't ignore me. I really would like to speak with you. This silence stretched between us mimics Hell."

Taylor stepped from the jukebox, passing through the back door leading outside. Sucking in a long deep breath of fresh air, she squeezed her eyes closed again, hearing him pass through the door behind her, steadying herself on the railing, her heart pounding like a bass drum against her ribs.

"I am confused as to how we got here from where we were. I really thought we had something Taylor. My feelings for you weren't a façade. This heartache has me reeling."

"Enough Garrett! I can't take any more of your lies! You have the nerve, the gall to bring another woman here, to my family's place and think I won't find out? Or worse, did you do it purposely to hurt me? You take me for a fool! But guess what? The real fool is you Garrett, not me! What we had was real! What we found in each other comes but once in a lifetime and you simply threw it away! In the end it will be you looking back with remorse. I don't appreciate being toyed with so please find yourself another puppet to play with. Oh wait I forgot, you already have! Go back to the new minion you found to amuse yourself with and leave me alone!" The veins in her neck bulged with hostility, heated words gushing forth. "You are no different than all the other men, you are simply well practiced."

"I wish you would tell me what happened to you that has men so tainted in your eyes!" Garrett quipped back in frustration. "Then at least I could understand why you think we are all the same, all out to destroy women!"

"You want to know? You really want to hear how I saved myself for marriage? How he swept me off my feet and made me believe we were 'soul mates'? Do you really want to know how long he spent pressuring me, convincing me that he was here to stay and that giving myself to him would demonstrate my true love to him? Or how about when he told me I really didn't love him and that he was done unless I offered my purity as confirmation! How about the night I spent two hours begging and pleading him to stay, or how I finally gave in, surrendering the most precious gift that I could offer to the man I was engaged to be married to, simply to validate my feelings for him!" Sucking in a quick breath she pressed on frenzied. "Quite possibly you may find it even more interesting that after all that I relinquished to keep him, he abandoned me three days before our wedding, and not alone, but with my best friend none the less!" Sobbing into her palms Taylor trembled with hysteria realizing that she had just blurted out the ugly truth of her past behind Donna's, to a man that had also broken her.

"Taylor, I am so very sorry! I have no words to express to you the anguish I feel for what that charlatan did to you! But he and I are not one in the same!" Grasping Taylor's arm, he turned her to face him as she started to walk away. "Listen to me I beg you! You are irrefutably the most incredible woman I have ever met. Beyond your breath taking beauty and utterly magnanimous heart you radiate resplendence and you deserve nothing but love and respect! He didn't deserve you! Taylor I want nothing more in the world than to be the man in your life. I tried to express that to you, proving it by wanting to wait. I am sorry if I somehow failed."

Taylor stepped back freeing herself from his grasp. "You sure have an interesting way of showing all that you feel! What was it, maybe a whopping three hours after I left before you had another woman? Proof that you are no different than he was, don't you agree?"

"Please let me explain Taylor! This is no more than a misunderstanding, please hear me out!" Garrett pleaded, taking her by the arms once again. "I don't know all that happened to you in your past but I am willing to listen, eager to help you through the pain. Please don't push me out! I realize things have gotten jumbled up, but you have to believe me when I say I am not at all like the man that hurt you. I love you! Please give me a chance to clear all of this up!"

"Get your hands off of me Garrett," she barked though gritted teeth. "If you will excuse me I really need to go!" Pulling away she pushed past him making her way inside. Nearing the bar she spoke aloud turning heads as she continued walking toward the front door. "I'm heading home Toby. Sorry I just can't do this!" Giving a quick wave of dismissal, her words barely audible above the music.

"Love you sis!" Toby watched woefully as she hurriedly slipped through the front door.

"Taylor please stop!" Garrett ran to her from the side of the building. Taking her into his arms he pressed his lips hard against hers.

Her knees buckled beneath her at the feel of his intense passion. Lost in the moment she languished in his lascivious affections. Pulling herself back to reality Taylor pushed her hands against his chest attempting to shove him away. "I am begging you Garrett, please leave me alone. I can't take this. You're destroying me. I fully laid my heart out to you, my whole heart. This game you are playing is simply too much for my soul to handle," her words falling with the weight of despair barely audible.

Pulling her to him he begged, tears stinging his eyes. "Take a ride with me Taylor. Just one last ride, then if you want I will never bother you again. I promise you, just give me this… that is all I ask. I'm all but on my knees here begging you… Take one last ride with me?" Holding her gaze he stood unmoving awaiting her reply in the glow of the neon sign.

Trembling with emotion Taylor nodded her head, unable to deny herself one last opportunity to hold him against her, to feel the sheer pleasure that riding with Garrett afforded her. "When?" Squeezing her eyes closed again, unsure of her brazen decision, hot tears streaming down her cheeks.

Garrett sighed with heavy relief. "Sunday. Sunday late afternoon would be perfect." Smoothing his thumb slowly over her cheek, gently brushing her tears away he smiled.

Taylor nodded her head in agreement. "Call and leave the time on my machine. I have to go Garrett." Pushing past him she hurried to her car, fearful she had opened herself to more pain than she could tolerate. Her stomach churned with raw emotion. Her mind playing a myriad of varying scenarios driving her fragile psyche into a tailspin. 'Just drive on Taylor, don't lose it here in front of him. Don't give him the satisfaction.' Pulling away she glanced back in her rearview mirror against her better judgment. Standing where they had been Garrett stared, seemingly stunned, watching unmoving as she drove away.

Chapter Sixteen

The days seemed to drag on and on while awaiting the final ride that she would share with Garrett. Now that the day had arrived, Taylor spent much of it debating her decision. Dredging through her closet she perused her blouses attempting to find something unforgettable enough to make his heart ache even a little over losing her. Hearing her mother's words echoing repeatedly in her head... 'Make them regret ever letting you go each and every time they see you.' Smiling at the memory of her mother brushing her hair back from her shoulders with feigned attitude as she offered her feast of wisdom.

"I sure could use your savvy knowledge this time momma," sighing at the sad reality that all she had were memories to hold fast to.

Shaking off the moment she held up a long sleeved deep V-neck sapphire silk blouse. Standing before the mirror she pondered the choice, her eyes meeting their own reflection. Searching her soul she contemplated her decision once again.

'Should I take this chance and trust Garrett even though I know he is seeing another woman? Am I playing the fool? Should I stand and fight for what I really believe in, or simply walk away?' Confusion swirling through her mind took her away momentarily. Shaking herself back to reality, Taylor stepped away from the mirror, dressing.

Only time would tell if she was making the right decision. No turning back now, she had committed. Never had she been one to go back on her word… so she convinced herself.

The doorbell rang. Glancing at the clock on the hall wall she shuttered for the unfolding of the night ahead. 'Let's get this ordeal over so I can get on with the rest of my miserably lonesome life,' she thought to herself, making her way through the house.

"Ready?" Garrett inquired as she opened the door in expressionless silence.

Moving through the door she pulled it closed after punching in the code, hearing the alarm pad chime as it armed itself. Making their way to his bike Garrett heeded her unspoken hint to refrain from speaking. Offering her his spare helmet, he then pulled on his own, sparking the engine to life. Slipping his foot beneath the kickstand, he steadied the bike watching her step on. Tightening her grip, he momentarily lay his hand over hers, their eyes meeting in the mirror as they steered onto the road. Pulling hard on the throttle, they leaned into the bike, rolling out of town at a quick clip.

Taylor scooted up close behind Garrett, soaking in every detail, every second. Closing her eyes she let the buffeting wind sweep her away. This was where she truly longed to be, wanted to stay always, with Garrett. Pushing away the reality they were facing, she immersed herself in the unbelievable heaven being near to him brought her.

Before she realized how long they had been riding, Taylor felt the bike gear down. Lifting her eyes, the barn filled her vision. So different from when she had seen it last, she blinked with surprise. The exterior had been sanded and bathed in a rich dark walnut stain. The dirt lot now covered in a thick taupe layer of Tuscan inspired gravel, edged in new rail road ties studded with large steel conches held in place by equally large bolts framing the drive. An amazing structure of dark stained twelve by twelve posts and two by two's laced together with massive metal plates and more steel bolts stood jetting off the right side wall of the barn. Beneath the romantically lit arbor stretched a rustic slate patio decorated with espresso iron and wicker furniture. Willow branch embellished tall cylindrical glass lanterns filled with giant cream colored candles, perched on every table glowed in the early evening light. Curvy iron hanging pots overflowing with wire vine and bright salmon petunias hung on each side of the posts, filling the air with the loveliest fragrance.

Taylor's eyes fell on the massive outer sliding doors, opened to reveal dark wood French doors adorned with elegantly rustic antique copper door pulls. In the fading light a new copper roof gleaming above caught her eye. From the ground she could see through the matching French windows above. Mesmerized by how the dusky sunlight streamed through the creamy gauze curtains pulled back on each side, she sighed. A large wrought iron window box graced the exterior frame, snowy white plumes of alyssum and glossy emerald ivy spilling over the sides. Taylor's eyes feasted on the breath taking transformation as she stepped from the bike. Momentarily dazed, she wandered without speaking across the patio, along the side, to the backside of the barn.

Countless half wine barrels dotted the grounds, stained to match the barn wood they stood here and there, crowded with rosemary circled in dripping pale pink flowering ground cover. A perfect row of Italian cypress angled away from the side of the barn casting stoic shadows across a meandering stretch of freshly laid brilliant green fescue. Staring out across the valley Taylor spied hundreds of rows of rain-birds drenching the grassy knolls with liquid diamond dust as it rained through the golden rays of fading light. Bookend stands of newly planted grapes angled away from the mountains beyond. Each row studded with flourishing pink rose bushes, standing proudly in full bloom.

Taylor caught her breath. The work had been done so quickly, but how, and even more importantly why?

The creaking of hinges echoed down from above her. Gazing up she spotted Garrett pushing open a set of French doors, stepping out onto a small balcony encompassed in ornate art nouveau metal work. Making his way to the edge he held Taylor's stare.

"Why did you bring me here tonight Garrett?" Taylor asked still stunned by the incredible alterations that had been done in such a brief time. "Who did all of this?"

"I did Taylor. I bought this place. This is my home now. That's why I asked you here for the picnic, last time. I wanted to share my excitement."

"Congratulations, I'm happy for you, really I am. I know this has been your lifelong dream, but again I ask, what am I here for?"

"Because I love you Taylor. I love you more than I can express. I brought you here to show you that I want you in my life no matter what it takes. That first night when we spoke on the phone… I believe I already knew you were the one.

Then nearly losing you before I met you scared me to death. That was why I came to visit you every single day that you were at the rehab hospital. Once we met face to face it was all over. Feeling you near me on that first ride, I couldn't imagine another being in that space. It was as if God had destined us to be together and we need only find one another here on earth. Once we were together there was no way I could walk away."

"What do you want me to say Garrett? We haven't spoken for nearly eight weeks, and within hours of being apart you had already moved in on someone new!" Taylor lowered her exceedingly ramped up voice, attempting to hold onto her composure. "Garrett, I too felt the stars realign that night we first spoke. I could think of nothing more than our first ride together. The torture of unknowing during my recovery nearly took my sanity. But now, the dynamic has changed, we are in a much different space. Too much water has passed under the bridge. We are no longer those love sick fools stirring passion in the hayloft. You've moved on and now it is time that I do the same. Besides, I bet your new girlfriend wouldn't appreciate hearing this from you," Taylor spewed, turning to walk away.

"Taylor please wait! Hear me out!" Garrett pleaded. "Please come here with me. Give me just a few moments, then if you want I will take you back to town, no questions asked." Garrett anxiously pointed toward the wrought iron spiral staircase leading to the balcony above.

Shaking her head in self disbelief she climbed the ornate stairs slowly making her way across the wood planks.

Taking her hand firmly in his, he led her to the bow of the balcony.

"As you know when I first saw this wonderful place I knew it was where I wished to live the days God would allow me." Gesturing toward the valley below, he turned taking her hands in his. Staring into her eyes he smiled. "If I had the words to express all the love I have in my heart for you woman... I wanted to bring you here this day, because it is the anniversary of our conversation that we shared that first night."

Kneeling Garrett slipped a tiny box from his pocket, opening it. "Marry me Taylor, make me the happiest man alive. Allow me to love you all the days of your life. Be my wife, let's build a family of our own. Share the future with me here, within these walls?"

Silence fell between them, Taylor's eyes brimming with tears. "I was not expecting this. You must be kidding me. You haven't even explained why you have been seeing that other woman. Why have you allowed all this time to pass between us? You want such a commitment with so many unanswered questions? Here you are on bended knee expecting me to accept your clever proposal without any clarity... with so much unfinished business dividing us? How little you know me." Taylor turned from him, wiping her cheeks as she stepped away.

"Her name is Erinn, she's my little sister. Taylor please listen, don't walk away." Standing, he rushed to her, taking the bend of her arm, he turned her to him pleading. "She came here to help me restore this place. To help me pull it together in an insane amount of time for you, for us. I was afraid that you would get suspicious and come around if you found out she was here and I had yet to introduce you, so I allowed you to think the worst. We all worked together to keep this quiet, so as not to spoil the surprise. I called everyone in I could. Outsourcing was the only way to make this happen in such a short time. It wasn't easy, but there was no other way to keep you from finding out. And I wanted this to be something to tell the grand children about. I'm sorry for the deception, please forgive me."

"All of who? Who else is in on this Garrett?" Taylor's face paled with bewilderment, attempting to find perspective. Desperately trying to understand the landscape of the truth unfolding before her.

Garrett led her to the bow once more, wolf whistling over the balcony. From the far side of the barn the mystery woman appeared, offering up a kind wave, smiling. Jake followed suit, then Liz, Toby and nearly half of the town.

Staring down on the ever growing crowd below, Taylor rubbed her furrowed brow. "What? Everyone I know has known about this, are you kidding me? Everyone!" Waves of frustrating confusion coursing through the confines of her fragile psyche. Marinating in the flashbacks of the past few weeks, her mind replayed all that she had experienced. Unanswered questions filling her disempowered heart with even more curiosities. "So you were compelled to purchase this place; the one place that means more to you than anyplace in the world, redesign it… convincing nearly the whole town to join in on the scheme, amassing even my own family so that you could meet a deadline? All with aspirations of proposing marriage to me following nearly two months of suspicious conduct?" Glancing over to Toby, and then to Liz, she paused. Toby offered an impromptu wave, his smile quickly fading as he looked to his shoes, sheepishly shoving his hands into his pockets.

"Guilty as charged. You were the inspiration to take this on with such determination, such discipline. You were my muse," nervously clearing his throat, he continued on, "yes I fully concede it was you and ultimately the magnitude of my feelings for you that motivated me to take this plunge, knowing still the potential for rejection was there. That is how

259

much I truly love you Taylor!" Holding his breath, Garrett stood frozen, his heart overwhelmed with longing for some sign of reaction from her despite her blank expression.

"You turned this dilapidated old barn into a home, all so that we can live out our days together here? Am I hearing you correctly?" Taylor stepped closer to Garrett staring intently, continuing on without leaving time for him to reply. "You somehow persuaded most everyone I know to collaborate in this elaborate attempt at domesticating me? You devised this magnificent plan all on your own thinking that you could win me over simply with the idea of being your wife? Putting in place a seemingly appealing proposal surely oozing with originality and complex elements of romantic mystery with merely the desire to win me? A proposal that precludes surrendering all my freedoms, putting upon me the weighty responsibility of loving you all the days of my life, through thick and thin, through hardships and disagreements? You thought by doing all this that you could seduce me into abandoning the life that I so valiantly fought for following the wreck, resigning my eternal allegiance to you and only you?" Taylor's tone flattening as she stepped even closer to him. "Spending the rest of your life with me being your only motivation in the execution of this intriguingly persuasive demonstration? You are claiming that me... myself and I alone were the inspiring factor for you all to finish this place in such a secretive fashion? Creating such a masterpiece while omitting the facts to me, this you thought would win my allegiance?" Moving closer still, antagonizing him she pushed on.

Swallowing hard Garrett wiped his ashen, sweat soaked brow with the back of his hand barely blinking. "Um... well, yes," his heart beats virtually visible through his white cotton dress shirt.

"It fascinates me how astonishingly unpredictable you operate. So I suppose you think that this handiwork of sorts is going to earn you an acceptance to your proposal, don't you?"

"I was hopeful... but now not so much," slipping the ring box back into his pocket, withering.

"You want an answer Garrett? Then ask me again," she said positioning herself exceedingly close to him, noses nearly touching.

"Taylor, will you marry me?" His voice cracking with sheer anticipation.

Positioning herself with deep purpose she moved closer still, until they were flush against one another. With momentary hesitation she stared into the warmth of Garrett's gaze. Closing her eyes she leaned in, her breath falling warm on his ear, offering him a final reply.

The crowd below stood unmoving, anxiously awaiting his reaction. "What did she say for heaven sakes?" Jakes baritone voice echoing up from below. Laughter moving through the crowd.

"The anticipation is killing us!" Toby called out in turn.

Garrett stepped back from Taylor, his face unchanging. Taking her hand, he led her to the very edge of the balcony once more. Meeting her eyes with a knowing glance he peered over to the eager assembly below. Meeting her eyes again he pressed his lips to hers. Taylor languished in the reverence of his warm, passionate kiss. The crowd below erupting in harmoniously amplified bliss. The air filling with wolf whistles, hoots, and frenzied applause. Parting they shared a mutually intense smile.

"You could have drawn it out a little more there just before you answered you know. It would have added much more drama to the moment," Jake called up, winking at her.

"I thought about it, but once I saw the veins in his forehead threatening to explode I gave it a second thought," Taylor quipped in turn.

Peering down at the exhilarating swarm below, they all laughed aloud. Wrapped in one another's arms they watched as strangers hugged one another, hands shakes and high fives abound. The buzz of laughter filled chatter floating on the cool evening breeze.

The night had proved to be more than Taylor could have dreamed of. Mingling about the crowd she spied Jake from the corner of her eye, standing alone on the sideline of the party. Seeing his arms crossed tightly over his chest, his face an undiscernible pallet of remorseful consideration and cautious jubilation, Taylor offered a sweet smile. Nodding he raised his hand in a slow wave. Lingering momentarily, he held her stare before disappearing into the shadows behind the barn.

Epilogue

The day seemed somehow much brighter than most. The brilliant sun cheerfully hung high in the azure sky above. Fluffy cotton white clouds dotted the horizon casting shadows here and there on the lush mountains standing in the distance. Brilliant emerald stands of glistening grapes stood proud in their perfect rows, offering a slight formality to the meandering meadows lying between.

Garrett had well watered the surrounding gardens by late in the evening the night before. Taking time to tend to the grounds after the raucous crowd of his bachelor party had cleared. Sparkling crystalline dew drops still lingered on the delightful spread of flowers blanketing the yard. Countless strands of fairy lights swaged from the arbor to the trees, across the lawn and patios, from post to post.

Stepping to the window, Taylor admired the rose petal lined isle below. The perfectly set rows of brushed platinum Chiavari chairs swaged in glimmering pearly white tulle, had Taylor's heart aflutter. Today she would marry the love of her life, this day she would marry Garrett... This very day she would marry her soul mate, marking the beginning of her new life with the man of her dreams. Taylor smiled from the window of the hayloft converted master bedroom at the sight of the lovely decorations Erinn had designed and so elegantly put in place with her make shift team of townspeople, even recruiting a dozen or so friends from rehab. Having an event coordinator in the family was more a blessing than she could have imagined.

Turning her eyes to the rim of the mountains she inhaled a long, slow, cleansing breath. Closing her eyes, she said a silent prayer of thanks to God above for the blessing of finding her soul mate in all the distracting noise of the world. Moving from the window she glanced across the loveliness of the creamy linen shrouded boudoir Garrett had created for her. How could he have known she would so love the ivory sheer gauze curtains that hung from the vaulted ceilings on each side of the thick barn posts standing in rows along the perimeter of the loft? How might he have foreseen how she would adore the iron tie backs, forged by Jake's hands into the ornate shapes of everlasting roses? How wonderful the details of this room she called her own, and soon would share with Garrett.

Grazing her fingers along the silken cream quilted duvet cover his great Auntie Penelope had created just for this very day, she recalled their first kiss, shared in this precise space. The passion stirring within for all she wanted to share with him, all she wanted to explore. Her dreams would this night become reality. How she longed for the moment they would finally share this bed, consummating their boundless love for one another. This night would be that night, this truth blushed her powdered cheeks.

Misty light streamed through the gauze linen gracing the windows, playing on the folds of her gown hanging from the massive creamy white washed, French cottage armoire Garrett had won at auction just one week prior. Such a spectacular piece, now and forever her beloved wedding largesse; the sight of which still took her breath. Staring at her reflection in the wardrobe mirror she held the delicately embellished sheath to her. "I wish you were here momma," Taylor whispered.

"I know that I'm not mom, but will I do just the same?"

Gasping she returned the gown to its padded hanger. Turning she rushed to her sister's arms. "Liz, you've made it! Thank you for closing the store today just for us. You being here is more important to me than you'll ever know," Taylor stepped back smiling, her eyes stinging with emotion.

"Don't get me started or we'll look like prize fighters by the ceremony!" Liz sniffled, dabbing her eyes with a lace edged hankie. "This is for you by the way," retrieving a delicate white box from her bag, laying it in Taylor's palm. "I promised mom that if anything ever happened that she couldn't be with you on this day, I would step in. So this is my first matter of business.

Taylor lifted the lid slowly exposing the most exquisitely tatted edged eggshell white handkerchief. "Oh Liz!"

"Mom had granny make it for you when you were born. It has never seen the light of day since... It's perfect for your something new," dabbing her eyes once again.

"Come see my something borrowed sis," Taylor smiled, taking her by the hand, leading her to the armoire.

"Oh Tay, it is spectacular! His grandmother did a fabulous job beading mother's gown, and those dainty sheer rosettes are stunning! I have never seen a more lovely dress in all my life. You'll look like a princess," standing in awe of the masterpiece. "Mother would be so proud that you chose to wear the very dress she married daddy in. Tears streamed freely from her eyes at the mere thought.

"Stop it!" Taylor laughed trying to lighten the moment, wiping her own tears away. "I need to pull it together before the stylist arrives to make me look good enough to even do that gown justice. Come on, you can dress back here," pointing toward the changing screen she'd once had in her home, leading Liz back behind it.

"Wow you already moved your things in?" Liz jabbed, sizing her up. "I never would have imagined you…"

"Garrett and Jake surprised me and brought the majority of my belongings over so we wouldn't have so much to finish after we return from Italy and Greece. I hear honeymoons are quite exhausting," Taylor gushed, batting her eyelashes.

"He's a great guy, I must admit. How is he adjusting to having another living with him? And you, more importantly how are you dealing with the change?" Liz unloaded her bag of beauty supplies onto the white marble counter in the dressing alcove behind the screen awaiting her reply.

"Actually… tonight will be the first," biting her lip, eyes sparkling at the sentiment.

"Really?" Liz stopped abruptly turning her full attentions to Taylor.

"It was his idea. He wanted to wait until I was his bride… so romantic. He has been bunking with Jake for the past two weeks. He wanted to give me the chance to nest I guess. We have never even been in this renovated room together. This is where we shared our first kiss in the hay bales Liz. Now it is where we will spend all the remaining nights of our lives together," twirling around in a childlike motion smiling.

"And tonight it will be your love nest. You really have found the man of your dreams Tay. I couldn't be happier for you," taking her tightly in an embrace.

"One day you too will find your prince sis... one day soon, you will too," Taylor whispered squeezing her tight. "He's out there waiting, longing to find you too, just wait and see."

Slowly moving to the aisle, Taylor watched as hundreds of guests rose at her arrival. Stepping forth Toby offered her his arm. Making their way through the guests Taylor felt her knees wobble. Toby steadied her and they continued forward toward the iron arch trimmed with snowy wisteria blooms, velvety tawny cinnamon sticks, curly lengths of variegated ivy, delicately topped with sparkling strands of clear iridescent beads. The delicious scent of her gardenia bouquet tickling her nose. The romantic glow of giant white candles set in iron stands holding large glass globes graced both sides of the pathway.

Taylor's eyes found Garrett awaiting her at the end of the processional, her breath catching in her chest. Her heart skipped a beat at the realization that he was soon to be her 'forever' and in turn she would be his. Life would never be the same again, and for this she could be no more pleased.

Garrett glowed with pride, admiring her head to toe before offering her his hand. "You are enchanting my love," leaning in close, his whispers sending chills pouring over her.

"And you more handsome than legal," she whispered back smiling as she lay her hand in his, entranced by his gaze.

Lost in one another they continued through the ceremony, savoring each and every second. As they finished offering their sacred vows they had written for one another, the pastor said a final prayer over them and excitedly announced their union. "With this, I present to you Mr. and Mrs. Garrett Larkin. You may now kiss the bride."

Turning to face Taylor, Garrett softly took her face in the palms of his hands pressing a long, slow emotionally charged kiss upon her lips. Parting, Taylor's cheeks flushed with utter delight. Lost in one another, the sudden cheering of their guests shook them back to reality.

In an instant two white butterflies danced across the yard, circling Taylor and Garrett before fluttering off once again. Taylor looked to Toby, his eyes reddened with emotion, as they shared the precious moment.

Making their way back down the aisle, Taylor spied Jake among the rows of guests. Offering him a knowing smile she prayed that he was finding his way through the sea of mixed emotions he must be experiencing in seeing her marry another. Her heart soared with glee seeing him blow her a kiss, a cheesy grin plastered across his face. Pleased at his reaction she couldn't help but wonder how he was in such great spirits… considering. Shaking it off, she followed Garrett to the side doors of the barn. Tugging one open he slipped inside pulling her in, quickly closing the door behind them. Taking her to him, he wrapped his arms tightly around her, kissing her with heated waves of passion. Without speaking he opened the door stepping out once again. Closing the door he ran his hand over his hair, offering her a sneaky smile before leading her to the reception site on the opposite side of the barn.

The night proceeded with traditions and laughter. After sharing their first dance, Garrett had mysteriously excused himself. Within a few moments Jake was standing before her.

"May I my lady?" His beautiful sea green eyes sparkling beneath the fairy lights, as he gestured towards the patio requesting a dance. Bowing he offered her his hand.

A girlish giggle escaping her, "yes you may dear sir." Placing her palm in his, she allowed him to lead her out onto the patio. The sun casting its last fiery light before sinking into the shadows of dusk, set the sky on fire. Jake pulled Taylor to his broad chest, candlelight falling across the stones, along the sheer hem of her dress. Candle glow offering a soft illumination all around.

"You look as if you stepped from the pages of a fairytale Missy. He's a very, very lucky man," Jake's words falling warm on her ear, "this time I believe he truly knows it."

"One singular 'very' would do I believe, my sweet friend," squeezing his hand, pleased for the compliment.

"That is a matter of opinion," Jake whispered, smiling.

"Thank you for offering Garrett a place to stay. Having time here alone has helped me to transition into this new chapter. You are the best Jake," meeting his gaze, "there will never be another that will hold this sacred place in my heart as you do, please know this."

"And you for me sweet Taylor," starring at her with great intensity, their feet stopping beneath them.

"Hey now, no ogling buff dudes in front of your new husband. What have we been married, barely an hour, and she's already shamelessly flirting? Liz, trade with my wife so as to spare me any more pain in watching this," Garrett chuckled spinning Liz away from him.

Taylor stepped back making room as Jake caught Liz in mid twirl, sharing a moment of laughter before moving across the dance floor. They stood watching in amazement as Jake twirled and spun her around the patio. Liz threw her head back laughing at the sheer thrill of dancing with Jake.

"That's the most that I have ever seen my sister laugh in… well, ever!" Taylor exclaimed as stared stunned.

Smiling, Garrett took her hand pulling her to the front of the patio, lifting two glasses of champagne from a side table, offering her one.

Nodding to the D.J., they waited for the song to fade out. The guests looked to Garrett realizing that he was about to give a toast and found themselves flutes of champagne as well.

"My bride and I would like to thank you all for joining us. You've shown us both such kindness and love. Thank you especially for helping to make this night possible. So here's to the gracious love of friends and to my beautiful new wife."

Lifting their glasses they all toasted, "cheers!"

Garrett moved around behind her. "I have something for you, come with me," breathing steamy warmth into the back of her hair, tickling her neck with each word as she walked ahead. Closing her eyes she inhaled deeply as he lured her away from the crowd. Stepping in behind, she followed. Setting their flutes aside as they moved through their front doors, locking them behind them, he flashed a wicked grin. Sweeping her off her feet Garrett carried her upstairs kissing her neck, nibbling her ear. Reaching the loft landing he stopped allowing her to take in the view.

"Oh Garrett, it's magical!" Her eyes feasting on the splendor before them. Curvy wrought iron hooks protruding from each post gleamed with glistening candlelight pouring from oversized leaded glass lantern globes. Tiny iridescent spectrums played across the smooth creamy walls mimicking glittering diamonds. Dozens of tall glass cylinders sat in groups here and there, a glow with beautiful eggshell colored candles. White rose petals strewn along the floor in a trail leading them to the beautiful brass and marble canopy bed enshrouded in antique lace panels. "Garrett, I..." Taylor's words stifled by a long impassioned kiss.

"Shhh, my love. This night you will know true passion for the first time. This night will be the first of a lifetime of nights spent showing one another all the love we carry within," his whisper tickling her skin. Setting her feet upon the smooth dark wide paneled wood floor just beside their bed, silently turning her away from him. Running his fingers along the line of her waist... her hips... he slowly unzipped her dress. Tilting her head back in sheer anticipation, moaning at the sensation of his fingers sliding beneath the edge of the beaded sleeve, as he slipped it from her shoulders sending her gown sensually sliding down the length of her body, pooling on the floor. Shuddering beneath moist heated kisses falling softly on her bare flesh... his lips lingering at the nape of her neck, suckling their way across her skin. His breath sensually feathering across her ear, setting her afire inside. Delicately trailing his electrically charged fingertips across her collarbone... along the line of her breasts... the inside of her arm, circling a finger inside the dewy palm of her trembling hand. Relishing her reaction to his touch he smiled hearing a hushed gasp escape her, pressing himself against her as she arched her back in sheer ecstasy. Stroking the curves of her breasts, smoothing his palms over the sweep of her ribs he firmly tensioned himself against her, unbinding the line of hooks securing her sheer ivory lace bustier, dropping it to the floor. Tracing his fingertips along the curve of her hips, Garrett sinuously slipped her matching panties down, hearing Taylor sigh.

Turning to him she lustfully peered deeply into his eyes. "Thank you for making this day so special. I'm so very glad we waited..." Taylor whispered, holding his stare as she began slowly unbuttoning his shirt, slipping it from his shoulders, kissing his chest as she ran her fingers along the muscular line of his ribs to the waist of his trousers, languidly unhooking the band. Garrett breathed deeply hearing the slow slide of his zipper, feeling his pants fall.

Standing face to face bathed in candle glow their eyes searching one another's, Taylor drew back the lace panel as Garrett laid her back ever so gently onto the silkiness of their down feather bed.

Laying himself over her he paused, "I love you Mrs. Larkin, this day and forever more. I don't ever want for you to doubt this... not ever," hungrily pressing his mouth to hers.

Shifting and sliding voraciously against one another, veiled in feverish yearning, Taylor felt the world tilt, her heart shift, the walls of unresolved trepidation falling, profound reverence filling her for the man she held so vehemently in her arms. This primal unspoken union of souls, the uniting of kindred spirits taking her beyond the realms of Heaven, as two became one.

Coming Soon....

Sparks

In the riveting sequel to 'One Last Ride'
Jake allows love into his life but one last time.
In the midst of his renewed faith in 'forever'
tragedy strikes and turns his world upside down
Struggling to find his way he discovers a new life
beyond any that he might have imagined for himself.
Will he once again trust in love, or will he turn
his back on the best thing that ever happened to him?

ALSO COMING SOON!!!

FULL CIRCLE